ATLANTIS
SHIP OF THE GODS
- A Trilogy -

-BOOK THREE-
THE PATH TO CREATION

Pat Laughy / David Shearer

Dedication

This book is dedicated to the four
musketeers: David, Jonathan, Brendan and Pat

<u>Acknowledgement</u>

Many people helped in the creation of this novel. We offer special thanks to Jonathan and Brendan for their input, perspective and advice during the planning stages and hours of reading. Suzy for her editing, behind the scenes support and her publishing expertise. Linette for her input, editing and encouragement.

CHAPTER ONE

- *Blind Faith* -

All the team's members had committed to getting a good sleep before the trip to retake Atlantis.

In truth, none had been able to manage that, with the exception of Brother Sebastian.

And now it was time.

Once the final decision to risk using the halftrack to breach the shield Marduke had raised around the ship had been made, Jonah's little Almie, Sal, had been up front with the team about the facts of the matter.

As they'd gathered together inside the machine, he'd calmly explained that, while he was confident that there had indeed been a pre-set emergency auto-return command transponder function installed in the halftrack, he didn't know exactly where that device was located on the machine itself.

Unfairly, at least as far as Sal was concerned, the others had then immediately turned on him and begun to argue among themselves and question the whole enterprise. Although surprised by this response, he could reasonably dismiss some of their comments by putting them down to the adrenalin rush they must have all been feeling at the thought of any delay, especially now that they had wholeheartedly committed themselves to the venture.

But really, what did they expect from him.

After all, the transponder was an after-market add-on to

the halftrack. It was only sensible for them to acknowledge that the locating of the initiating device would take some effort on his part. It wasn't as if the manual told him where the thing was. He would have to work to locate it - that was only reasonable.

He sighed deeply and then, with some difficulty, forced himself to ignore the ruckus and demeaning remarks that were being directed at him as he wormed his way down into the cramped space beneath the dashboard to begin his search.

The hullaballoo above and behind him continued as he worked at isolating the wiring circuits to determine exactly where the add-on wiring for the return system was located on the machine. It took a few moments for him to narrow it down to one of two switches; however, both of these appeared to be *add-ons* and there was no way he could be absolutely certain which of the two would initiate the transponder and thereby transport the halftrack to Atlantis. He had absolutely no idea what the other switch might do, although he feared that it might be some sort of self-destruct mechanism.

While he was trying to differentiate between the two switches, his though process was shattered by a last frustrated silent command from Jonah filling his brain.

"For the love of Solar, Sal, do it before we lose our nerve!"

Sal looked from one of the two switches to the other.

Only one had a locking mechanism that had to be physically removed prior to the throwing the red switch below it, which would then complete its circuit. It seemed probable to Sal that such an override device would be fitted to the transporter system in order to prevent an accidental activation. It was also quite possible that such a protective step would have also been installed for a self-destruct.

However, the placement of the protected switch was easier to access than the other unprotected one. It seemed reasonable to assume that it would therefore be the right one.

Sal hated to act on assumption; experience told him that it was both rash and impractical. But that was what was coming down to, like it or not.

It was a guess, but Sal considered it the better of the two options. All things considered and very aware of the urgency, he removed the locking mechanism, placed one spindly finger on the switch and flicked it closed.

The kibitzing from above and behind him suddenly ceased. The others were now quiet. He considered that a good sign.

Although, buried below the dash where he was he had no way of knowing for sure, it appeared to Sal that he had made the right selection. It felt to him that the machine had successfully made the transition from the planet surface, passed through the protective shield surrounding Atlantis and into the transporter room and had done so relatively quickly and smoothly.

The resulting wave of relief that initially filled the little Almie as a result of that accomplishment was, however, to be very short-lived.

Bedlam now erupted behind and around him. The decibel level was suddenly much higher than the earlier round of complaints from the team members.

No other expression could better describe it.

It was very apparent to him that all hell was breaking loose around the machine.

He was pinned underneath the dash, his way out blocked by the numerous legs clamouring about inside the cab of the halftrack as the others in the party struggled to make their way clear of the vehicle.

While the team had had no way of knowing exactly what type of reception they'd be likely to receive upon their sudden appearance in the transporter room on Atlantis, each member had been pre-designated a specific task to accomplish, right off the mark.

Sal's job had been to stick with Jonah and under his direction, lock directly into the computer at a security access terminal and look after dealing with any changes that had been made to the protected door entry codes. This had to be done before the team could have assured access to the several security-enhanced portals that members of the team would have to pass through to complete their mission, the first of these being the doorway leading out of the transporter room itself.

The shouts, curses and racket Sal could now hear going on around the machine served to magnify the importance of his quickly joining Jonah. Unfortunately, at least until the others got clear of the halftrack's cab, he was penned in by limbs, whether he liked it or not.

After what seemed to him an eternity, the number of offending legs was reduced down to two lanky limbs - obviously these belonged to Duanna.

With pent up frustration and just a tinge of satisfaction he reached out, grasped both of them and gave a determined shove, effectively, tumbling her over backwards and out of his way.

At any other time, he would have expected her to immediately communicate her displeasure at such an affront.

Luckily for him, Duanna's main assigned task throughout the attempt at retaking Atlantis was to mentally construct a two-way communication lock on Marduke's Almie, Bellum. In order for their invasion to be successful, she would therefore have to diligently use her full concentration on this task of jamming in order to ensure that Marduke was unable to take any defensive action against the team.

Sal therefore had good reason to believe that Duanna would be so occupied with maintaining that task that she would be unable to chastise him for the insult of his knocking her off her feet.

Finally free, he scrambled out from beneath the dash, clawed his way up onto the passenger seat of the halftrack, and there briefly exchanged glances with Duanna, who was now ducked down below the back of the driver's seat.

Despite the deep concentration going on inside her head, indicated by her fluttering eyelids, she managed to flash him a very frigid look.

Sal paid her no heed and swiftly swivelled his head in an attempt to assess the fractious scene surrounding the halftrack. His naturally large eyes grew even bigger as he attempted to take it all in.

CHAPTER TWO

- *Team Effort* -

All about Sal there was what appeared to be a small army of worker Almies, at least thirty in all. Uncharacteristically, the lot of them seemed to be aggressively piling onto the other members of the team, who in various locations throughout the room, were separately and furiously struggling with the belligerent little imps.

Jonah, who was about halfway across the floor between the halftrack and the doorway of the transporter room, was currently giving immediate combat to four of the small creatures, all of whom were tenaciously locked onto and determinedly attempting to stop his forward progress by doing their level best to anchor his legs. A fifth had somehow clamoured up off the floor and was currently draped precariously over his master's back.

Jonah was frantically trying to buck the little devil off but it was hanging on for dear life and had clamped its little hands over Jonah's eyes, leaving him no option but to fight blind.

Sal had difficulty in understanding and believing what was going on.

The whole scene was ridiculous. It made no sense. Almies had never been designed to fight. And yet that was exactly what these worker Almies were attempting. For several moments, Sal struggled to rationalize what his eyes were telling him.

Obviously, someone had taken the time to reprogram the Almies currently in the room, but if that were the case, why had they not been provided with even the simplest of weapons. Realistically speaking, in a hand-to-hand combat situation, they could be considered as little more than a temporary irritation. They were certainly no physical match for the members of the team; however, he had to admit that they did outnumber them.

While he could rationalize that a horde of attacking worker Almies, despite their numbers, was unlikely to be too much of a challenge to the team over the long run, it was becoming readily apparent to him that they were certainly capable of slowing the team down considerably.

A trail of bedraggled and semi-conscious Almies were splayed out over the area now separating Sal from Jonah, as he jumped down off the halftrack and began to work his way toward his master.

Conscious of the fact that he could be grabbed as he attempted to pass through the still twitching forms he was forced to step carefully over and around the steadily increasing pile of discarded combatants.

He slowly inched his way through the fray in his attempt to close with Jonah.

As he stepped over an inert, but still twitching body, he spotted movement out of the corner of his left eye and ducked just in time to avoid being struck by one of the attackers who went flying across the room just inches from his head before crumpling to the floor several feet away. In so doing, his gaze settled briefly on Gabe, who was currently encircled by a large group of determined assailants.

The big Neanderthal was waylaid by the onslaught without doubt; however, he was grinning broadly and having no particular difficulty in dealing with the numerous little blighters, despite the fact that they were scrambling all over him.

During the few seconds Sal spent watching this particular confrontation, several of the tiny devils had gone sailing off into the air only to bounce off wall or floor, whichever they came in to contact with first.

As planned, Gabe's first detail after their arrival was to handle any problems the group might face upon setting down in the transporter room. As such he was armed with one of the machine guns taken earlier from the group of SS troops who had attempted to snare his grandmother. Jonah had also been so armed. Both of them were now using these weapons as clubs.

Sal could understand why this was the case. One didn't have to be programmed for advanced physics to recognize the fact that both of these weapons were, under the current circumstances, useless. The close-quarter struggle forbade their being used as designed.

To Sal, the initial plan of expecting Gabe to take care of this unforeseen manifestation of wild Almies was now quite obviously out of the question. He could see that everyone was going to have to pitch in at this point or they were not even going to get out of the transporter room, let alone move on to successfully retake the ship.

He took a moment to access the full situation, shifting his gaze from one to the other of the individual team members.

Juno and Venus were standing back to back, surrounded by a large group of the small spritely figures. According to the plan, Juno was supposed to be teamed up with Gabe at this point and Venus should have been with Duanna, protecting her from any interruption in her concentration on Bellum.

Obviously, this crazy Almie attack had thrown a monkey wrench into their plan from the onset and Juno was now trying to help Venus break free so she could work her way back toward the halftrack where Duanna had sought safety.

Venus herself was putting up a vigorous defense against the small armada encircling them, but of the two, it was Juno who was the more effective in making progress. She was wearing heavy, if stylish, knee-high leather boots and her feet were in continuous motion. All around her, little worker Almies were soaring off right and left with great regularity.

Their progress toward the halftrack and the protection of Duanna was steady if not rapid.

Sal determined that they would be there to support her

shortly.

Sebastian, whose preliminary assignment had been to cover Jonah's back, had now reached the door and was maintaining his position with his back to it as he waited for Jonah to reach him. The monk's staff was at times nearly invisible as it snapped and slashed about, sending worker Almies tumbling across the floor in all directions.

As a whole Sal deemed that the team seemed to be slowly gaining the upper hand; however, time was of the essence and was quickly passing by. Something had to be done to deal with the problem swiftly. That said, Sal wasn't exactly sure what part he could play in helping.

He certainly didn't know how to fight.

In the end, it was Gabe who had the presence of mind to take definitive steps to turn the tide.

As the big Neanderthal tossed yet another unconscious Almie into an attacking line of his cohorts, he spun around and then quickly crossed to the spot where Jonah was doing battle.

In short order he ripped the clinging Almie off the Atlantian's back and tossed it across the room. The two of them then each removed one of the remaining rascals off Jonah's legs and sent them reeling across the floor. As the little devils soundly rebounded off the far wall, Juno and Venus had made it to the halftrack and Venus had immediately climbed up into the cab.

Once she had managed to protectively station herself next to Duanna, Juno turned her attention away from the two of them and began to work her way back across the room toward the others. Sal reached the group just in time to overhear Gabe addressing Jonah as he gestured upward with his hand.

"They keep coming back for more. We need to pen the little beggars up instead of just bouncing them around. Do you know how to operate that thing?"

In response, Jonah lifted his eyes to look up toward the ceiling, some forty feet above.

At first, he wasn't sure what he was looking for and then, near the roof he spotted the massive rope cargo net. The net was attached to and dangling from a large mobile crane whose track appeared to run the length of the cavernous chamber.

He looked back over at Gabe and shook his head.

"No, but I'm sure Sal can figure it out."

Both of them then turned to face the long-suffering little Almie and with a deep sigh, Sal turned his big eyes upward as Gabe shouted out instructions.

"Bring the crane over to the center of the room and then lower that rope-basket thing down to about four feet off the floor. The rest of us can form a bucket brigade and I'll stand closest to the net. As they pass them to me, I'll bonk the little blighters on the head to stun them before I toss them inside, then all we have to do is close up the top of the thing to trap them inside and use the crane to crank them all the way up to the roof."

Jonah grinned broadly at the thought.

"Yup, that should do it.

"Go ahead Sal, get it done and then head over to that door Sebastian is covering and get us the codes we'll need to make our way to Marduke and the main keyboard. If these crazy Almies are any indication, it would seem that we are going to have to do a good deal of reprogramming in order to undo what changes have recently been made around here and get things back to normal and fully under our control."

Sal could see the compact control box at the end of the heavy cord hanging down from the crane. He hurried across to it as the others turned their attention back to deal with the crowd of Almies who had now regrouped and were obviously preparing for a renewed onslaught.

He unhitched the box and unwound several feet of cable so he could comfortably examine the array of buttons and switches covering the front of it. He had no idea of which did what and immediately decided solving the problem would have to be left to trial and error.

Ignoring the sound of the renewed battle on the other side of the room, he began to experiment and within a few moments he had mastered both the back and forth movement of the crane and narrowed down the choices to the specific buttons that lowered, raised, opened and closed the huge cargo net.

His first attempt at carrying out Gabe's instructions didn't go perfectly of course; after all, this was all new to him. He realized, unfortunately too late, that the net had a tendency to stay in motion briefly after the crane itself had stopped moving.

As a result, he'd not only brought the crane forward just a smidgen too far, but, as a result of the cargo net continuing to swing afterward, he'd managed to drop it all the way down onto the floor.

The result being that it was now draped solidly over Gabe, who was now flat on the floor thrashing about under the weight of the heavy rope basket.

And the language that the obviously displeased Neanderthal was currently using, although most of it was unfamiliar to him, was clearly of a profane nature and very disturbing.

A panic stricken Sal immediately moved to correct his error, but he wasn't able to do so in time to prevent a further extensive string of curses, which were clearly being leveled directly at him from the center of the room.

Then it was Jonah who was berating him, due in no small part to the fact that during the next tumultuous few seconds the attacking Almies, whose greatest threat was now writhing helplessly under the cargo net, had managed to succeed in pouncing firmly upon the remaining members of the team.

By the time Sal managed to lift the net and free Gabe, allowing him to rejoin the conflagration, the little Almie was nearly frantic and completely exhausted.

Before he could regain his composure, Jonah was shouting at him again.

"The codes Sal, for the love of Solar, get those bloody codes so we can get out of this madhouse."

CHAPTER THREE

- *World War* -

Von Jaeger, who had recently been promoted to the rank of Feldmarschall by the Rector, stood stiffly to attention as Eisen paced slowly back and forth on the raised dais behind his desk.

"So what is the current situation?"

Von Jaeger responded somewhat tremulously.

"Well it appears that, in the name of the faith, the Devi has declared a holy war against us. Emissaries from the Holy See have spread out over the other states of Olympos and armies are being rapidly raised in support of her request."

Eisen stopped his pacing and settled into the oversized chair at his desk.

As he did so, Von Jaeger, who was now becoming uncomfortable standing at attention, let his eyes shift from the Rector to one of the armchairs facing the desk in hopes that his master would allow him to be seated as well; but it was not to be.

"How soon will the Devi have an effective force at her command?"

The Feldmarschall allowed himself a shrug, more to relieve the strain in his shoulders than for effect.

"Our agents in the various states have been able to provide some indication of what is transpiring militarily. We have solid reliable reports from Billan Kalam and Saibutan, the states ringing Almeca. All three have already responded with fairly large forces, which are at this moment on the march toward the Holy state. Our information from other states is sketchy at this time but in view of the fact that the belief is the largest religious formation on the planet, there is no doubt that the leaders of all of them will be answering the Devi's call.

Eisen pursed his lips and brought his hand down solidly onto the top of his desk.

"So be it then. We may not yet be ready to make our move but we no longer have the luxury of waiting for our forces to reach optimum levels. We will have to go with what we've got and rely on the fact that the weapons that that turncoat Marduke has supplied us are sufficiently advanced to provide us with the balance of power.

"It is time to empty our warehouse of wonder weapons von Jaeger.

"I will give you a week to have your men made familiar with those superior armaments and then we will make our move. I gave the Devi every chance to accept us but the fool has chosen to push us into a military thrust. We must take Almeca and execute the Devi and sack the Holy See before Aabha can build up any more strength in numbers."

The Rector raised his eyes and locked his gaze with von Jaeger. The Reichsmarschall was instantly chilled by the steely glint registered there.

His heels cracked together and he raised his arm in salute. Eisen sat back and nodded.

"The very first task I have for you is to find our good camp chaplain and have that pompous representative of the Faith shot.

"And, once that is done, we will take Almeca and simply mop up the rest of the states on Olympos one at a time. Each will pay the price of not having accepted us. In a matter of months, I will not only rule Indus, but the entire planet.

"All will be under the heel of my boot!"

* * * * *

Aabha was finding that she had little time for the general maters of state.

The Devi was giving all her attention to the organization

of the armies of the Faith that would soon have to face the fascist war machine that Eisen would send against the states of Olympos. All other tasks had been delegated to her cabinet of Mitra Varuna.

Shortly after dawn, she found herself sequestered in her office alone with Brother Jacob.

She waited until honeyed tea had been served and the server had left before she spoke.

"Before Brother Sebastian left us he mentioned to me that he had suggested to you some kind of plan that may allow us to cut off the head of that snake who currently holds the state of Indus in his clutches and win the war without need for further bloodshed. Could you advise me of what this plan is?"

Brother Jacob set his teacup in its saucer and nodded.

"Yes of course. I would have advised you on it earlier but time has been short and you have had a rather full plate.

"It is a rather ambitious plan that I personally have my doubts about, but relatively simple in nature.

"Prior to leaving us, Brother Sebastian approached me with a slim possibility that had occurred to him.

"From his earlier experience with the Eisen phenomena, he is of the opinion that the entire ruling party of Indus could well fall into ruins, if the Rector were to be eliminated. With that end in mind, he felt that a small group of individuals could take the captured air machine, fly it to Indus and use it as a base from which to destroy the Rector.

"There is a small weapons stash on the ship as well as a supply of destruction devices that are apparently designed to be dropped from the airship onto a target below which would, as a result, be obliterated in an explosion of some type."

The Devi's brow furrowed deeply as she tried to get her mind around such advanced concepts.

"It sounds rather farfetched to me..."

Brother Jacob raised a hand to stay her further comment.

"As it did to me at the time, but after spending an afternoon aboard the airship with Brother Sebastian, I have to admit that, if not convinced it would work, I was left with the feeling that it just might.

"I have since spent several days in further evaluation of the concept and have concluded that if we were to successfully train a small group of brothers of the golden ring to fly the craft and to use its weapons, we might well be able to pull it off.

"When you summoned me, I was actually on my way to arrange an appointment to see you in order to suggest that we give this plan a try. We have little to lose if it fails, but a success could well save tens of thousands of lives."

Aabha shook her head slowly and sighed.

"It seems unlikely to me that such a plan could work. I think perhaps we would be reaching for straws if we gave it any further serious consideration."

Brother Jacob shrugged his shoulders and let his gaze hold hers.

"Perhaps it is necessary for us to be reaching for straws, in view of what we know of Eisen."

He paused briefly to let that statement hang in the air before continuing.

"He has a whole warehouse full of unimaginable weapons of war and apparently fully intends to use them on us. If the airship and that tracked fighting vehicle we have seen are any indication of the threat these newfangled machines will level at us…perhaps we need to think outside of the square in our response to such threat.

"Would you at least allow me to attempt to train up a team to see if the idea should be given further serious consideration?"

Aabha had long had reason to respect Jacob's loyalty and expertise. She valued his opinion. She had also picked up just how much Jacob obviously wanted to continue with his evaluation of the project.

She raised her four hands palms up and smiled.

"Yes Jacob, as always you give good council.

"If such a thing can be accomplished, then we should not dismiss it out of hand. You may train up your men and if you and your team can provide me with some sort of demonstration that gives such an undertaking even the smallest possibility of success, I will consider such an authorization for a direct attempt on the Rectors life."

CHAPTER FOUR

- *Uncertainty* -

Adon and Gaia shared a small table in the dining hall for the morning meal.

Although it was not in the nature of Atlantians to express strong public emotions, Adon was very much aware of the fact that there was tension in the air among those around him. He lowered his fork and keeping his voice low, addressed his lifemate.

"It seems so long since they left. You would have thought that we would have heard something by now."

Gaia nodded and then let her eyes meet his.

"Yes. And I'm certain that the rest are thinking the same thing. I'm sure you've noticed that despite the number of us here one could hear a pin drop in this room."

Adon shrugged and looked around the before speaking.

"I'm convinced we will hear from them soon; however, I think we should perhaps organize something that would include everyone and help to take their minds off the waiting. Any ideas?"

Gaia thought for a moment and then smiled.

"Actually, now that you ask, I have.

"You remember when we told Jonah and Venus that we would allow the younger generation to take the lead on the creation on life of the new planet?"

Adon nodded and she continued.

"Well, it occurs to me that we haven't discussed that possibility with the elders yet. Perhaps this would be a good time to have a meeting to seek everyone's support for such a plan? That would give them something else to think about and also serve to affirm our personal belief that all is currently going well up there on Atlantis."

Adon nodded enthusiastically.

"We are in agreement then. Considering the subject of our discussions, we will need to have privacy. Perhaps we could ask the Devi to provide us with a suitable hall, well away from curious ears. I know she is very busy now but I'm sure she would acquiesce if we ask her."

* * * * *

Sebastian appeared at Sal's side and rested his hand on the little Almie's slumped shoulder as he spoke softly to him.

"Don't sweat it my son. No one is perfect and under the circumstances, you're doing fine. They'll have the little devils all wrapped up in no time now. I'll watch your back. C'mon let's get over to the door and see if you can get those codes for us."

Sal surveyed the scene and satisfied that the others were indeed showing definite signs of successfully corralling the waring Almies, he turned back to the task at hand.

Soothed by Brother Sebastian's comforting words and confident that he would indeed cover his back he quickly crossed to the access panel, opened it and thrust the middle finger of his right hand into the sensing outlet.

Information began to flow immediately into him and he quickly concentrated the download to recent updates, rapidly ascertaining exactly what changes had been made in the various door admittance codes.

There were too many of them to tackle on a one by one basis and he decided to simply remove all the recent changes by doing a restore of the computer bank link back to the day before Marduke had arrived aboard. He then and rebooted the system, thereby returning all computer controlled systems to what they had been prior to that time.

That accomplished he secured the panel and turned back to evaluate what progress the others had made in the interim.

He was pleased to see that apparently the restore had not

only returned the door access codes to their previous allocations, but had also removed whatever adjustment had been made to the programming of the working Almies remaining in the room.

The previously belligerent little devils suddenly seemed no longer interested in arraying themselves defensively against the other members of the team and were now standing frozen in place obviously attempting to understand what was going on around them.

Sebastian had left his side and moved across to the center of the room to assist the others and Sal noted that nearly all the stunned Almies had now been manhandled along the production line and unceremoniously tossed into the net.

He moved quickly across to the crane's dangling control box and once the last of the little creatures had been corralled he closed the top of the large cargo net and let the crane haul the all but unconscious bundle upward toward the ceiling.

Jonah watched the raising net for a moment and then urged the others into action.

"Right, that little interruption having been dealt with, let's get moving. Gabe you come with Sal and I. You'll may have to do your invisible thing until we have Marduke under control, and while Sal and I will not likely attract any undue attention from any of the Almies we run across in the halls, they would certainly be at least unnerved by the sight of the rest of you wandering about.

"Sabastian, you and Juno, remain here with Venus and make sure that Duanna does not exhaust concentration and holds the jamming in place with Bellum. We fail to maintain that and we're going to lose our chance. Marduke is very probably not far from one of the two main computer stations and if alerted, he could quickly undo what Sal has just accomplished.

"Unless I miss my guess, Marduke is ensconced within my dad's apartments. If Gabe, Sal and I take a direct route there, we should arrive in about six minutes. Based on our intelligence, Marduke and his friend Eisen appear to be on the outs and because he knows that the planet is going to die very soon, I doubt that Marduke will have any of those bloody SS troops up here on Atlantis with him.

"Besides, if that were the case, there would have been no need for him to have put the blast shields up. We will just have to play it by ear, but all things considered I think it should be relatively smooth sailing from here.

"Once we get Marduke shackled and Bellum off line, the rest of you can join us. Duanna will know when Bellum is shut down and she will let you know. Once that happens, Duanna can drop the jamming and communicate with Sal and the rest of you can join us. In case I'm wrong and Marduke is not in dad's apartment, we will have to look for him and that make take some time.

"I'm fairly sure however, that in view of the way Marduke was hitting the bottle the last time I saw him, he will still be tucked up in bed and it is only logical that he will be using my dad's apartment, so expect to hear from us shortly.

"Let's get this show on the road."

* * * * *

Von Jaeger stood on the rise of the hillside above the major port on the south coast of Indus.

He had not slept for twenty-eight hours but a sense of anticipation filled him and he paid this lack of rest little concern.

Time was working against them; he knew that. However, the warehouse had been emptied and there could be no denying that the machines and weapons now moving in convoy toward the ships below him were impressive and beyond question unmatched by the forces he would currently have to face.

The six large, steam-powered transport ships that Marduke had earlier provided were now settling deeper into the water as their holds were filled with troops and weapons.

Loading was scheduled to be completed by evening and

the Rector, who would be taking personal overall command of the operation against Almeca, would be arriving in the morning just before they sailed.

* * * * *

Aabha managed to meet with Adon and Gaia shortly before noon and was pleased to grant them the use of a large conference room for the proposed meeting of the Atlantians under her protection.

Although she was somewhat curious as to why they needed to gather for a private meeting, her current schedule did not permit her the time to give the request any further thought.

From this short consultation with the Atlantian leaders she went directly to the large balcony off her personal apartments and met with Brother Jacob who passed her the strange looking brass-tubed looking glass that had come from the airship and explained how it worked as he spoke.

"It magnifies what you are looking at. It will be blurry at first. You can adjust the focus by turning the end-piece. If you look out over the bay, you will see the airship. It is under power and moving out to the opening of the port. The Brothers have been training diligently and seem to be in full control of the machine. An old barge has been anchored well clear of the main port. It will be the target for our demonstration.

We have ten of the large destruction devices, and are using just one for this test. As soon as the craft is over the barge, they will drop it.

The Devi took a few moments and with Brother Jacob's assistance, soon had the scoping device adjusted and in focus. She could clearly see both the Airship and barge floating at anchor well below it.

Neither of them spoke as they watched the test unfold with some anticipation.

They did not have long to wait.

Once the airship had reached positon and had stabilized Aabha saw a small door in the side of the craft open and moments later two Brothers leaned out and released a thick cylindrical object which dropped swiftly downward.

The object had several flanges affixed to the upper portion and it soon became apparent that the purpose of these seemed to be to maintain a controlled fall. They caused the object to spin slowly as gravity took hold and increased the speed of the descent.

In a few moments the object struck the barge just off center.

The intensity of the resulting blast caused Aabha to gasp and swiftly lower the looking glass.

She no longer needed it. The destruction caused by the demonstration was sufficient in power to be easily seen by the naked eye, despite the considerable distance separating her from the barge. A few moments later, after the formation of a massive fireball, there was nothing left of it but a fog-like cloud of raining debris.

Brother Jacob turned to her with a beaming smile.

"May I assume you now see your way clear to authorize our little endeavour."

Aabha simply nodded and handed him the looking glass.

CHAPTER FIVE

- *Hope Renewed* -

As foretold by Jonah, Marduke had indeed been imbibing heavily of intoxicating beverages well into the early hours of the new day and was currently fully clothed and spread-eagled on his back on what had previously been Adon' sleeping pallet.

Before collapsing in a drunken stupor just three hours before the team had landed, he had given Bellum clear instructions that he was not to be wakened for any reason. He would get up when he was recovered.

He was in a deep sleep and snoring loudly.

His little Almie had sensed that something was wrong the instant Duanna had reached out to him, overloading his capacity, disrupting his though processes and transfer systems, with a steady incoming barrage of primarily intelligible information.

His first thought had been to wake Marduke. It seemed the right thing to do - but then there had been his sharp instructions not to do so for any reason - and of late there had been numerous alcoholic-fired rages. Things had been broken for no reason and his master had even gone so far as to strike him a few days back.

He did cross over to where Marduke slept but was quite simply afraid to attempt to wake him.

Perhaps, if he could only think more clearly, he could understand better what was happening to him. He would fight against the overload, perhaps it couldn't be sustained for a long period of time and he could sort it out for himself without waking Marduke.

* * * * *

When Adon stood up at the head of the table the sound of muted conversation among the others gathered in the large conference room ceased.

H stood quietly for a few seconds letting his gaze move over those present.

All the members of the Council of Advisors were in attendance, with the exception of course of the one member who had been designated as overseer duty for the confined Demeter and her personal Almie.

"As you know we have not conducted a monthly meeting since Marduke banished us from Atlantis. As we wait for word of the successful retaking of our ship and home, we must prepare for our return and with it, the resurgence of our responsibilities for the preparations of the creation of life on the new planet that will form once Olympos reaches its end.

"While, of necessity, we have already made much of the necessary preparation for that eventuality, we have had our duties interrupted due to Marduke's breakdown, his subsequent actions and we have also lost Demeter from our team.

"It is well that we had done so, for although we do not know exactly when Olympos will meet its end, we do know that time is growing short, probably a matter of less than two weeks, and we must be ready to immediately concern ourselves with the challenge of fulfilling our responsibility to renew life in our solar system."

He turned to look over to the table next to him where Enoch and Persephone were seated side by side and he raised a hand to indicate them as he continued.

"We have been very fortunate to have capable replacements among us to take up the vacated responsibilities of both Marduke as Military and Police advisor and Demeter as Economic Development advisor.

"These two relative youngsters have, of necessity, willingly stepped into the void at a very early point in their lives.   They have smoothly agreed to accept full responsibility for their new duties as permanent Advisers and have already proven themselves more than worthy to hold these positions. I'm sure that all of you will join me in expressing our undivided confidence in Enoch and Persephone, who now sit within this circle."

Adon released an immediate flood of warmth and love directly channeled toward the young couple.

Gaia stood up beside him and turned her full attention toward Enoch and Persephone and in short order everyone in the room, with the exception of Enoch and Persephone themselves, who were obviously embarrassed at all the attention they were receiving, were also on their feet and openly offering supporting waves of warmth and affection.

* * * * *

Bellum was still struggling to clear his mind as the door behind him opened.

The change in ambient heat plus the resulting movement of airflow resonated against the sensors in his skin and the little Almie turned around to appraise its cause.

He expected to find that someone had entered the room. Something he would not have expected but which was the only explanation for the sensations he'd felt.

The doorway, which had been closed, now stood open. However, no one had entered the room.

While he was still attempting to evaluate what this meant, Jonah, accompanied by Sal, stepped through the opening. One look at them shocked Bellum thoroughly and he spun around and made to quickly wake his master but before he could move, he found himself clamped in a vice-like hold and lifted clear of the floor.

As Gabe tightened his grip on Bellum, he released his concentration on invisibility and instantly materialized.

A dumfounded Bellum, still occupied with fighting the overload-jamming of his thought processes, began to struggle but the massive Neanderthal had no difficulty holding him firmly. It required the use of only one arm to do so.

Jonah, with Sal trailing behind him, quickly closed on the bed and a stupefied Marduke had been placed in restrains within a few seconds.

Sal then gave a sigh of relief and quickly opened a channel of communication with Duanna.

"We have him. It is done. We are in Adon's apartments. Join us now."

* * * * *

At dusk Brother Jacob, surrounded by a ten-man crew made up of Brothers of the Golden Ring, boarded the airship in the harbour and immediately began to cast off. Aabha, watching from her balcony observed the machine turn slightly into the wind and begin heading north out of the bay against the backdrop of a darkening sky.

Before turning away, she paused long enough to offer up a brief prayer for the safety of those aboard, asking Solar for His blessing on their perilous mission.

* * * * *

When Adon raised the suggestion that those of the younger generation of Atlantians within the team be allowed to play the major role in bringing to life the new planet, those sitting at the tables put aside their other concerns and actively participated in the lively discussion that followed.

This would be a stark modification in the standard procedure normally used when it came to the processes used in the creation of life process for newly born planets.

There had therefore been some thoughtful questions, some honest concerns and a good deal of exchanged opinions expressed. This was to be expected and did not surprise Adon.

And, as he had anticipated, after a half hour of discussion, a consensus of general agreement began to hold forth. The overall decision to go ahead with such a plan, albeit with some provisions, was soon reached.

Satisfied with that outcome, Adon was about to close the meeting when *'One'*, his little Almie, quietly sidled up behind him a touched him lightly on the elbow. *'One'* remained mute when Adon turned to face him, silently communicating his message directly into his master's mind.

"Sal reports that it is done. Atlantis is now fully under the team's control. Jonah asks us to immediately prepare for direct transport to the ship. As soon as we are ready, we are to notify him and he will then lower the blast shields in order to facilitate our return."

* * * * *

A flurry of activity was taking place aboard Atlantis.

Venus was in the large control room, which was located on one of the massive ship's lower levels.

Here she supervised Duanna, who was leisurely running a complete check of all the ships mainframe computer systems to ensure that Sal, in his earlier rush to get access and change the codes, had not overlooked revoking any of the changes that Marduke had made and had not inadvertently made any other changes to the systems. Changes that could prevent the normal flow of activity aboard the ship from continuing as planned and at the correct pace.

Jonah and Sal were back inside the huge central transportation dock.

Sal had lowered the cargo net down with the crane and released the Almies who had been trapped inside. Having been reprogramed, the little creatures meekly left the room and quickly moved to take up their previously assigned duties.

Once they had gone, Sal raised the net back up to the ceiling and then he and Jonah hurried across the room and climbed up into the glass-fronted control booth situated above and overlooking the special transparent cover that roofed the raised dais of the transportation dock itself.

Here they began to familiarize themselves with the apparatus necessary to successfully launch the return transport of the other Atlantians up to the ship from Olympos.

Juno and Sebastian had been detailed to ensure that Marduke and Bellum were temporarily secured and could pose no further problems. Jonah had suppled them with an encapsulation unit to safely contain the Almie.

This unit was made from a special combination of metals that ensured the now deactivated personal aid unit would remain immobile and uncommunicative until it could be safely dealt with. It, with Marduke, who had been completely blindsided by the team's arrival and was furious, had then been moved to a secure room, the only door to which was now being carefully watched by the two team members who had taken charge of them.

As Gabe had completely exhausted himself both physically and mentally by having to remain invisible for longer than expected in order to facilitate the taking of Marduke, the young Neanderthal was forced to rest and Juno had seen him safely tucked up in Adon's bed before joining Brother Sebastian to stand guard over the room containing their prisoner; Marduke and his encapsulated Almie.

CHAPTER SIX

- *Homecoming* -

Although fully aware of the fact that the return of the Atlantians to the ship was paramount now, Adon knew that before he left, he had to take the time to personally thank the Devi for her unbridled sanctuary and support, which had been given after Marduke had unceremoniously expelled them from Atlantis.

Although there was a considerable array of individuals already waiting impatiently to see her in the antechamber leading into Aabha's office when the two Atlantians arrived, the Devi immediately gave him and Gaia audience, once she had been informed of their arrival.

Time for all parties was short and after warmly embracing Aabha and expressing heartfelt appreciation for the part she had played in rescuing them, they hurriedly left and returned to the conference room to gather the others together in preparation for their imminent transport back to Atlantis.

* * * * *

Shortly thereafter Sal received the coordinates for the conference room in Almeca from '*One*' and provided them to Jonah who immediately left the control booth, descended to the transport chamber and entered them into the panel affixed to the wall therein.

He took the time to double-check them for accuracy and then quickly returned to the control booth. The two of them then, with some trepidation, stared downward through the transparent cover of the dock's ceiling in order to observe the physical transition of the transport itself.

Jonah looked to Sal briefly and the little Almie responded.

"All is in readiness…should I have Duanna lower the blast shield?

Jonah took a second to review their preparations and then offered up a short, silent prayer to Solar before giving out a deep sigh and nodding his head.

"Yes, do it, but ask her to be ready to bring it back up again as soon as we have everyone on board. We'll tell her when, and also let her know that she is to do nothing else until we get back to her and ask her put the shield back into place.

"We have no idea what kind of knowledge Marduke has supplied to Eisen and we can't lose sight of the fact that that evil bastard might somehow know that we have dropped the shield and that he can somehow manage to get some of his men up here when it is down.

"Needless to say, that we do not need.

Sal shared the information with Duanna who did as she was asked and moments later confirmed with Sal that the blast shield was down.

Sal promptly closed the massive door to seal the transporter dock as he spoke.

"The shield is down. As soon as the door has closed we can commence the transport."

Once the airlock had ceased hissing, signifying the dock was completely sealed off from the rest of the room; Jonah nodded and as the lighting in the massive room shut down, leaving it in complete darkness, illumination below, within the dock itself, became distinctly more intense.

Jonah threw the switch to initiate the procedure.

Almost instantly, the bright light in the dock below began to defuse and then, what had temporarily been black and white patterns of matter, began to transform into various shards of colour.

Both Jonah and Sal were mesmerized by the changes taking place below them. The whole thing was so intense that they found themselves immobilized, segregated and disconnected from the world around them.

For a few seconds nothing was solid, everything was blurred to their perception as the interior of the dais within the dock began to grow considerably brighter and within a millisecond after that the transition of the trillions of atoms that made up the large group of Atlantians being transported, began to fuse and take individual shape below them.

Seconds later it was done.

* * * * *

Brother Jacob had plotted a direct course from Almeca to the island state of Indus. Due to the season, he was expecting to have excellent weather conditions and tailwinds throughout the trip.

It was his desire to have to travel over water for as short a time as possible. The route of the voyage he had thereby chosen meant that the airship would reach land directly above the area where the most southerly port of Indus was situated.

Coincidently, this was the port that the Rector's invasion fleet had just recently sailed from.

Eisen, aboard the largest of the six ships making up the invasion fleet, and very conscious that time was no longer on his side, had ordered that the course for the fleet must take the most direct route to Almeca. It was to travel at optimum speed and arrive unerringly at the port of Pag in order that the massive port facilities there could be used to rapidly disembark so that upon arrival he could instantly employ his forces against the Holy See.

* * * * *

Jonah instructed Sal to open the big door of the transporter dock and as it began to move, the illumination within the big chamber surrounding the dock came back on, bathing the huge room in bright light.

Jonah hurried down from the control booth to welcome the

Atlantians who were now beginning to move forward out of the transporter dock.

Once he reached the floor and mixed with the cavalcade exiting the dock, the overwhelming sense of relief that had swept through him following the successful transport was strongly amplified by the fact that, due to their natural abilities in energy transference, this sensation of relief was also being individually shared by all of the arriving Atlantians.

Greetings were exchanged and Adon allowed a few moments for these to take place before he spoke. Gaia had joined him and they exchanged smiles before Adon verbalized, raising his voice slightly to enable himself to be heard over the muted conversation of the others.

"Everyone! Your attention please. You all know that time for us to get things back on track is very short. With the exception of Jonah, I want all of you to return to your offices to make a quick appraisal of what you must individually accomplish in order for us to be in a position to execute the planet change procedure.

"I will be calling a meeting to be held in the conference room in approximately one hour. At that time, we will discuss the situation and prioritize our immediate needs. Please waste no time; we've none to spare."

He paused long enough to ensure that there were no questions. There were none and as the room began to empty, he turned to Jonah who had by this time been joined by Sal.

"Where are the others?"

It took Jonah a second to realize that his father was referring to the other members of their team. When he did, proud of their success at retaking the ship, he grinned broadly.

"Venus is in the control room. She and Duanna are checking to ensure that anything the Marduke has changed in the computer systems has been removed and that all the auto systems are functioning as they should be. We can join her there if you wish."

Adon frowned and shook his head.

"I was referring to the others who assisted."

Assuming that his father was seeking an opportunity to thank them, Jonah nodded.

"Right, well the humans, Juno and Brother Sabastian are currently standing guard over Marduke and Bellum and I'm afraid that Gabe, due to the fact that doing his invisible thing drains him, is currently resting in your bed. He will probably be out for a while. That invisible thing he does worked like a charm. We couldn't have taken Marduke without him and doing it really drains him and..."

His Father cut him off.

"Jonah, surely you realize that they must leave Atlantis and return to Olympos at once. We cannot allow them to stay on board the ship any longer than is absolutely necessary.

Have you forgotten who you are and what responsibilities we have? Olympos has no more than two weeks left before the process of dying begins. We must be ready in half that time to play our part and while we owe these beings who assisted you with the retaking of Atlantis a strong vote of gratitude, we must not forget that they are aliens and must be returned to their own planet before they get any inkling of what is about to take place there."

Gaia rested her hand on Adon's forearm and he felt a strong flow of gentleness at the contact.

"Your father is not expressing himself too well, Jonah; however, what he is saying is true.

"We will thank them for their help before they leave of course, but what they did does not alter the fact that they must go as soon as possible. We have much to do here and any understanding of what we do by them will not serve either Olympos or us.

"Your father and I will be very busy over the next few hours and we are counting on you to see to it that your three compatriots are properly thanked for their parts in allowing us to return to the ship and are quickly and safely transported back to Almeca. Under the circumstances, I can understand why the fact may have slipped your mind, but believe me when I tell you that their continued presence here is a danger to everyone involved."

Jonah found himself at a loss for words, a situation that he had rarely faced during his lifetime. He looked from his mother to his father and his shoulders slumped.

"Sure, of course. I'll have to arrange for someone to replace Juno and Sebastian and it may be awhile before we can safely wake Gabe. It seems that he goes into a kind of short-term coma state when he comes down from the invisibility thing - but we can all stay in your apartments until Gabe comes round.

"Although I have to tell you that this is really hard for me to understand and I know that Venus is going to be really pissed about it."

Adon could see no conflict in the need to return the Olympoians back to the plant as soon as feasible. A look of incomprehension formed on his face. Gaia, who had immediately understood the meaning lying below Jonah's statement, nodded her understanding.

"Ah, your sister has become very attached to the handsome young Neanderthal. Well, then it will then be necessary for you alone Jonah, to take on the responsibility for their return.

"Your father and I will see to it that Venus is otherwise occupied in the interim.

"Go now, see to this task as quickly as you can and let us know when they have been successfully transported back to the planet. It is for their own good. To do otherwise would cause unnecessary upset, pain or confusion upon their return to Olympos.

Away with you now. We have much to do and little time to do it."

CHAPTER SEVEN

- *Time Is Short* -

Adon and Gaia had joined Venus in Atlantis's large control room.

The three of them and their personal Almies were alone within the vast utilitarian facility. Venus sat behind Duanna, observing as the small creature scrolled though a seemingly endless stream of computer systems with complete concentration, pausing periodically to make small adjustments before continuing.

Gaia crossed over to her daughter and the two exchanged a few seconds of warmth and support before she spoke.

"I don't wish to interrupt. Please continue. Has there been much damage done?"

Venus raised her shoulders slightly and frowned.

"It appears not. Sal restored the system to what it had been pervious to Marduke's take over and then rebooted it.

I've been looking for any incidents where changes have been made during Marduke's tenure so that an assessment can be made as to what effect this has had on the initial plans. Some programs have been modified slightly but there has apparently not been any attempt to interfere with, or to slow down the automated programs for preparations that had been previously input to the main computer.

The changes he made appear to relate mostly to the reprogramming of some of the worker Almies aimed at creating a sort of security force here on the ship to prevent an assault from Olympos. However, as I'm sure you know, there are many programs that I have no previous knowledge of and I have marked these down as we go through them so that you and the elders may review them to ascertain what they might mean in relation to the overall project."

Gaia nodded and took the chair beside Venus.

"Yes, perhaps you could give me a list of those that have been changed and I will do the necessary review as you supply them. We need to make any corrections necessary before we can continue our preparations."

Venus nodded and handed her Mother the tablet that she had on her lap as she got up.

"Now that you are here to take over, I'd like to get back to the other team members."

Gaia shook her head.

"No, time is of the essence. It needs the two of us working together now. We must get this done quickly so we know where we stand overall. We will accomplish that far more rapidly if you continue doing what you have begun and I concentrate on checking the programmes that you have marked as altered. You have no immediate need to worry about the others. Jonah will take good care of your friends until we finish up here."

Venus, obviously disappointed, frowned deeply and a pout formed on her lips, but she did return to her seat, if with little enthusiasm.

Adon took in this exchange and, satisfied that Venus had been deterred at least temporarily from joining the others, he shifted his attention from them to the massive map of Olympos that he had brought up on the large screen that filled a good portion of one wall.

He moved to a control station at some distance from his wife and daughter, sat down to the keyboard, and began to enter a series of commands. Gaia leaned back in her chair and waited for a few seconds to ensure that Venus's attention had returned fully to Duanna and the scrolling screen in front of her before she allowed her gaze to shift briefly to the large screen.

As her eyes settled on the small window that had now opened at the bottom right corner of the immense screen she immediately picked up on what Adon was doing. Within the tiny image was a time countdown clock and she took in the content of the steadily decreasing number reflected there.

While the clock would have little meaning to Venus should she happen to notice it, Gaia knew exactly what it reflected.

Although the assessment procedure in place for making the determination of the commencement of the degradation of life on a planet, its first steps toward extinction was not an exact science. The timing was approximate and based on several varying factors. It warned her that in approximately a week and one-half, the countdown clock would reach zero.

Within a few hours of that occurrence, Olympos would begin its predetermined shift away from Solar and with that movement would come the natural death march of the planet as a whole. After that, the inevitable processes leading to the total destruction of all life on the sphere would follow in short order.

Time was indeed running short for the Atlantian's unit to prepare for that eventuality.

* * * * *

Jonah was very much conflicted over his being seemingly at odds his responsibilities.

On the one side was his fealty toward his Father and the Atlantians in their appointed task and on the other, to the team members to whom he now owed so much.

With the limited knowledge that he had been given, the rough idea of what was soon to happen to Olympos, a rising sense of guilt filled him in relation to what he was about to do and he couldn't help but inwardly struggle to try to justify it all in his mind.

As he, followed by Sal, joined them in Adon's apartments, he did his best to hide his conflicted feelings from the others.

He found Sebastian taking in the elegant surroundings offered by the Atlantian living unit with great interest. Up since being transported up to Atlantis, the Brother had found little time to wonder at the construction of the huge facility and was now taking advantage of the current lull in activity to do exactly that.

Juno was otherwise employed. She had managed to find an emergency medical kit and was swearing a blue streak as she followed Sebastian about the room, ineffectually attempting to disinfect and treat some of the small wounds that he had incurred during the conflict with the worker Almies.

She stamped her foot in frustration.

"For the love of Solar, will you stand still long enough for me to finish with you?"

Jonah's attention shifted to Gabe who was still lying on the bed. He noted that that his clothing had been adjusted, suggesting that Juno had and waved him over.

"You'd better let me have a look at you too, once I've finished with this damn uncooperative representative of the faith. Those little beggars seemed to like the taste of Humanoid flesh and busily munched on the lot of us while we were battling them. Admittedly they were too small to cause a great deal of damage, more like a swarm of blood-suckers they were, but I'm worried about the possibility of infection from the bites."

Jonah raised his hand brushing away any concern.

"You don't have to worry about that. They're robotic creatures and their bites would not be infectious"

He turned his gaze back to Gabe as he approached the bed.

When he next spoke, he did not address anyone in particular.

"How is Gabe doing...any idea when he's going to come around?"

It was Sebastian who responded

"Hard to tell. We have been practicing the invisibility trick a lot over the last little while and he seems to require less and less time to recover from each session. That is - providing he doesn't do it repeatedly over a short time frame. In view of the fact that we stopped experimenting with it four days ago so, I would imagine he will pull out of this one fairly rapidly."

Jonah nodded absently and stood quietly watching the impressive breadth of Gabe's exposed chest rise and fall rhythmically for a few seconds before offering his next inquiry.

"How can you tell how his recuperation is going? Are there indications suggesting that he will soon come out of it or does it just happen without warning?"

Sebastian who had now moved away from a frowning Juno in order to examine the advanced fixtures of the en-suite bathroom turned slightly to reply.

"Well, based on what I've observed so far, I would expect that another hour or so will probably do it. It takes a while for his breathing to return to normal and heartbeat and pulse to settle down. But once that happens the resurgence in his system is quite rapid."

Jonah nodded and moved closer to the bed. He spoke his thought out loud.

"Another hour or so. Right."

He then did a mind lock with Sal and silently passed a message to the little Almie who was standing quietly by the door.

"Sal, communicate with *'Two'*. Ask her to advise mother that she will have to keep Venus occupied for approximately two hours and also tell her we will let her know when the others have safely transported back down to Olympos."

CHAPTER EIGHT

- Parting Comrades -

Anxious to have the aliens removed from the star ship as soon as possible, Adon granted Jonah permission to attend the Atlantian emergency meeting in the conference room late, once his task of returning them to Olympos had been completed.

Gabe regained consciousness just over one hour after Jonah had joined the others in his Father's apartments. In order to ensure that their trip from Adon's apartments to the transporter room would go unnoticed by other Atlantians, Jonah waited until he was certain that the meeting was well under way before venturing out.

They came across no one in the halls as they made their way to the transporter room, other than the odd worker Almie, who took little notice,

Once they arrived, Jonah thanked them profusely for their assistance in retaking the ship.

After promising them that he and Venus would see them shortly, they said their goodbyes and he and his little Almie took up their positons in the control room above the transportation dock.

Jonah then had Sal enter the coordinates they had used for the earlier transport up from the stable courtyard in Almeca, drop the blast shields and throw the switch.

To Jonah's immense relief everything went smoothly and when it was done, he beamed over at Sal.

"You know little buddy; I'm getting pretty good at this!"

Sal, who was still smarting over what had been expected of him during the retaking of the ship, had to struggle to keep from firing back some type of smart-ass remark. Experience had taught him that doing so would serve no purpose, as it would have been given no serious credence whatsoever by his master.

Instead, he reinstalled the blast shield and then the two of them immediately left for the conference room.

* * * * *

Because the addendum for the meeting was holding her entire attention, Venus had taken no notice of the fact that Jonah had not joined the others of the Atlantian Advisory team in the large circular conference room.

The first topic listed for discussion was the suggestion that the elders grant the younger generation the right to play the lead role in the determination of how the new planet would be formed and colonized.

For some time Adon and Gaia had been preparing the way for this possibility, privately raising the prospect of such a decision with several other elders and pointedly offering their own positive thoughts in that regard. Given that this had been done, none of those present were surprised to find it on the addenda and all had been given sufficient time to mull the idea over before the meeting.

Given the fact that it was general knowledge that both Adon and Gaia were in support of the idea, it was not surprising that a confirming vote by all present, albeit with some provision for oversight, was a given.

The following addenda topics had to do with the practical steps needed to be taken by the individual advisors with regard to ensuring that all systems were brought up to speed for the imminent change in planets.

As Venus had not been previously privy to many of these and did not completely understand what they entailed, her attention had begun to wane somewhat by the time Jonah entered the room and took up the empty seat next to Adon.

Realizing that he was unaware of what had gone before,

she shifted closer to her brother and in a whisper, began to bring him up to speed about the decision that had been reached prior to his arrival. That done and having a very enquiring mind, she then questioned his previous whereabouts and tardiness.

Jonah, had no intention of telling her exactly what he had been doing to prevent him from attending the start of the conference, instead immediately went on at length about how pleased he was about the positive vote to give them the lead on the planning of the new planet. Venus, who was still very excited by that particular turn of events herself, was easily led away from pursuing the second part of her question and it quickly drifted to the back of her mind.

Usually pretty fast on the pick up, as absorbed as she was in listening to him, she completely missed revisiting his reasons for not attending at the commencement of the conference.

At that point, the two of them were drawn into the general discussion as their Father suggested to all present that in view of the fact that it had been decided that the other younger members of the group would be taking the lead in overall planning, they should remain behind to immediately form a committee under the chairmanship of Gaia.

It was then agreed by all present that the younger Atlantians remain behind in the conference room to decide among themselves specifically which members from their ranks would make up this new small working committee.

Adon then brought the meeting to an end.

It wasn't until the meeting was breaking up that Venus found an opportunity to ask her brother where Gabe, Juno and Brother Sebastian where.

Try as he might, Jonah could think of no way to avoid answering this direct question and he bit the bullet and told her that they had been transported back to Olympos.

It was then that he found out that his earlier prediction, offered to his parents, had rung very true.

Venus made it apparent to him in no uncertain terms that

she was very definitely displeased that the rest of the team had been transported back down to Olympos without her knowledge.

It wasn't until the elders had left and all the young Atlantians present in the room had physically begun shifting their positions in order to form a smaller grouping that Venus was forced to restrain her verbal tirade against Jonah, compose herself and turn her attention to the business now at hand.

Very relieved to have that happen under the circumstances, Jonah quickly got to his feet and took the lead even before some of the members of the younger generation had settled into their seats.

"What we have to do now is select a small number from those gathered, who we all feel will be best placed to represent the others. In my judgement, we don't want too many on the committee itself, as all that will do is lead to endless meetings leading to a good deal of bickering about what needs to be done and getting very little accomplished.

We do not have a lot of time to achieve our task and I would suggest that we limit the number to four, with Gaia as chair, to offer input on matters that we do not yet fully understand.

Additionally, those who make up this foursome will have to realize that they will have very little free time available to them in relation to their own specific assistant advisory duties after the committee is formed. Once those on the committee have determined a basic plan, all of us will, as a matter of course, meet again, discuss it and then amend and vote for overall acceptance. The majority will have the final say.

It seems likely that committee members will find that they will be fully involved in doing that specific work.

With this in mind, can I please have suggestions from the floor as to how we make our selections?"

Enoch was the first to respond.

"It goes without saying that both you and Venus need to

be on the committee. You each have a predetermined responsibility to step into the leadership roles of the entire program should, Solar forbid, your parents be in some way incapacitated."

General agreement with this observation was immediate and both Venus and Jonah accepted the decision. Venus then spoke.

"In view of the fact that two of the others here will have very little demand in both their areas of responsibility with relation to the future of Olympos, and in order to have a gender balance on the committee, I would suggest that it should be Enoch and Persephone who fill the other two vacancies. The specific advisory nature of their areas of responsibility will be very necessary in the creation of the new planet. Additionally, as they have both been permanently appointed to these positions by the elders, their input will be both invaluable and readily accepted by those same elders as we reach our final decisions as to exactly how we are going to proceed.

Some discussion took place, but this offering too, was soon agreed upon.

In less than a half hour the selection of the committee members had been affirmed and as everyone else had much to do, the four chosen members soon had the huge room to themselves. It wasn't really until that time that Jonah, Venus, Enoch and Persephone each took the first step toward the realization of just how large a task they had taken on.

Gaia had asked them to contact her when the members of the new committee had been formed and they did that now.

* * * * *

When the three of them materialized in the stable courtyard on Almeca, they congratulated each other on having made a safe passage and agreed to meet for the evening meal.

Sebastian then took his leave and hurried away to seek

audience with the Devi.

Gabe was eager to check on his grandmother and together he and Juno veered off in the direction of her temporary quarters.

As the two of them made their way through the streets, they became aware of the massive troop buildup that had occurred while they'd been away. The stable had been full of horses when they arrived in the courtyard and now as they moved through the streets and lanes they found themselves competing for space with large groups of out of state soldiers.

* * * * *

Once she had been notified that the election of the committee members had been completed, Gaia agreed to meet them. She had suggested the use of a small meeting room, normally used for minor discussion groups, for their first gathering. She told them she would meet them there in fifteen minutes.

She then spent ten minutes with Adon, discussing the parameters of her position as the chair. They were of the same mind on this and quickly agreed that in situations other than those where they specifically asked for her direct input, she should simply provide to the young group a full understanding of their responsibilities and take little or no part in the actual decisions they reached.

It was with this understanding that they parted company. Adon to spend one on one time with each of the advisors involved in the preparedness of the individual systems that would come in to play once the time had come for the shifting of the planets; Gaia to fulfill her obligations as the chair of the new policy making committee.

* * * * *

When Brother Sebastian arrived at the antechamber to her

office, he was informed that Aabha was in conference with an ambassador from a nearby state.

He took note of three additional ambassadors already seated in the waiting room and then quietly informed the Devi's secretary that he needed to see her as soon as possible. He was advised that she would squeeze him in next and asked him to take a seat.

CHAPTER NINE

- A Call to Arms -

Gaia had arranged to have a light meal sent to the small meeting room.

The others had already arrived and when she entered the room, she invited them to share a brief snack before commencing their discussions.

She immediately picked up on the prevailing mood in the room. There was a definite sense of unease among her young cohorts.

As they picked silently at their food, Gaia did her best to put all at ease, sending out a steady flow of warmth and confidence. While doing so, she took the time to individually weigh the prospective effectiveness of those the young Atlantians had voted to represent them.

She was pleased to see that both Venus and Jonah had been chosen. It was to them that leadership would eventually fall in the end and their presence in this room had been anticipated. As well, she could not fault the other two members who had been chosen. Both Enoch and Persephone had already demonstrated sound decision-making and the ability to hold firm to their beliefs.

All in all, she was very pleased with, and confident about what these four working as a team, could be expected to accomplish.

* * * * *

By the time they reached his grandmother's rooms, Gabe was functioning well enough, although he had not completely recovered from his last bout of invisibility.

He didn't feel particularly sick or anything, but just very tired. He figured that the adrenalin that he had been running on for the past twenty-four hours or so probably had a lot to do with his sense of listlessness.

They found the spirited old woman in good spirits and pleased to have them back safely.

Within minutes of their arrival she was bustling about preparing tea and chatting happily. She had the two of them laughing in no time and her upbeat mood went a long way to easting Gabes stress level.

By the time they were sitting down to steaming honeyed tea and freshly cooked biscuits, he felt himself releasing the tenseness that had filled him during and after the taking of the Atlantis.

When they said their goodbyes and left her, he was once again at peace, if still feeling somewhat drained, and very much in need of some rest and tranquility.

Juno's mind was oriented toward a slightly different purpose. She was looking to take advantage of the fact that Venus was, at least temporarily, out of the picture. She fully intended to use this period of separation from the Atlantians to do her best to solidify her relationship with Gabe.

Although she was reasonably sure she that she had the edge in that department, Venus had certainly been an ever-present complication in that regard to date.

That said, up to this point she felt that she had done pretty well in holding the majority of Gabe's interest and with Venus temporarily at least out of the picture she was resolved to make hay while Solar shined.

They now had a couple of hours of free time before they would meet Brother Sebastian for the evening meal and Juno decided to make the most of what one on one time was available to them.

War was coming; there was little doubt about that. Before the war started and all the horror of what that meant began, she wanted to make certain that Gabe had moved solidly past the simple state of perpetual lust, around which their current relationship had been built. It was past time for him to move on to an understanding of what a serious commitment to real love would mutually offer - the promise of a better, more secure future.

From this point on her main task would be to concentrate on weaning of Gabe from his current enjoyment at having two women competing for his attention.

She did not fault Gabe for the partaking fully of the enjoyment of that dual availability, any more than she faulted Venus for bedding with him. Both situations were quite understandable.

Gabe was, in every sense of the word, a male after all and all real men seemed to have to go through that stage. Additionally, Atlantian or not, Venues was a woman and very capable of appreciating how desirable a lover, the young Neanderthal could be.

She was no longer prepared to share him with any other woman. Gabe must be made to realize that he could have only one true love, and she fully intended to be that one. She therefore intended to demonstrate beyond doubt to him that, on her own, she was more than capable of meeting all his needs in that department.

Over the free time they now had together, she would see to it that Gabe was a very happy boy, as long as he recognized that there was a price to be paid to the provider of that happiness and that a real relationship was a two-way street.

Her short-term goal was simple enough - to have him fully committed to her alone by the time Venus next waltzed into the picture.

If he could see the value in that, she would give her all. If not, he was about to become a very frustrated boy.

* * * * *

Aabha stood before the large window overlooking the bay

and port below. She was attempting to take in everything Brother Sebastian was telling her and endeavouring to make some sense of it.

"...and where they live is quite futuristic. It is a massive complex, sterile to a great degree, but very well appointed. Clean, spotless even. Machines play a big part in their daily life. Little real labour is required of them and as you know, they each have a personal Almie.

"The mundane tasks on board this massive structure are taken care of by another form of Almie. These are under the control of a central artificial brain of some kind into which the Atlantians feed instruction to the little fellows. They call them worker Almies and only Solar knows how many of them they have up there. I saw only a few but understand that there are hundreds if not thousands of the little robotic creatures diligently working away around the clock..."

Aabha swiveled around to face him, her brow furrowed deeply and her lips pursed.

"Did you gain any understanding as to why the immediate return to this complex was so important to them? Why there was such urgency?"

Sebastian shrugged and settled back a little deeper into his chair as Aabha moved back across her office and sat down across from him at her desk.

"Well it is where they live after all and it is not hard to understand why they would want to return to it. However, I too was set to wonder why it seemed to be so urgent to accomplish it so quickly. The Atlantians usually appear so calm, so in control, but in this instance there almost seemed to be a shared anxiety over getting back up there.

"I kept my ears and eyes open you may be sure, but I was not able to ascertain exactly what made the retaking, of what they call the ship, so pressing.

"I can tell you that it was not just the wish to retake the ship per se - once they were back on board there was an absolute flurry of activity by all concerned, not characteristic of those individuals at all. No, I got the distinct impression that it was something other than that. That time was running out for them in some way - that something big had to be accomplished and there was little time left for them to achieve it."

Aabha nodded and let out a withheld breath.

"I think we see this in parallel lines.

"After giving it a good deal of thought it seems to me that the only reasonable answer to this quandary relates to the current conditions here in Olympos. I believe the Atlantians are our creators in some sense. For time immemorial, they have overseen our daily lives and visited with us, sent their children to our learning establishments, shepherded us through problems and concerns. It therefore seems understandable, that due to the impending war, they will be in a heightened state of concern.

"If I am right on this, it probably means that they are going to involve themselves in some manner, hopefully to the point of putting a stop to it."

She raised her hand as he opened his mouth to speak.

"I know...in the past, they have always made a point of refusing to step in when states disagree and raise arms against each other. But this time we are looking at a global war. That fact may well push them to act in this case.

"We have seen and heard about all these fantastic super weapons that are available to them. Surely they have the capability to intervene and bring this threat of full-scale war to an end.

"That being the case, perhaps we have less to worry about than we think."

Brother Sebastian shook his head slowly before speaking.

"You may well be right, but in my opinion, after spending what little time I did up there, I just don't believe that is what they are worried about.

"It is something worse.

"Much worse.

"I will be the first to admit that I have no idea what it is, but whatever it is, it's much more serious than we know and very probably, than we can possibly imagine."

Aabha paused to consider this suggestion and her shoulders sagged.

"Yes, it may just be wishful thinking on my part. We must find out what it is then. In Solar's Name we must find out and quickly."

Sebastian sighed deeply.

"I know.

"Jonah and Venus indicated they will be returning to Olympos in the near future. I am hoping that the relationships I have built up between us during our adventures working as a team will be strong enough to make them feel a moral obligation to enlighten me as to what has them all so upset. Such may not be the case, but at the moment it is all the hope I can offer."

The Devi raised her four hands slowly upward off her desk in unison in a stark reflection of her frustration and despair.

"Then, that being the case, my prayers will be for that relationship to bear fruit and serve to supply us with the knowledge we seek."

CHAPTER TEN

- *The Beginning of Enlightenment* -

Gaia waited until honeyed tea had been poured for all, and the five Almies in the room had moved to the walls and closed down to recharge, before she began to speak.

"As the chair of this committee I would like to begin by placing some parameters around how it will function. I will not, nor should you expect me to, take an active part in the discussions when it comes to decision taking. You will do that on your own. It has been agreed by the elders that this will be the case. You should also understand that they did not reach that conclusion without some pressure being put upon them. This concept is unprecedented and therefore agreement was only reached after a good deal of discussion"

Gaia allowed for a response and received the nervous laughter she had expected. She beamed around the table then picked up where she had left off.

"You should know that I refused to accept the position as chair of the committee unless that stipulation was acceptable to them.

"I also want you to recognize that I have every confidence in your abilities to reach sensible and proper decisions on your own. However, it must be said that it would be booth foolish and very unfair for we older Atlantians to expect you to do this, without first being given a full understanding of what you are about to take on.

"For example, none of you is even aware of the existence of the secure areas located within the core of Atlantis, let alone what marvels go on there. Nor do you have any idea of how long the planet Olympos has been in existence as a home for life forms, nor what that means in relation to the very serious responsibility that we the elders have given you.

"That is why I have accepted this chair. In order that I can offer to you a complete and factual overview of what we, and I might add, the entire Atlantian realm expects of you"

When she paused, Jonah piped up.

"Secure areas within the core of Atlantis? We..."

He glanced around at the others before continuing.

"...all of us here have grown up on the ship. We've been everywhere!"

Gaia laughed and silently picked up all but one of the small pile of printouts that were neatly stacked in front of her.

"No Jonah, you have not. You have been given the freedom to wander everywhere on the upper six deck levels, but none of you have ever been on the lower twenty-four nor in the massive enclosure at the very center of this ship. There, representatives of every type of life form we Atlantians have ever created multiply and thrive in small groups and have done so since the day this interplanetary ship took flight.

"But far more important is the fact that all of you realize that the planet Olympos has existed for very nearly four billion, six hundred thousand years and that despite our personal Atlantian longevity, few of those you now identify as elders were initially involved in the preliminary decisions that went into developing the life forces on this planet.

"That was done many, many generations ago. And for all those generations of Atlantians that evolved up to this point in time, the decedents of these original creators have done no more than act as caretakers, just as your progeny and their progeny and their progeny's decedents will do for billions of years. What you create now will therefore last long after you are dead. Even the smallest of choices and decisions you will have to make can have tremendous and unforeseen positive or negative ramifications over time.

"That should be a sobering thought to you and it will

hopefully instill in you the grave responsibility you now share. If you should get it wrong with your initial planning, many generations will pay the price for your mistakes. So please take the time to carefully analyse each and make as few missteps as you can."

As she spoke, Gaia picked up the printouts and stood up. As she did, *'Two'* immediately opened her eyes and began to move toward her but Gaia waved her back to the wall with a toss of her wrist and began to circle around the small table handing each of them a copy.

This done she sat back down and glanced down at the printout in front of her.

"Contained within this document is an overview. An overview only - mind. It will give you a very general idea of what you are about to take responsibility for.

"It is a fairly long document, as you can see, and to be honest with you it would be foolish of me to expect you to absorb everything it contains, here and now. That being said, within the next two weeks you will have to make a plethora of decisions, decisions that will then lead to the creation of an entirely new living world."

The four pairs of eyes facing her had grown in size considerably and Gaia laughed.

"There is no need to be unduly concerned. It is far from an impossible task you face. The groundwork for this entire process has been ongoing for some time, so you will not be starting from scratch here. But you will be offered many options to choose from when you make each of the necessary decisions that will be needed to go forward, and you will have a very short timeframe in which to accomplish this task.

"For today, I would like you to return to your individual apartments and read through the briefing notes I have provided for you. I would then like you to take this evening's meal on your own, the four of you only, and please do this within the privacy of one of your own personal living areas so that you may have complete seclusion. There you can openly and freely discuss the contents of the document, air your concerns, ask for support in understanding the contents - whatever is necessary for you all to come to our first full meeting here at eight in the morning.

"At that time, I will act as a sounding board, answer any questions that may have arisen during your discussions and then take you, as a group, on a tour of the chambers that make up the entire bottom twenty-four deck levels of Atlantis. I do this, in order that you will all fully understand the importance of what you are about to be privileged to undertake.

"If you have any questions now before we break up, please feel free to ask. I know it is a lot to take in and, let me be honest with you; you will really still have no idea of the scope of the job after reading the documents I have given you. But once you have accomplished your task and have the leisure to look back on the wonder of it, I promise that each of you will firmly and unquestionably believe that it was worth every ounce of effort you gave.

"I expect that I will have to do a lot of explaining over the next couple of days, but after that I will only offer information when you request it of me and from then on, it is my intention to do a great deal of listening rather than instructing. "

Staring at the stack of paper in front of them, the four young Atlantians were a little overwhelmed and humbled by what seemed to be expected of them.

Gaia could feel their unease and with it; she sensed the shaken aura of confidence that had filled the room earlier, before she had begun to speak. She immediately unleashed a very strong flow of warmth and understanding to each and smiled to demonstrate her own confidence in their ability to do what was being asked of them.

All four were struggling to assimilate what they had been told and there were no questions.

* * * * *

As they had walked together companionably, Juno intentionally brushed against Gabe from time to time. On each occasion his skin tingled where it had been touched. Tired and preoccupied, his thoughts had been wandering listlessly through the corridors of his mind as they moved, but now, when her swinging arm grazed his side lightly, he began to become more keenly aware of her physical presence beside him.

He glanced at her out of the corner of his eye, drinking in her beauty and his nostrils filled with the delectable scent of her. Uniquely Juno, gently suffused by the soft sensuous perfume that she used sparingly but effectively.

It occurred to him that he had not bedded her for what seemed to him like a very long time. Not surprisingly, that realization took precedence in his previously rambling mind and his awareness of events occurring around him as they walked paled in comparison.

It occurred to him that the dinner engagement with Brother Sebastian was a least a couple of hours away and as far as he was aware, he and Juno had no other commitments during that time.

What was to prevent them from enjoying some personal time together?

With this thought in mind, Gabe found himself reflecting back to the last time they had slipped between the sheets. A mental and much animated picture of that last tryst formed and as an active remembrance of the scene took shape in his mind, he smiled broadly as he relived and savored it.

A very interesting prospect of how the two of them might spend the unencumbered time before dinner occurred to him and any thoughts of his previous need to seek quiet and tranquility over the next two hours were swiftly swept away.

By the time he and Juno had reached their own quarters Gabe was feeling very much better.

Alas, his much-anticipated tryst was not to be.

CHAPTER ELEVEN

- Frustration -

Brother Sebastian had arrived early and already secured a small table in the far end of the cafeteria. He'd been watching the main door and stood and waved as Juno and Gabe entered.

As they spotted him and started toward him, Sebastian recognized that all was not well between his two friends. Something had had obviously transpired between them since he'd seen them last.

He briefly watched them moving across the room, doing his best to ascertain what might have arisen between them to cause their current state of unease, then sat back down and did his best to keep his curiosity to himself.

Juno, smiling and seemingly contented enough, led the way, with the handsome Neanderthal, who looked frankly disillusioned, following listlessly in her wake.

Whatever it was that was amiss between the two of them, Sebastian was pretty sure Juno was not the one suffering any serious concern. Gabriel, on the other hand looked like his whole world had suddenly and unexpectedly been turned upside down.

* * * * *

In view of the fact that Jonah's apartments normally looked like a disaster area, despite Sal's attempts to keep it in good order, it was agreed between the two of them that it would be Venus who would host the evening meal for the four young Atlantians.

Enoch and Persephone, with their two Almies in tow,

arrived together and as Venus welcomed them, she sensed that their relationship had advanced to a new stage. While the two of them had obviously been attracted to each other in the past, there appeared to be a new and much stronger aura of warmth surrounding them now.

Venus liked them both very much and she was pleased to note this change.

The three of them had no more than been seated in the small greeting area when there was a sharp knock on the door and Jonah, followed by Sal, let themselves in.

All three of them had brought their briefing notes with them and once they had set their Almies to the preparation of the meal, exclamations and concerns over the contents of the document were soon being exchanged among therm.

It became apparent that this initial round of excited observations was more a venting process than an indication of any major trepidation. If anything, all concerned were notably energised at what they had been able to understand from the handouts Gaia had earlier provided for them - anything but briefly daunted by the immensity of the task they had been given and eager to begin the challenging process and forge ahead.

* * * * *

Juno, with what appeared to Sabastian to be a pronounced attempt at appearing her routine happy outgoing self, dominated the conversation while they ate. The Brother did notice however that her effervescence lacked its normal level of sincerity and seemed to be intentionally engineered to make all seem as it should be.

Gabe came across as preoccupied and ill at ease. The Neanderthal had been quiet, offering little comment and even then, only when a direct question was asked of him. And on those rare occasions, the response more often than not, was a half-hearted nod or a shrug.

When they had finished eating, Juno gathered up the dishes from the table and headed over to the serving area to place them into the bins for washing. The second she was out of hearing range Gabe spoke.

"Females! The more you think you understand them the less you do."

Sebastian bit his lip to prevent a smile and did his best to appear surprised at the comment.

"You and Juno have a disagreement?"

Gabe shrugged.

"If we did, I don't know what in Solar it was. Everything seemed to be going along great and then suddenly she tells me that she thinks we should slow things down a little. Says she needs some time to think. Apparently I have been abusing our relationship, that while wanting each other is normal and a wonderful part of any liaison, true and meaningful shared love is necessary to achieve an enduring relationship."

Sebastian let out a deep sigh and nodded.

"Well she's very likely right. I may not have a great deal of expertise in that area, but it seems to me that any long term relationship has to be based on a mutual love of one another."

Gabe, who had been expecting support for his positon from the good brother, bristled and shrugged.

"Well I told her I loved her and all that stuff, but she still wouldn't…"

The Neanderthal blushed.'

"…well you know."

Try as he might, Sabastian couldn't repress a small smile before he responded.

"Ah…yes, I see."

"She says she wants me to think overnight about what our future holds and then we will have a further discussion over breakfast in the morning. I have no clue what she expects of me - I just want things to go back to how they were before she started in on this foolishness."

Gabe spotted Juno returning to the table with a tray holding three honey teas. He raised his finger to his lips to silence Sebastian as he whispered.

"If you have the time, I would like to meet you in your rooms in an hour. I don't understand what has suddenly come over Juno and could use the benefit of your experience to help me to sort this whole thing out."

"Of course. I will be glad to give you whatever advice I can. I will be waiting for you."

* * * * *

At the end of a far-ranging discussion, it was Enoch who was chosen by the others to elucidate in simple terms, a recap of the facts offered by the briefing notes.

"We Atlantians have the responsibility of introducing life to appropriate planets in our assigned specific solar systems.

In the case of ours, cyclically over time, the planet where Olympos is now positioned away from Solar begins to shift outward, away from Solar and is then replaced by the second, which is subsequently supplanted by the first, which is then itself supplanted by a newly formed planet.

This process takes billions of years.

Within roughly two weeks, the planet we know as Olympos will be slowly pushed out if it's orbit in our solar system. It will be propelled slowly but steadily away from Solar.

The atmosphere on the planet will become weaker during this ongoing process. In simple terms, this will result in less oxygen being generated as the plants begin to die. Olympos will then suffer droughts and, over time the death of all living things.

In the end, everything on the entire surface of Olympos will turn to lifeless dust.

This process is inevitable and nothing can be done to prevent it or slow it down.

During this progression, what has been the second planet from Solar will then take up the position previously held by Olympos and will also take up what has previously been that planet's current orbit.

Our sole purpose for being in this solar system is to prepare this usurping planet to receive life, determine what that new life will consist of and then to manage and oversee the development of what we have created.

Once this new planet has reached and taken up the orbit currently held by Olympos as both move further away from Solar, it will begin the cooling process. Billions of years will then pass before atmosphere and water, the necessities of life, form.

Within the core of our ship is a large area where life forms of all types have been created over time. While aboard Atlantis these, like us, do not age. Worker Almies daily tend to the care and feeding of all that is confined there.

From this assortment, we will be asked to choose the specific species that we want to place on the new planet, once it is ready to receive and support lifeforms.

In relation to humanoid lifeforms, we are to choose approximately one hundred each of the specific groups from those on offer and which we decide are suitable for transfer to the new planet. Fifty of each gender will be placed on the planet and over time, these will multiply and move in groups until they are eventually spread over the entire planet.

We are also to choose the plants we want and the animals with which we wish to populate the planet.

The plantings will be done en mass and in great numbers. The animal life to be limited initially to one hundred of each species and they too will be selected on equal terms when it comes to gender.

Over the long term, our job as Atlantians is to manage the development of what we have created. There are no strict guidelines as to how we organize this process. However, in a general sense it is suggested that the less intrusive we are, the more likely it is that those inhabiting the planet will evolve to self-govern, learning from their own successes and failures."

Heads nodded all round.

* * * * *

Juno appeared pleasant but somewhat distant as she allowed Gabe to escort her to her door.

He was still confused and feeling hurt by her recent behavior toward him and he was being very careful not to somehow, inadvertently, make matters worse.

As she had obliquely indicated earlier, Juno, holding to her decision that he should sleep on what she had imparted and that they would discuss the matter further over breakfast, made no offer to invite him inside.

Gabe was petrified over the thought of that exchange and knew he was not going to get any sleep that night due to the trepidation he felt over coming up with some sort of response for her - one that would make things all better again.

At this point in time, he was satisfied to accomplish nothing more than to part from her on good terms and then seek Brother Sebastian's help in determining how he was going to deal with her change in attitude come the morning.

When she tilted her head up to him he lowered his and he was not particularly surprised when he received nothing more than a light brush of her lips across his cheek instead of what had become the norm between them, that being a passionate meeting of their mutually hungry mouths.

Under the circumstances, it was enough and he immediately stepped back as she opened her door and went inside leaving him in the hallway.

He crossed to his own rooms where he spent the next half hour pacing and looking at the clock.

* * * * *

Sebastian stood back to allow Gabe inside and with a wave of his hand indicated the bottle and two tankards that rested on the small table beside his bed.

"I thought you could probably use a small libation before

we discussed your problem my son."

Gabe was in full agreement with the suggestion and readily accepted one of the tankards after the brother had closed the door and crossed over to pour out hefty helpings of the mellow, yellow intoxicant that was favoured by the majority of Almecans.

CHAPTER TWELVE

- A Wee Drop of Courage -

Gaia found the four young Atlantians already ensconced within the small meeting room when she arrived. The Almies were at rest against the walls.

The group was actively involved in a discussion as she entered but paused to welcome her before continuing.

It was obvious that the others had arrived significantly early, as the remains of a working breakfast were apparent on a sideboard.

A large pot of what Gaia guessed was honeyed tea stood in the center of the circular table and each had a mug of steaming liquid in front of them. A fifth mug had been placed where she sat and unasked, *'Two'* immediately picked it up and filled her mistress's mug half full of the sweet concoction.

As Gia moved to take her seat at the head of the table, placing her copy of the briefing document in front of her, her Almie pushed her chair in before moving to the wall behind her. Gaia shifted slightly to a more comfortable positon and then smiled.

"Please continue. This is your committee and from this point on, I'm just here to answer any questions you may have. I would ask you to keep this first real meeting as relatively brief as possible, as we will have to take our tour of the secured areas at the core sometime today and due to its complexity it will take some time for us to assimilate all that entails. I note that you've had an early start and that bodes well for the task ahead."

Venus, Enoch and Persephone all shifted their gaze to

Jonah and he took in deep breath before speaking.

"We started early primarily because after spending most of the evening going over the briefing document a couple of questions arose that we felt had to be dealt with before we proceeded with any of the actual planning stages.

"There was nothing in the document to give us any direction on these two points and we reached the decision that we would need to pose the two problems to you and ask if what we wish to do is possible or not."

All four of them now turned their attention to Gaia. She nodded her understanding before responding.

"There are few if any absolutes as to how you go about accomplishing the undertaking you have been assigned. However, I would be pleased to provide guidance if needed. What are these two concerns that you want out of the way before we procced?"

Adon shifted a little uncomfortably.

"Are we restricted to selecting all the lifeforms we wish to use to inhabit the new planet from those that will be on offer in the secure areas we will tour today, or can we choose at least some of them from those that currently live on Olympos?

"We ask this in reference to the Humanoid life forms not the plant life.

"Additionally, are we empowered to make changes in those who will hold the specific advisory positions we put into place for the new planet?"

Gaia raised her mug, took an experimental sip and finding it cool enough, further indulged in a mouthful before she responded.

"In regard to the first matter, may I assume that you wish to save some of your intimate contacts from Olympos, by including them in the numbers that you use to inhabit the new planet? While I understand why you might want to do this, I must warn you that to do so would mean that these people, if not adjusted, would naturally take their environmental history of the old planet with them to the new planet and, inherent in that are a great number of concerns.

"Each new planet must be allowed to evolve on its own and at its own pace. Historically we Atlantians have always been very careful about how rapidly we allowed scientific discoveries to be made over the process of development among the Humanoid life forms. A prime example of a failure to do this appropriately is apparent on Olympos today, a world going to war, thanks to Marduke's insane provision of advanced weaponry, thereby creating a military imbalance.

"Before you ask, we have the capability to brainwash or remove portions of the memories from those you may choose to select from Olympos, so what you suggest is not out of the realm of possibility. However, this type of procedure was not created, nor intended, to completely remove the massive recall that those who have already experienced life on a previous planet would have built up. Its effectiveness in blanking memories accrued under those conditions has never been attempted due to the complexity involved. The outcome would therefore be at the very least unpredictable.

"If you should decide to do this despite the risk, you may do so, of course. But, if that is to be the case, I would very strongly recommend that you take a very small number and only those who you feel you can trust implicitly not to use any historical knowledge learned on Olympos that might inadvertently carry over to the new world, to their advantage over others."

What had been a frown on Venus's face slipped away and was instantly been replaced with a beaming smile. Gaia was pleased but gave no indication of the fact as she continued.

"In answer to the second question, I would require some additional information before I am able to give an informed response. There is some past precedent for what you suggest. However, it has never been done without a very good reason and I would be staunchly advising against doing it on any large scale, as that would be a definite harbinger of disaster.

"There is good reason that we chose to organize these positions over a long period of time. We do so in order to ensure that those who take up these positions are fully expert in their chosen field. Exactly how many of the current advisors would you want to replace?"

Jonah responded.

"Well, only two actually. And we would not be replacing people exactly, just swapping positons between two of us who now sit at this table.

"Both Enoch and I feel that we should switch advisory posts, he to take mine and I, his. Quite frankly, I don't want to take on Father's responsibilities over time and have already found that I am more inclined toward action than planning, while Enoch is a far better choice for that advisory position and he would have plenty of time to take instruction from Father over the next centuries, while the new planet is evolving.

"We have all discussed this idea a length and given up a good deal of sleep in the process and we are all in agreement about making this particular change."

An eerie silence filled the room.

Gaia received expectant expressions from all four of the young Atlantians.

She sensed that this was a trial balloon being floated and aimed at reaching a firm view on how much real control the committee was to have in the undertaking they had taken up.

She knew that, generally speaking, they were pleased with the resolution of the first point, but were on tenterhooks awaiting her response on the second.

"If you are both in agreement as to the change and are sure that you will have sufficient time to learn the specific intricacies of each other's areas of expertise prior to the beginning of the natural progression of the races placed on the new planet I can see no reason why you should not make this adjustment. In the end it would mean that each of you will have the benefit of both perspectives and that can only be a positive development.

* * * * *

As the first beams of morning light entered into his room, Gabe woke with a start.

He immediately raised his hand to shield his eyes from the brightness and just as instantly regretted the rapid movement. His mouth dry and his head pounding, he swore and grimaced.

It took him a few moments to clear his head enough to seek an explanation for his condition and as the memory of the night of drinking came into focus, he groaned and carefully, very carefully, raised his upper body and swung his legs out from under the covers until he was in a sitting position.

The resulting elevation of his head only compounded the thudding drumbeat centered in his temples and he blindly fumbled around with his left hand in search of the glass of water that he normally kept beside his bed.

In his eagerness to sooth his parched throat and with eyes still tightly closed against Solar-beams, he groped out in the general direction of where the glass usually was.

After a little searching, he managed to find it, but his hand was shaking so violently that instead of being able to grasp it firmly, he inadvertently pulled it off the edge and it dropped directly into his lap.

The tepid contents emptied out over his crotch and give the edge of the bed a thorough soaking.

Both the resulting decibel level and the number the number of choices available in his repertoire of explicit expletives, instantly reached a new high.

As he shakily lurched to his feet and shook the water off, his pain-muffled brain struggled to understand how he had come to this lamentable state of affairs.

Slowly, a hazy memory of the previous hours managed to push through the fumes and register and with it a commitment.

Juno! Breakfast!

He raised his bloodshot eyes to the clock on the wall.

Only eight...praise Solar, he had an hour to get himself into presentable shape.

It was no wonder he felt so rotten.

If his muddled memory served, he'd only been in bed for about an hour and a half. Additionally, at that time he had been unable to make it back under his own steam. He'd required Brother Sebastian's assistance to make his way back to the apartment even at that late hour.

But there was some hope. He could vaguely remember what had taken place.

Right. Despite the fog of consumed spirits, they had come to agreement on a plan of action as to how he might deal with his problem with Juno.

Now what was it? Oh yes! Sebastian had left him a potion to consume when he woke up. Something to ease the effects of the alcoholic intake, he'd said.

Yes, there it was on the table.

Praise Solar!

Now if he could only remember what conclusion it was that he and Sebastian had decided might serve to bring Juno around.

He looked at the clock again.

Less than an hour...

CHAPTER THIRTEEN

- Revelation -

Gaia led the committee members, with their trailing Almies, down to the main control room of the huge ship where they found Adon waiting for them. He looked up from one of the computer data entry ports and smiled.

"Ah, here you are. I am almost ready for you; just give me a second to bring the overview up on the large screen"

Gaia pointed to seating facing the massive screen, which covered almost one entire wall. As they sat, she nodded over at her life partner and he entered a code into the keyboard in front of him.

The screen, which currently reflected an aerial rendition of Olympos, flickered slightly and was replaced with a birds-eye view of the massive cavern that made up the core of the interstellar starship Atlantis.

Gaia began her commentary.

"What you are seeing now is an overview of the secure facilities I referred to earlier. As you can see, the chamber is dived into many individual units, each of which is used for a specific purpose. Within each of these are additional compartments, which are individually responsible for the various species native to each of the units.

"To give you an idea of the size of the space you are seeing up on the map; it takes up almost a half of the entire space available below the surface of Atlantis. It will be hard for you to imagine exactly how large an area we will begin touring shortly. We will start by looking at the screen, but be warned that it will take us a good day to physically observe all that goes on there, even with the use of motorized transport.

"You are very privileged to be allowed to do this. Under normal circumstances, no Atlantian is allowed to enter this controlled environment.

"There are two main reasons for this. Firstly, the entire area is administered by specially trained and programmed worker Almies who have been carrying out their duties without interruption since this interstellar craft first left the Atlantian home solar system and took up its mission of responsibility in our current one. Any instructions that are deemed required to be delivered to these workers are passed on through the ship's main computer frame, which oversees the automated workers below.

"Secondly, there is a concern that the sight of any living being, by the life forms existing within the area might cause unease in some of those forms, all of whom have only ever seen, or had to relate to, nothing but their own kind. The Almies who work there possess internal night vision ability and never expose themselves to the life forms, at least not while they are in a conscious state and then only in emergencies.

"In my lifetime, no occasion has ever arisen when it has been necessary for an Atlantian to enter these spaces.

"If you had been given previous knowledge of what goes on here, as all Elders have been over time, it would not be necessary for you to go there now. Your learning curve will of necessity have to be short and therefore we have decided to allow you entry, but I will be with you and in direct contact with the computer the entire time to ensure that no accidental sighting is made by those members of the life forms in residence occurs.

"Additionally, we will be doing it in the dark and you will be given night googles to allow you to observe without being seen in return.

"For the occupants, who are used to a routine of living with both day and night, cyclically as occurs on any life-supporting planet, there will be nothing unusual in the darkness and for this occasion we have every intention of seeing to it that they will notice no change in their day to day lives. We have the capability to zoom in on all areas and we will do that after I answer any primary queries you may have.

"Now, if you have any questions, feel free to ask and if not we will get started with this visual overfly as we have a great deal to see and little time to accomplish it.

"Once we have finished doing that I will ask you all to go and get whatever rest you can and then meet me back down here in eight hours' time. We will then begin the actual hands-on physical inspection of the facilities so you are able to get a better idea of what species you will have to choose from.

* * * * *

It took until ten to eight for a bedraggled Gabriel to finally track down Brother Sebastian who was awaiting a meeting with the Devi.

Sebastian took one look at him and shook his head.

"My Solar, man, you look like something a shapeshifter dragged in. What are you doing here? I thought you were to meet with Juno for breakfast this morning."

Gabe raised his arms in frustrated subjugation.

"I forgot what the plan was! What did we decide? For the life of me I can't remember."

Try as he might, Sebastian could not hold back a smile and as it formed on his face Gabe flushed and he snapped back.

"There is nothing funny about this; my whole future may depend upon it."

Sebastian forced the smile off his face and reached out to take both the young Neanderthal's shoulders and gripped them firmly.

"Yes of course, it is no laughing matter. Please forgive me. It's just that you look so disheveled and very much like death warmed over. Come my son, let's just step out into the hall for some privacy and I will refresh your memory as to what course of action we had decided on, which if memory serves, occurred just before dawn."

* * * * *

Venus was both relieved and excited as the four young committee members left the large central control room.

The prospect of there being a possibility to save their team members from the demise of Olympos and instead to offer them a chance at being part of the creation of a new world had pushed her adrenalin levels high. They had no more than left the room when she took Jonah's arm and asked to speak with him privately.

Jonah who had no other thought in his mind than that of getting some much needed sleep in preparation for their upcoming all-night session to learn the secrets of the wondrous facilities located deep within the core of Atlantis, was distinctly unimpressed at the though of any further discussion.

He wanted his bed.

Knowing Venus as he did however, he accepted the fact that she would not be put off and he let out a sigh of displeasure and nodded. After the two of them had said their goodbyes to Enoch and Persephone, they stood silently in the hallway until the other committee members had rounded the corner at the end of the passageway leaving him and Venus alone.

Jonah was frowning deeply and when she looked over at him, she gave him a dismissive look and started right in.

"We have to find time to drop down to Almeca and let the others know the whole story about what is going to happen to Olympos. Once they know what is going to happen we can offer them sanctuary with us and a place on the new planet."

Jonah, who had been half expecting this suggestion, shook his head.

"Look Sis, I don't know about you, but I for one think that

both of us have other priorities at the moment. Anyway, we would have to discuss all this with Enoch and Persephone before we did anything like that and then run the specifics, things like exactly who we chose and why, by Mother as well.

"We have too much on our plates to do it now. It will just have to wait until we have more time."

Venus was having none of it. Not that he'd seriously expected she would.

Venus placed her hands on her hips and squared off with him.

"You promised to help. You did. And after all they did for us, my Solar, how can you be so cruel and cold about this."

Jonah's shoulders sagged and then he sucked in a deep breath and smiled down at her."

"All right little sister, as per usual, you win. I gather you want to do it this minute. I don't suppose there is any possibility that we might manage to grab just a couple of hours sleep and then..."

Venus features softened instantly and she promptly popped up onto her tiptoes and gave him a little peck on his cheek.

"I think it best we do it now and sleep later. I couldn't possibly sleep anyway, not until this is done and out of the way."

He nodded.

"I had a feeling that would be the case."

Sal and Duanna were standing a short distance away from their master and mistress while this conversation unfolded.

Duanna received a short silent message from Sal.

"I see no good coming from this."

CHAPTER FOURTEEN

- Woes and Wonders -

As Gabe, tray in hand, joined Juno, who was already seated in the cafeteria at a secluded table, he was still struggling with his foggy mind as he rehearsed for the hundredth time exactly how he was going to phrase his position to her.

A look of self-satisfaction filled her features as she took note of his disheveled condition.

He had very obviously taken her earlier comments to heart and that boded well for her chances to set the rules for their future relationship.

Her first comment to him was delivered with a hefty degree of contentment.

"Heavens, you look like the wrath of Solar has been delivered upon you. You poor thing,"

Any solidly formed thoughts as to how he wanted the session to go drifted to the back of Gabe's mind and he was momentarily at a loss for words.

Was she making fun of him, attempting to tease and arouse him with her feminine wiles or was she sincerely concerned over his wellbeing?

Juno's features were now filled with what appeared to Gabe as honest anxiety for his welfare and he immediately found he was chastising himself for even considering that she might be making fun of him.

Picking up on that fact, Juno instantly moved to strengthen that premise.

"You look as though you got absolutely no sleep."

She placed one hand on his.

"Has something terrible happened? What is it? What's wrong?"

As Gabe responded to the warmth of her touch, he was completely flummoxed.

"I…um, was just doing a lot of thinking. I also might have had a little too much to drink as well and I…um, just couldn't seem to sleep."

Her hand tightened on his.

"Poor baby. Why don't you tell me all about it?"

An expression of confusion flooded across Gabe's features.

What the hell?

The day before she had made it clear to him that this breakfast meeting would be for the sole purpose of sorting out her concerns over the basis of their relationship and their future together and now she was all worried about how he was feeling and his lack of sleep?

Women! What on Olympos was she thinking? What was going on in the devious female brain? He was of two minds. Instead of having the conversation that he had so carefully planned, she had turned all warm and cuddly. It was throwing him offside. She had been so standoffish last night and now this. In response, he was acting like some juvenile and had instantly melted and was completely under her spell.

This was not going the way he'd planned at all. Firstly, he was supposed to be giving her the impression that he had given the whole problem a good deal of mature thought and secondly, he was supposed to be taking the lead role in the entire discussion. That was what Sebastian had strongly recommended as necessary. He was to deal with her from a position of combined strength and sincerity.

He took deep breath and gently but firmly pulled his hand from her grasp. He had to get it all out while he could still remember it.

"Look Juno. I didn't get much sleep last night because I was doing what you asked me to. I was giving serious thought to our future together and what you had said about all the lust versus love stuff and all that…"

Keep it short and to the point Sebastian had counselled. Right.

He straightened up in his chair and stared directly into her eyes as he spoke. It came out rather more forcefully and louder than he had intended but he wasn't about to change step and risk forgetting something or letting her take the lead away from him.

"…and I came to the conclusion that you were absolutely correct. I have been selfishly and blissfully floating along and unfairly taking for granted just how wonderful the physical part of our relationship was. Without doubt, despite that fact that I do love you very deeply, I agree with you. Therefore, I have decided that I will immediately forgo any further enjoyment of that wonder and determinedly staunch any future such lustful thoughts about you.

"As I understand it, what you wished for was for us to experience a period of a deeply loving, but physically platonic bonding, over a period of time to ensure that the basis for our relationship was more than just physical. A period of time during which we could both reflect upon on what a true loving affiliation should be based."

Sebastian's words sounded stilted to him as he began to repeat them.

"So, when it comes to our relationship, I'm determined to be celibate until I have fully matured and done away with the overpowering and all-encompassing desire I have to make passionate love to you, which is pretty much all the time, at least until such time as we officially become life-partners"

He managed to get them all out before she could interrupt. He was very thankful for that but now that it was done he had no doubt in his own mind that at all that the brother's words had sounded very foreign, even to him and he couldn't help but wonder if Juno might just pick up on their origin.

He'd firmly held her gaze throughout his little speech and now that it was done, he continued to do so, doing his best to gauge her reaction.

Gauging female reactions to things had never been something that he'd ever been very good at and this case was no exception to that general rule. Despite trying his best, he really had no idea what she was thinking.

If anything, she just appeared dumbfounded to him.

He sat silently, painfully awaiting her response.

Gobsmacked.

Juno, who had just lifted her cup to hear mouth to drink, choked on it and when the contents went down the wrong way, she snorted several times.

What in Solar's name was he going on about?

Celibate?

When it comes to our relationship. Celibate!

What about other relationships - celibate period, or just celibate with me. Where in Solar's name had that idea come from? Had he suddenly turned into a besotted idiot?

This was definitely not going according to plan.

No.

It was not going to her plan at all.

For several seconds Gabe wavered in his assessment as to exactly how the little speech had gone over. But then he realized that Juno's reaction appeared to be just what Sebastian had predicted it would be.

'She will be so impressed that she will be at a loss for words.'

Juno definitely appeared to be speechless. Now if the remainder of the good brother's prophesies came true - all would indeed be well again in his world.

Time would tell.

He reached out and took her hand and delivered the final portion of the carefully rehearsed phrases.

"I'm so glad you're pleased with my decision. "

* * * * *

Venus, Jonah and their Almies arrived in the stable court-yard and quickly made their way to the building where Gabe and Juno had their apartments. Before they had transported, Jonah had asked for and received her promise not to say anything about the situation until everyone was together. Venus had also agreed to allow him to take the lead in explaining to the others what was on offer.

Coming from different directions, the four of them chanced to meet at the entrance of the building and then together, they went in search of Brother Sebastian.

Eager to break the news to them, Venus had been bubbling with anticipation and talking a blue streak to Gabe and Juno on the way over. Subsequently, Jonah had been doing his best to offer a calming presence until they had found Sebastian, who was in his rooms.

In short order all had found seating within the brother's compact salon and the two little Almies were at rest against the far wall. Sebastian offered refreshment and he and Juno briefly left the others in order to prepare a large pot of honeyed tea.

While they waited, Jonah, sitting directly across from his sister, held her gaze firmly, willing her to hold her peace and keep her part of the bargain.

When Sebastian and Juno returned with a tray and Juno had passed out steaming mugs, Jonah cleared his throat and began to speak.

"Venus and I have something to tell you, but before we do I have to ask that all of you give me your word that what I am about to tell you will be kept secret among us and no word of it will leak out to any of the other inhabitants on Olympos. "

Sebastian's ears perked up. It sounded to him like they were about to be told what it was that had all the Atlantians so worked up.

"That sounds rather ominous. What could be so important to us but have to remain secret to the rest who share this world?"

Venus couldn't resist getting into the conversation.

"This information is very important. It could save your

lives and offer you a wonderful new future."

Jonah let out a deep sigh.

"Please bear with me.

"What Venus says is correct.

"We are about to offer you a way to save yourselves from a fate worse than anything you could possibly imagine. But before we can do that, we must have your solemn oath that no word of what we tell you ever leaves this room.

"If it will help you to agree to do that, I can tell you that each of you will have the option to reject our offer once you hear what it entails, if that is your wish. But, whether you decide to accept our offer of not, before I reveal it to you, you must give us your assurance that no knowledge of what we tell you, will become general knowledge among those on Olympos."

Gabe and Juno exchanged looks and both responded, Juno first.

"I agree."

"Me too."

Venus nodded eagerly and both she and Jonah turned to face Brother Sebastian.

He met their gaze and slowly shook his head.

"Regrettably I am not in a position to make such a promise despite the fact that I accept your warning that this is a matter of great importance and that it may cost me my life if I refuse to do what you ask.

"I thank you for your concern over my wellbeing, but I have a sworn fealty and duty to the Devi and cannot agree to withholding information from her under any circumstances."

Venus turned to Jonah and implored him.

"One more. Just the Devi. And, it is only right after all she did for us."

Jonah shifted his gaze back to Sebastian.

"If the Devi was included in our offer…do you think that she would be prepared to give Venus and I the assurance that she would not share the information with others?"

Sebastian paused to consider.

"I can not speak for her of course, but if you are open to such a possibility, I could ask her if she might agree to such a proposition."

Time was of the essence for both Venus and Jonah and they made that clear.

Subsequently a private working luncheon for their party with the Devi, slated for an hour hence, was hastily arranged.

CHAPTER FIFTEEN

- *Reprieve Offered* -

Adon and Gaia shared an early brunch before she got some rest in preparation for the nightlong vigil with the committee in the secured area of the starship.

Gaia shared the outcome of the earlier meeting as they ate.

Adon listened without comment until she'd finished and then thought for a few seconds before offering his observations of what had transpired.

"Well, I'd have to say that the concept of Jonah and Enoch switching advisor roles initially surprised me.

"But, when you take their individual characters into consideration, I will admit that there is a reasonable argument in it. Jonah is far more a man of action and Enoch seems to have the benefit of sober second thought before he acts. In many ways it is a better fit for each of them."

Gaia smiled.

"Yes, they were all in agreement to do so and as I told them, there is precedent for such changes in responsibility."

Adon nodded his agreement with the suggestion and then shook his head slowly.

"This other thing, the transferring of specimens from the old planet to the new - that seems to be contrary to anything that has ever been done before."

Gaia placed her teacup down and pursed her lips.

"Yes, I agree and I advised them of that as well.

"Inherent in doing so is a risk that the transferred lifeforms, despite steps taken to prevent it, will take with them knowledge that is far advanced from the norm. I specifically advised them of that. And suggested they reconsider.

"However, since then, I have had time to think more deeply on it and although I still have my doubts about the idea, I've had to admit that some good things could come from such an arrangement.

"Those of this ilk placed on the new planet would bring with them some experienced leadership ability from the beginning, which has not been the case in the past. That just might be a positive development over past situations and serve to counterbalance any negative carryover. "

Adon settled back into his chair and both *'One'* and *'Two'* moved in to clear away the dishes as he responded.

"Possibly. Exactly how many are they wanting to transfer?"

"I believe just the group that was involved with them in the retaking of the ship."

Adon nodded.

"Three then.?"

"Well in the case of the young Neanderthal and the human girl, I suppose it could be argued that they are basically relatively simple specimens and therefore hardly in possession of, what could be considered, advanced information. They both appear to be of good character and physically hearty.

"The brother is somewhat older but he too seems to be in very good health and in excellent physical condition.

"Perhaps just the three specimens, out of the two hundred humanoid species that will be placed on the planet, would be of a sufficiently low risk to allow such a concept.

"There are complications with this idea of course.

"We would have to bring them up to the ship. If we do that, we certainly can't have them wandering about freely among us. And to safely do so, we would have to place them in an isolated enclosure within the secure holding area until the planet was ready for life forms.

"Once aboard they would not age, but I have to wonder in view of their concept of time, at how well they would endure the abject boredom of such an arrangement."

Gaia smiled.

"We think very much alike.

"I gave that concern a great deal of thought too, and I agree with you. I don't think they would do well reliving their daily lives over and over again for such an extended amount of time.

"In answer to that specific problem, if the committee members are determined to go ahead with this idea, I believe it would only be sensible for their wellbeing and ours, that those chosen should be placed into some form of isolation until such time as the planet is ready to support lifeforms."

Adon raised his arms and shrugged.

"The only sensible course to take. However, if I were in their shoes I'm not sure I would agree to it. They would have to possess a great deal of trust in us to agree to such a concept."

Gaia frowned.

"Yes, I completely agree. I believe we must make it quite clear to the committee that it is the only way such a suggestion will be allowed.

"Having said that, I have to point out that the three of them have certainly been prepared to trust Jonah and Venus with their lives on several occasions already and when faced with the alternative of dying on Olympos, perhaps they will find the idea at least cautiously acceptable."

* * * * *

They met in the small dining room adjoining the Devi's apartments.

Brother Sebastian had spoken briefly to Aabha before the others joined them.

Once they were seated and had been served, the brothers in attendance left them alone in the room. Aabha then spoke.

"Brother Sebastian tells me that you have some information to share that may save us from some horrific fate that is imminent here on Olympos and that you require from us a solemn declaration that we will not share this information with anyone outside this room, before you are able to make it available to us. What you ask is very hard for me, not personally but in my position as Devi of the Faith.

"However, for the sake of all of us and because I do have a responsibly to shepherd the Belief's flock and this knowledge may make it easier for me to do so, I am willing give you this personal solemn pledge. But I will only do so if you recognize that, while I will not share this information, I may well act upon it in some form to save others of the Faith."

Venus glanced briefly at Jonah and then responded.

"As you will soon realize, there is nothing that you will be able to do in relation to those currently living on Olympos. Because of that fact, your promise not to share the information will be sufficient for us to offer it to you. I'm sure that Sebastian told you that the offer we are about to make as a result of what is about to take place, is an open one. You may accept the offer or choose to turn it down. Needless to say, Jonah and I and in fact all the Atlantians owe you a great deal. We therefore hope that you will allow us to offer you personal sanctuary just as you did us.

"Juno and Gabe have already given us the necessary assurance. Brother Sebastian would not do so unless you agreed that he could."

The Devi nodded and looked over at Brother Sebastian before she answered.

"I am prepared to give you my agreement to keep this matter to myself and release Sebastian to accept your generous proposition."

Venus beamed.

"Thank you.

"While the news we bring is certainly not good for Olympos, we are in a position to offer you an option in relation to your personal futures. Although very saddened by the fate of Olympos, I am very pleased and a little excited by the whole prospect of what we have to suggest to you, once you know of what is to come.

"Now, I think it best if Jonah, who is less emotional about the enterprise and therefore more focused on the intricacies of the operation, explains the whole scenario of what will take place over the next two weeks' time."

Jonah, who had carefully rehearsed how he would deliver the offer of a new life to them, began to speak dispassionately.

A deepening sense of astonishment and disbelief filled the room as he outlined the facts in relation to the fate of Olympos and the chance for them to escape the upcoming apocalypse.

When he'd finished, he asked them for their decision.

It immediately became apparent to the Devi that the other Olympoians had been left speechless and in no position to respond without further consideration and evaluation.

She said as much and in view of the fact that the two Atlantians were pressed for time requested that all involved be given until the morning to mull over their decisions regarding the offer at hand.

While Venus for one was a little disappointed by this delay in response, she understood the gravity of situation faced by the Olympoians. While neither she nor Jonah, who obviously did not enjoy the idea of another twelve hours of little if any sleep, welcomed the deferment of the decisions, both agreed to meet with them in the morning.

Once the Atlantians had left, the Devi, who was clearly very upset by what they had been told, asked Brother Sebastian, Juno and Gabriel to remain behind.

She'd then bade refreshments be brought and the four of them settled in for some serious discussion.

In consideration of her position, Aabha had taken the lead.

In order to ensure that everyone in the room was on the same page, she'd begun by providing a synopsis of what had transpired. Repeating what Jonah had told them and reliving with the others their initial disbelief. The very idea that

Olympos was about to suffer what Jonah had described as an imminent catastrophic cycle of events leading to the death of all living things on the planet had been very difficult for all present to accept out of hand.

This initial inability to appreciate the seriousness of what was to come had then morphed into dismay at the very prospect. A raft of questions from the Olympoians had been the result, all made in an attempt to lessen or question the irrevocability of the demise of life on the planet.

Fully expecting this type of reaction, Jonah had dismissed any and all suggestions that something could be done to change the inevitable. He had done so without rancour, but with a firmness that pushed them toward acceptance. That done, the group had grown silent and it was then that Venus had intervened to explain their plan of how to offer those in the room an escape from the devastation that was to come and a chance for a new life on a new world.

When she'd finished offering her understanding of what had taken place she asked the others if they were in general agreement with what she had taken from the earlier meeting.

Solemn nods all round had been the result. The food arrived at that time and Aabha suggested that they eat before the debate moved on to what response each would make to the Atlantian's offer.

CHAPTER SIXTEEN

- *Decision Time* -

The changeover from day to night, which the ship's central computers matched to what was taking place on the planet below, had begun just before the committee reconvened in the small meeting room.

Gaia noted that although both Persephone and Enoch seemed well rested, her two children exhibited signs of being anything but. She made no comment in relation to this observation when they arrived however, and after sitting down to a light meal, the five of them returned to the main control facility, where Adon once again brought up the overview of the secure areas located at the core of the interstellar craft on the big screen.

Gaia then drew their attention to the three separate areas that made up the massive complex.

"As you can see there are three distinct work stations encompassed within the facility. The regularly programmed change in illumination of the entire area from day to night has already begun. This happens daily in order to match the current orbit of Olympos around Solar so that such changes in light are natural occurrences and to be expected when they arrive on their new home, which will move in the same orbit.

Adon will individually isolate each of theses areas for us now so that I can explain the purpose of each."

The screen image zoomed in on the first of the three distinct sections.

"Depicted now is the plant developmental vegetation unit. It is here that all plant life is created and tended. As is the case with all three areas, many eternities of experience and research have allowed Atlantians to generate plant life in a variety of forms, shapes and sizes. Central to this development is the necessity of creating a progressive food chain and symbiotic relationships with the other life forms that will inhabit and develop as each new planet evolves."

Enoch heaved a sigh and shook his head.

"The section is absolutely massive and the number of plants depicted is beyond grasp. How in Solar's name can we be expected to select from all of these, a reasonable number of plants in the restricted time frame available to us?"

Gaia smiled and turned to Adon.

"Adon, will you please blank the screen for a moment."

He did so and Gaia stood and turned to face the sitting committee members.

"An excellent question, and the answer to it resides inside the huge memory banks that reside within the starship Atlantis. When we do our tour, you will reasonably and undoubtedly find the sheer size and scope of the facility daunting. But, because all your choices for the new planet must, and I stress that word *must*, be both part of the food chain and symbiotic in some degree to all the other lifeforms selected, you will find that it will steadily become less depressive in nature as the choices are reduced. Once you have made your very first selection and entered it in the *'Creation Registry'*, the main computer with ensure that all you succeeding choices have to be made from a continually reducing list of options. In other words, each specific individual specimen that you choose will determine what your future options are and these will be shortlisted each time you have made a choice. As you select each new lifeform, your list of other possibilities in that particular category will become shorter and shorter until you eventually have no further selections to make in that given area.

"I realize that on first glance, the process seems to be impossible, but I will tell you now that it is not as complicated as it appears. It should in fact take you no more than eight hours to accomplish, providing you are disciplined and can all agree upon each choice you make without a great deal of unnecessary discussion.

"What you have to understand before you begin the process is that you will not be working alone. The main computer will assist you through the entire progression, guaranteeing you a millennium of experience, which has been garnered as a result of previous actual trial and error.

"With that in mind, we will now go down and enter the secure area where darkness has now descended. With the use of night vision eyewear, you will tour all three of the areas. We will begin with the vegetation development section and move on through the animal development and end with the Humanoid section.

"Once you have seen all there is to see, you will take some rest and then begin to make your choices."

* * * * *

Due to the intensity of what had just transpired for them, both Gabe and Juno were independently quietly running the meeting with Jonah and Venus, through their minds, as they walked back to their quarters. Understandably, the acceptance of what was about to take place for Olympos and all who dwelled on the planet, was weighing heavily on them.

For each their personal relationship problems had been at least temporarily put on the back burner.

Without any conscious intension, they held hands as they moved slowly and silently across the paving stones, each lost in their own thoughts. Just past the halfway point Juno broke the silence.

"It is hard to comprehend, hard to accept...surely there must be something that can be done?"

Gabe sighed deeply and frowned.

"If the Atlantians say it is going to happen and nothing can be done about it, who are we to question it. My first thought is for my grandmother. I don't know what to do.

"We all agreed to keep the information to ourselves and the reasoning for doing so, as delivered by Jonah, is pretty strong. Can you imagine what would happen if everyone on the planet were to be told what was going to happen. There would be chaos."

Juno frowned and nodded.

"Yes, he is right in that, and yet it doesn't seem fair to the others - to leave them in the dark like this, when we know what is coming. I really have no one now, but you have your grandmother and I know it must be hard for you not to tell her. "

Gabe shook his head angrily.

"At the same time, what would it accomplish if I told her? The Atlantians have made it quite clear that the offer for a second chance is only to be made to the four of us. Not to any others. If I could not give my grandmother the same chance as us to have a new life, then what would be the point in telling her? She is not a young woman and has few years before she passes. Would it not perhaps be better to let her enjoy what time she has left?"

The large building appeared suddenly out of the darkness and as he reached to open the door and held it for her, she responded.

"All things considered, it would probably be best for us to keep this to ourselves. I assume that you will want to accept the chance to start over again on a new world?"

Gabe nodded and followed her inside, closing the door firmly behind him and reaching for her hand again.

"Yes, I think so. I mean it would be crazy for us not to jump at the chance, wouldn't it?"

She accepted his hand and smiled up at him.

"Yes I think so, a chance for us to do this together on a brand new planet. A new beginning in a new world. Despite the horror that has led to this opportunity, it is a very exciting thought."

She turned to him

"Would you like to come to my room? I don't want to be alone to think on this and it would help me if we could discuss the whole thing together, just between the two of us."

* * * * *

When Juno and Gabe left for their rooms Sebastian stayed behind with the Devi. He spoke as soon as they had left the meeting.

"What will you do?"

Aabha, looking very tired, sat and waved him into the chair across from her.

"Well, firstly I will do as I promised and not share this knowledge, and then I will do my best to dismiss it from my own mind and concentrate on my responsibilities. We face a holy war and it is my duty to lead the armies of the Faith.

If this horrible future end is indeed imminent, and I have no reason to believe it is not, then my place is to face it with everyone else on Olympos. I will not accept this offer from the Atlantians. It would be wrong for me to do so. I have a duty to the Faith and I will fulfill it until the end, whenever that may be."

Brother Sebastian nodded sombrely.

"I kind of figured you would see it that way. Well then, I'll be turning them down too. My place is at your side and that's where I will be when whatever happens, happens."

Aabha shook her head.

"No, you will not.

The new world will require a leader of faith of some type and I can think of no one more qualified to take up that challenge than you. You will accept the Atlantians' offer, just as I am confident that your friends, Juno and Gabriel will accept it."

The colour drained from Sebastian's face and he raised himself up from the chair to look down at her.

"But, the faith has always been led and overseen by Ogres – female Ogres, to be exact.

I am neither an Ogre nor a female!"

The Devi smiled up at him.

"Yes, in this world it has, but that doesn't mean that in a new world a male human could not do just as well, perhaps even better. No Brother Sebastian, your loyalty is to me and so it shall remain.

"You will take up the Atlantians' proposal and you will present this future innovative world the benefit of an organized religion.

"They will sorely need it, I am sure. Life will not be easy under the conditions you will find on a virgin planet. It will be a new beginning for all things, as it should be."

CHAPTER SEVENTEEN

- Revelation -

Gaia asked them to put on their night vision goggles, scanned her handprint to open the large door located deep within the ship, and led them into the humongous chamber.

As the heavy door slid silently closed behind the group, it took them a few seconds to become used to the effects of the night vision apparatus in the complete darkness. It wasn't until then that they were able to take in and fully understand the sheer size of the area.

Despite the depth of the description of the restricted area at the core of Atlantis that Gaia had offered the young members of the committee, they were having a great deal of difficulty in accepting that such a massive structure could have existed on the ship all along and they'd had absolutely no knowledge of it.

It was like being in another world entirely.

All the other areas of the ship were austere, functional, practical and colourless. This was very much different. It was like they had dropped down into a new reality. It was a world within a world.

Looking upward, they were offered what appeared to be a dark sky filled with a million stars, a single moon and drifting clouds. Although they knew that they were within a single chamber divided into various specific units, at ground level there was no sensation of that fact.

No matter where they looked they could see only an endless expanse of lush landscape running to a distant horizon.

The headset each wore as part of the night vision equipment also contained earbuds and it was through these that they heard Gaia's voice.

"Wonderful isn't it? It isn't real of course, but no matter where you are within the facility and it is extremely large, all that can be seen is an endless expanse of rolling hills under an endless sky.

We are now in a central hallway, which runs down the middle of the entire chamber. Its walls are constructed of a thick one-way glass. Both the interior and exterior of these walls normally operate as large screens. For those inside they reflect a mirror image of their world. For us in the hall, a window into their worlds.

We will board a floater and use it as transport as we move along the hallway and as we travel along the walls, the area we are immediately facing will become a one-way window allowing us to look in through to whatever is behind it. Any living thing on the other side will see only what you see now, an endless landscape appearing to run to the horizon.

We may see worker Almies here and there, both in the hallway and occasionally working on the other side of a wall, dealing with emergencies. The are all programmed to take no notice of us.

Those lifeforms inside the various compartments are unable to ascertain the presence of the workers who must, on occasion enter the chambers. All of those contained within, be they animal or humanoid, are temporarily placed into a form of suspended animation during these incursions by worker Almies and they always take place at night. This precaution is of course not necessary in the areas where only plants are present."

Parked along one of the walls was a line of floaters, small truck-like vehicles that were propelled silently on a cushion of air. Gaia led them to the first in the line and climbed into the small open cab.

"Hop in back.

"I apologise for the mode of travel. These floaters are used by the worker Almies normally, for the transport of materials and are not designed to carry passengers in any sense of comfort. We will be cramped; however, we have to make the best of what we have at our disposal. We can take regular breaks so that you may get out and stretch your legs periodically."

"We have a long way to travel and about nine hours to cover it all. We had better get started if we want to be finished by the time daylight rolls onto the stage.

"We'll begin with the vegetation. Varieties will be available on both sides of the hallway and later, when you are making your selections, I would suggest that you consider a precedent that was set long ago. It is best if you initially select vegetation that will flourish in a tropical environment, as that will allow for the easiest early evolvement over time for the animal and humanoid species that you later choose to inhabit the regions on the new planet.

"Once you have viewed the entire plant section we will move onto the animals and finally the humanoid offerings. In all the areas, you will find familiar specimens to what you have known on Olympos as well as many others that will be completely foreign to you. This is due to the fact the planet lifeforms evolve in stages.

"The very first choice you will make will be the humanoid lifeforms you want on the planet. Once that is done all the other choices will be somewhat mandated by that first choice in that the lifeforms initially placed there will of necessity be those which will eventually evolve into the Humanoid species that you have already chosen to inhabit the planet once it is ready for them.

"Do not allow yourselves to be overwhelmed by the number of each species. Remember that once you have selected the Humanoid species you want, the main computer will aid you in your other choices and each choice you make will narrow the possible choices that follow.

"Just one other thing. A food chain and that of the necessary symbiotic nature of the process also means that the initial Humanoid choices you jointly make, will also curtail whatever animal and humanoid species that will subsequently be available for your consideration. "

* * * * *

When they reached her rooms, Juno silently prepared honeyed tea and they settled onto the small settee with their steaming cups.

They both then spoke at once overriding the other.

Juno laughed and leaned over to kiss him lightly on the lips.

"I'm sorry for what I said earlier. After everything that we learned about what is about to happen, it all seems rather petty, very childish immature and insignificant really."

Gabe kept his silence. He didn't know exactly what was coming in relation to that subject as it had been temporally pushed to the back of his mind but so far, he liked the way the conversation was going.

He simply nodded and Juno continued.

"It's just that I love you and while I understand why you were happy with the current relationship, I was jealous of the time you spent with Venus and I didn't want to share you. I wanted you just for me. Silly really, when you think about it. It's not as if we were designated life partners or anything, but because that's what I wanted for us and you didn't seem to feel the same way, well I…"

Gabe gave a silent prayer of thanks to Brother Sebastian and cut her off.

"Why didn't you say something? I feel like an idiot now. I love you too. When I think back, I always have. Venus was just the icing on the cake…"

Her features darkened a little and her brow furrowed. He quickly began to back-peddle.

"You know, she was so available - ready willing and eager. It was completely different from what you and I had, though. There was nothing serious about it, just a little harmless fun and I didn't even give it much thought at the time. I should have known better but it simply didn't occur to me that it would in any way change anything between us.

"I know now how wrong I was and I'm sorry if I hurt you."

Juno's brow had progressively unknotted and her features softened again.

Gabe recognized it was time to let sleeping dogs lie. He leaned forward, took her into his arms, and kissed her deeply and she melted into his embrace.

*　*　*　*　*

Sebastian was in a word, confused.

He was torn between what he felt was his responsibility to remain at the Devi's side to face whatever fate Olympos was destined to suffer and the challenge of what wonders a new world would hold.

He spent a good half hour pacing back and forth in his rooms thinking about what he should do and then, no firm decision in his mind, he threw on his cloak and headed across the quadrant intendent upon speaking with Gabe in the hopes that a second opinion could help solve the dilemma for him.

Lost in his own thoughts, he hadn't even considered that the Neanderthal's door would go unanswered but that was what happened. He knocked a second time, a little more firmly, but got the same result.

Concluding that Gabe is not in his rooms, he turned, crossed the hall and raised his hand to knock on Juno's door.

Before his knuckles could make contact his ears picked up on the sounds coming from inside.

He was immediately suspicious as to what kind of activity was taking place beyond the stout wooden door and he pulled his hand back abruptly.

Straining to hear, he quickly confirmed his initial assessment of the situation and despite his agitated state of mind, he had to stifle a chuckle.

I guess all must be right with the world again, at least for Gabe. Giving them an hour or so to themselves wouldn't make a great deal of difference to him. I'll just leave them to enjoy the moment; Solar knows there is little joy on the horizon.

CHAPTER EIGHTEEN

- Information Overload -

After repeatedly reflecting on just how intense the activity behind Juno's door had been, Sebastian had allowed himself a good two hours before he'd turned up back at that door.

However, the extended time he'd allowed had apparently not been quite enough for those inside, in that, after a breathless...

"Just a moment."

...it took some time before the door was opened. And when it was the two of them appeared to be rather dishevelled, if distinctly exuding a sense of sated satisfaction.

Obviously their minds were on more important things, nothing small like a global war or the end of the world.

Gabe appeared especially content and the first words out of his mouth were almost giddy.

"Sebastian, my good friend! Great, I'm starved, lets all go grab something to eat."

Sebastian grinned.

"Yes, and while we're at it, perhaps we can talk over what Venus and Jonah have suggested. If it's food you want, I suggest that we go back to my place. While the cafeterias will have slim pickings at this time of the night, I have a certain amount of pull around here. Even at this late hour, I think I can arrange for us to have reasonable sustenance delivered there."

An hour later, the three of them stacked several demolished platters up on a side table and then settled down with mugs of steaming honeyed tea to talk.

Juno, who had been effervescent and bubbly from the start

of their search for nourishment blurted out her happy news.

"Gabe and I have committed to life a partnership. We wanted you to be the first to know."

From his own observations, Sebastian had gathered that things had been sorted out between them but he was still a little taken aback at the announcement. Publicly sharing an expression of life partnership was little short of an actual official coupling under law. It was a life commitment and not something that was treated lightly on Olympos.

The delight shared by the young couple was contagious however, and he was sincerely pleased that his friends had chosen him to first express their pledge to a joined future.

"Well, congratulations! I am very happy for you both.

This calls for celebration and I have just what will serve. I've had a bottle of aged honey wine stashed away for a special occasion for over a year now and I can't think of a better reason to break it out."

* * * * *

Gaia edged the floater back into line against the wall and the five of them climbed out and stretched.

The four young Atlantians were conjointly suffering from an overabundance of processing mental input and making the resulting assessment this entailed. They were exhausted and yet too keyed up and bubbling with exuberance at the marvels that they had viewed to notice just how tired they were.

Enoch was the first to speak.

"It is wondrous beyond words. A whole separate living world. A plethora of species, living in different environs, rain forest's, sup-tropical, temperate, tropical; rivers, lakes, oceans and all within the bowels of the starship."

Gaia smiled.

"Well put. It contains all the raw material needed to bring life to a new planet once it is ready to receive it. Now, as a group, all you have to do is select exactly what individual

Humanoid species will begin the new world and what rules will be set in place to manage how it then evolves over time."

Venus frowned.

"I noticed that some of the species are represented in larger numbers than others. Why is that?"

Gaia nodded.

"Yes, the lower they are in the food chain, the more numerous and more prolific they are.

This allows for their absorption by the species higher up in the chain, in a manner that assures they will not face rapid decimation and will be able to manage to keep pace with the need. At the top of the chain there are only one hundred of each of the Humanoid specimens per species that will actually be placed on the new planet. In order that the food chain will meet their needs, the lower species have to be placed on the planet in much higher volumes.

"It is one of the millions of things that the computer will help automatically sort out for you once you begin making your choices.

"You will begin the process by choosing the various humanoid species and once you do that the others will be chosen with a view to evolving to the point of maintaining the food chain and the interrelated symbiotic relationships that will allow for successful development overall when the Humanoids are introduced to the new planet.

"You have absorbed a great deal and as I said earlier, the experience is bound to leave you feeling overwhelmed. It is time for you to get some rest and then we can begin making our selections.

"Let's meet again in eight hours in the main computer room to begin the process of making our selections."

* * * * *

Sebastian awakened with the dawn of the new day.

The previous night's celebration had lasted well in to the wee hours of the morning.

The Brother did not welcome this sudden affront offered by the morning brightness but despite a pounding headache, he forced himself to commit the energy to rise to a sitting positon on his bed. He then sat there holding his head in his hands for some time, hoping, yes even praying that it would stop spinning long enough for him to begin his day.

As the fog in his brain began to clear, he struggled to recall what had transpired after the three of them had opened that first bottle of aged wine. There had been a good deal of toasting, that memory was solid enough, but then they had moved on to another topic…yes it was coming clear to him now.

They'd all decided to take up the Atlantian's offer of a new life in a new world.

After that had been determined, they'd gone on to wonder at exactly what that concept would mean for them. What would the new world be like? What part were they to play in its development and exactly how developed would it be? Would they be starting from scratch? What facilities could they expect if any? What would be the makeup of the place? Would everything be foreign to them or would some, or even most things be similar to what was on Olympos?

Round and round they had gone and in addition, he now recalled that at lest two more bottles of wine, wine definitively of a lesser quality than the first bottle, had been consumed before they'd exhausted themselves with questions that had no answers and decided to call it a night.

He vaguely remembered that they had also agreed to meet together for breakfast at nine in the main cafeteria.

It was at this point that he raised his bleary eyes up to look at the clock on the wall facing the end of his bed and groaned as he noted the early hour.

Two hours away from breakfast. He could maybe get at least another hour of sleep.

No. If he was able to close his eyes again and find sleep, an accomplishment that was highly unlikely in consideration of his pounding head, he would never wake in time for breakfast.

Like it or not, he was going to have to get up and get moving now, if he expected to be fully mobile by the time nine rolled around.

CHAPTER NINETEEN

- *Bond Enhanced* -

Jonah shook his head.

"Nope...no way. If you want to go down and talk to them again, you go right ahead. Me, I'm going to get some bloody shuteye."

Venus got that look on her face that he knew so well but, knowing it was coming, he had steeled himself against her and now held his ground.

That said, when he spoke again, he had softened his words.

"Look, it doesn't need both of us down there. Either they have made up their minds what they are going to do or they haven't. If they have, then you can handle it by yourself. You don't need me for that. If not, well, so be it, we haven't the time to fool around with this. If they don't agree to accept the offer now, then they stay behind and accept the consequences of that indecision."

With so much else going on, Venus wanted this decision out of the way so she could concentrate on the work the committee had to do, without continually worrying about saving them. As tired as she was, she was determined to transport down to Olympos, seek out the other members of their team and do her best to get their agreement on accepting the offer to escape and have a chance at a new life in a new world.

Although she would have liked Jonah's support, he was right. She could manage it on her own and up to now he hadn't really been all that committed to the idea in any event. Besides, after the all night session, she didn't have the strength left to argue at length with him.

She threw up her hands in frustration and her eyes flashed.
"Fine, you go and get your precious sleep. I'll look after it myself."

* * * * *

Gabe and Juno hadn't managed to get a lot of sleep, but both of them were so fired up about their commitment to each other and of the shared delight of her bed after they had returned from Sebastian's, that neither of them seemed to be suffering negatively from the lack of rest.

After a rapturous several hours under the sheets, they were starving yet again and bright eyed and bushy tailed, they'd appeared for breakfast early.

By the time Sebastian, obviously a little worse for wear, joined them they had already heaped their plates and found a table. Gabe took note of the rather sparse offering on the monk's tray and couldn't resist commenting on it.

"Porridge and a heel of bread. That won't take you far."

Sebastian set his tray down and slumped into his seat lethargically.

"My stomach isn't really interested in food this morning. I will be lucky to keep even this down."

He took in their hearty spread and managed a grin that looked to the two of them to be more like a grimace.

"You two don't seem to be suffering. There must be something in that old saying *'a night of love makes for a glorious day'.*"

Juno, despite her dark complexion, managed to flush and at the sight of it, the grimace-like expression on the brother's face managed to make it to a full smile.

"I'm really very happy for you guys. Don't mind me. I celebrated a little more than I should have last night but it wasn't the first time. I'll perk up in no time."

Venus, followed by Duenna, appeared in the doorway and when she spotted them she smiled, waved, and crossed toward them. Although the appearance of an Atlantian and an accompanying Almie had grown relatively common over the past few weeks, the conversations within the large cafeteria did lapse as they passed, politeness preventing anyone openly staring.

If Venus noticed, she gave no sign of it as she slipped into the empty chair across from Sebastian and Duanna came to rest against the wall behind her.

"Good morning everyone."

Her gaze rested on Sebastian.

"Brother Sebastian, you look as though you've been up all night."

Sebastian, by this time beginning to feel the first signs of relief provided by the earlier intake of his wonder powder for hangovers, let out a sigh and nodded.

"Juno and Gabriel shared some good news with me and we did a little celebrating last night. We didn't get much sleep I'm afraid."

Venus turned to face the others.

"Good news? What good news?"

A little uncomfortable with both women at the small table, Gabe avoided looking directly at Venus as he reached over, took one of Juno's hands in his, and beamed across at her.

"We've committed to be life partners."

Venus pursed her lips slightly as she shifted her eyes away from Gabe to face Juno.

"Life partners. Well that is good news. Congratulations to the both of you."

Eager not to dwell on the subject, Gabe shifted the conversation.

"I guess you've come to ask us if we have made a decision to accept your offer or not?"

Venus turned to face him.

"Yes, I don't want to press any of you, but we really don't have much time to waste. Have you decided one way or the other?"

Gabe nodded.

I can't speak for the Devi or Sebastian, but Juno and I are

very interested in taking you up on your proposition."

Venus let out a spontaneous squeal of delight.

"That's wonderful."

She looked to Sebastian.

"How about you and the Devi, Sebastian? Will you be joining them?"

Sebastian hadn't really made up his mind what he was going to do, however in view of the fact that Juno and Gabe were had committed to the idea, he responded without giving the matter any further thought.

"The Devi feels that she has a duty to remain here with those gathering for the holy war against Eisen, but she has instructed that I accept your offer.

"I have to admit that I was initially hesitant to leave her side but all things considered and with thanks, I'm in."

* * * * *

After some anticipated ups and downs in the learning curve, the makeup crew of the airship had found the machine surprisingly easy to handle and after several hours of fair winds and clear cloudless skies, the running of the craft had become almost routine.

Cradling a steaming cup, Brother Jacob was on the bridge of the airship conversing with the helmsmen when the lookout spoke.

"Is that smoke?"

Jacob turned to look at the brother.

"Smoke? Where?"

"Out there on the horizon - almost directly in front of us. At first I thought it might just be a dark cloud, but the longer I watched it the more it seemed like smoke and it is getting closer to us over time."

Jacob squinted out the front window of the cupola.

He could see nothing but the vast expanse of water and clear sky.

"Smoke! In the middle of the ocean?"

The lookout lowered the looking glass and raised his hand to point ahead. He held out the glass."

"Here, use this brother."

CHAPTER TWENTY

- *Selection Begins* -

Before returning to the ship, Venus had decided that she would go back down to Olympos in order to arrange for their transport back to the starship later that evening.

She'd told them that they needed to bring nothing with them by the clothing on their backs as they would be starting their new life from scratch and would come into that world as naked as any newborn would, bringing nothing but life itself.

Although the idea of that was initially very difficult for them to grasp, they were prepared to accept it, although there did seem to be some necessities they felt should accompany them.

Juno was concerned that she would be unable to find her favorite scent...Gabriel expressed dismay at the thought of complete nudity and Brother Sebastian asked if he could at least bring his staff.

Venus had indulged them after responding with a suggestion that they should not worry.

"By all means bring whatever you feel you must have, but believe me it will all soon be irrelevant.

"Nothing other than life itself may be brought to a new planet. It is written and so it must be. I'm sorry I don't have time to explain everything to you now. I must get back, but we will have lots of time to talk things through once you arrive at Atlantis.

"Don't worry. I will see you tonight. You'll see - everything is going to be wonderful!"

* * * * *

Despite the calm seas, Marduke was suffering from yet another bout of seasickness. He had given von Jaeger strict instructions that he was not to be disturbed.

Following these instructions, the Feldmarschall had decided against informing his leader of the brief, earlier sighting made in the distance above the horizon ahead of their column of six ships.

It was probably nothing at any rate. Only one lookout had seen anything at all and that only for a split second. There had been no further reports of anything despite an order for greater scrutiny.

It had probably just been a wisp of cloud.

* * * * *

Jonah was roused out of bed by a pounding at his apartment door. He blinked several times and managed to fully open one eye long enough to watch Sal leave his position against the bedroom wall and cross the room to respond to the irritating banging.

Seconds later a jubilant Venus was pacing furiously as she shared her news.

"The Devi declined with thanks, but the rest are all coming! They all said yes!"

Sal answered the unspoken, obvious question, almost before his master had completely formed it in his own fogged mind.

"Eleven-thirty."

Jonah groaned and rolled over pulling his covers up over his head as he mumbled.

"For Solar's sake Venus. They are coming, wonderful, but enough already. Let me get some sleep, we have much to do later today."

Venus frowned, picked up a pillow and before Sal could deliver a word of warning, whacked Jonah soundly over the head.

"Aren't you at least a little excited. Its fantastic news!"

Jonah protectively crossed his arms over his head beneath the blanket before he responded.

"OK Sis! Its great news! I'm overjoyed! Now, please let me get some more sleep."

She let out a derisive snort and tossed the pillow at his motionless form before spinning on her heel and heading out of the room.

* * * * *

Brother Jacob had immediately ordered a change of course once the smoke had been confirmed and it had become apparent that the airship had been pretty much on a collision course with what looked to be a small formation of large seagoing vessels.

It was not normal to come upon other vessels at sea this far from the shoreline and the very fact that they looked to be on an interception course with the airship strongly suggested that these vessels were headed toward Almeca from Indus. One had to assume that it was something to do with Eisen.

The course change Jacob had ordered as a result had taken them off course at a right angle and as the airship was travelling at least twice the speed of the fleet of closing ships, the maneuver instantly opened the distance between them.

The helmsman had also been busy plotting the course of the spotted ships and from that Jacob had been able to determine exactly how far he had to travel on the current course before he ordered a second turn that would put them on a parallel path to the vessels but at a distance that would keep the airship directly out of line of sight from their easily spotted trails of rising smoke.

Satisfied, he handed the glass back to the lookout and commented to the gathering of brothers now surrounding him in the cupola.

"We'll let them pass us then turn and come up on them

from the rear and in darkness. Their lookouts will be less worried about what is behind them and it should allow us to approach and evaluate them before they know we are there. There is little doubt left as to what they are, but if it turns out to be something else, we can simply turn about and return to our original course.

However, if, as I suspect, it is an invasion flotilla, we will have the advantage of surprise when we attack."

* * * * *

Gaia was already in the main computer room with Adon when the young Atlantian committee members arrive at two in the afternoon.

Adon brought up an overview of the secured areas below onto the large screen and as Gaia raised her hand to indicate the row of seats facing it, he enlarged the Humanoid area, allowing it to fill the screen.

Gaia turned to face it.

"Right. Well let's get at it. I will answer any questions you have as we go along. These first choices will be the most difficult.

"You will note that there has been a small, supplementary window added to the bottom right corner of the screen. That is where the computer will come into play. Once you have made the Humanoid selections and move on to the process of selecting the other specimens, your list of subsequent picks will be listed in that box.

"The computer will help you determine each additional choice you make and as you progress your options will begin to narrow, making each easier."

The first choice from the six available species was unanimous.

Human.

The second involved some discussion, but Venus pushed for Neanderthal.

Her argument was strong, pointing out to the others that it

had already been agreed that Gabriel and Juno would be taking part and that quite obviously if Gabe was to be there, the inclusion of his species had already been decided.

Neanderthal it was to be.

The computer raised no objection. The little window simply highlighted the two choices made from the list so far.

Three of the four remaining species were rejected out of hand as unacceptable, leaving only the addition of Ogres to be discussed.

Enoch was in favour of adding this species, explaining that they had played an important part in the early development of Olympos. Jonah, attentive, but grumpy and yawning from lack of sleep, had little to say on the matter and Venus, pleased with the inclusion of the Neanderthal, was willing to go along.

It was Persephone who raised an objection.

"I would suggest that although they did play a helpful role initially, over the long term they have proven themselves difficult to motivate and very self-absorbed. To be honest, I think it would be more sensible to simply limit it to the two species that we have already agreed upon. Just the two species, Human and Neanderthal."

Gaia interjected.

"It is not my choice to make of course, but I should point out that the two you have chosen so far are capable of mating with each other. In the case of the others, the individual genetic makeup is too different, making cross-mating impossible, in that they are only able to mate with their own kind.

"If you do as Persephone has suggested, you will begin with two slightly different genetic species and which are capable of cross breeding. This would serve to enable them to pass on to each other some very positive genetic improvements over time."

Enoch pursed his lips and nodded slowly.

"Can you give us an example of what a specific type of benefit that might be?"

Gaia thought for a moment before responding."

"Well for example, the Neanderthal species has an inherent and strong tendency to naturally produce a higher level of androgens in their males than does the human.

"Androgens are the hormones responsible for the physical male features and the reproduction stimulus of a given species. They are responsible for the sexual development in males and are produced by the testes. Females have smaller amounts of androgens too, which are produced by the ovaries.

"The primary group of androgens are called adrenal androgens and they function as weak steroids.

"The most familiar androgen is testosterone, which is responsible for developing the secondary sex characterises in males and in the case of the Neanderthal male, makes him more easily able to adapt to temperature change due to increased body mass. Another is dihydrotestosterone.

"If dihydrotestosterone is present in a developing embryo, it instigates the formation of the penis, scrotum and prostate.

"Once the males of a species reach puberty, androgens are partially responsible for the production of sperm and this production is ongoing throughout life.

"High production of androgens is therefore likely to mean an enhanced sex drive in males, which in turn can lead to a stronger determination to procreate very actively."

Stimulated by the turn in topic, Jonah stirred, let out a deep sigh and roused himself to sit upright as he glanced over at Venus.

"Well imagine that, Sis. Neanderthal males have a higher sex drive than humans. Who'd have guessed?"

Venus held herself aloof, choosing to ignore him and quickly moved to shift attention away from herself and back onto the topic at hand.

"All of which means that if Neanderthals and humans cross mate, the resulting exchange of genes will in all probability lead to a heightened sex drive in both species over time. Something that would obviously assist in their overall capacity to procreate. A good thing in consideration of the fact that it is our intention for them to go forth and multiply with a strong and deep-seated motivation to do so."

Gaia nodded in agreement.

"In simple terms, yes.

"Additionally, the androgens produced by Neanderthals tends to make them a more muscular and physically stronger race, thereby helping them to deal with the difficulties of making their way in warding off the inherent challenges of beginning life on a new planet.

"By sharing this particular genetic advantage through inter-race relationships, the two species that you have so far chosen would therefore likely both benefit over time. Having Ogres in the mix would do nothing in this regard."

Convinced of the argued advantage offered by the restriction of only the two species already selected, Enoch retracted his suggestion and all agreed to go ahead on that basis.

The first step had been taken.

Humanoid life on the new planet would evolve from a limited initial assemblage of two basic specimens: Human and Neanderthal.

CHAPTER TWENTY-ONE

- The Mechanics of Creation -

With the exception of one small meal break, they had kept at it for almost ten hours.

As Gaia had promised, the assistance of the main computer had indeed continued to simplify the work. The number of choices they had to make in each phase were many but once accomplished, each one brought about a less tedious numerical assault for the next in line.

After the first hour they had gotten into their stride. Toward the end of their individual choices, more often than not, they had confidently relied on the computer to quickly select the correct picks for them.

They were all exhausted by the time Gaia pronounced that the job of selection had been completed.

Of the four, it was Venus who was suffering the most from a distinct lack of sleep.

Despite that fact, she had then taken the time to discuss the situation regarding the addition of the three Olympoians to the mix with the other committee members and that out of the way, was secure in unanimous support for their inclusion in the initial groups to be sent to the new planet.

She'd then spoken to Adon and Gaia and explained that it was her intention to immediately bring the three Olympoians on board Atlantis. That had initiated some intense discussion, during which she'd agreed to their suggestion that upon their arrival, her parents would be responsible for arranging the shepherding of the Olympoians, looking after their introduction to their future situation on board the ship.

Adon and Gaia had promised to be present in the transporter room for the arrival.

That accomplished. she immediately had Duanna transport the two of them down to Olympos.

Duanna in tow, she arrived just in time to be invited to witness the *'Joining Ceremony'*, which Aabha had agreed to personally provide for the young and now publicly committed life partners.

Her offer had been both unsuspected and an unusual occurrence, in that historically only heads of state had previously received such an honour.

Both Juno and Gabe, inwardly pleased at receiving the privilege of such special treatment, were understandably nervous during the brief but resplendent ceremony, which was far more involved than the normal joining which was handled by far lesser members of the Faith.

It was conducted within the ornate surroundings of the Devi's personal Chapel. In addition to Venus and Sebastian, the entire entourage of Mitra Varuna also gave witness to what, in the eyes of the Faith, was henceforth to be an unbroken bond between a male and a female.

A half hour after the ceremony, Venus and her Almie arrived back in the Atlantis' transporter room accompanied by Gabriel, Juno and Brother Sebastian. Her parents were waiting to welcome them and Venus, who was by this point almost asleep on her feet, advised them of the fact that the Devi had just life-joined Juno and Gabe and promptly excused herself to return to her apartments.

* * * * *

Adon and Gaia escorted the three Olympoians directly down to the secured area at the core of Atlantis.

Here, on Gaia's instructions a new section, isolated, but comfortably so, with well-appointed quarters which were separate from the remainder of the operation, had been hastily created to house them.

Once the new arrivals had been given a tour and were acquainted with their habitat and the limits of their secure enclosure, they were given into the care of a group of worker Almies, who would now be available, around the clock, to provide whatever necessities might arise.

The two Atlantians and their personal Almies then left them to settle into their new surroundings. Once they had returned to their own apartments, Adon and Gaia settled down in her quarters to review their day over a pot of honeyed tea.

Adon spoke first.

"I still think we should have placed them directly into the memory-cleanse vessels with the others and left them there until it was time for them to transport."

Gaia smiled across the table at him.

"The two young ones were just joined Adon.

Can you not remember what it was like when we were first joined?"

Adon reached out to take her hand and offered a husky chuckle.

"Yes my love, a period of wondrous delights and one that I often reflect upon."

Gaia's eyebrows raised and she smiled warmly.

"Well then, let's at least give them time for that.

"What can it hurt to allow them a short while before we put them under? Their whole world has just been turned upside down. A short breather will serve them well. Besides, we haven't discussed that part with Venus and the other committee members yet and it would be unfair to place them there before they were aware of the need for all of the Humanoid lifeforms to undergo such brain adjustment prior to their colonization transport.

"In the case of Sebastian, Gabe and Juno, it makes sense to hold off on completing that procedure until we are all but ready to proceed with the settling of the new planet. Until that time and while they are on board the ship, it is very likely that they will be hearing and seeing many more things of a nature that will eventually have to be removed from their memory banks. However, there is no reason why this cannot be done just before colonization in order to ensure that they can be free of preconceptions and more easily accept their new environment.

Adon shrugged.

"Perhaps you are right and when it comes to discussing with the committee the need for them to go thorough memory cleansing, I will leave that part to you. Based on what I have observed over the past while; it seems that Venus has built up a strong attraction for the Neanderthal boy. Knowing our daughter as I do, I would not expect her to be easily convinced of the need to have his memory altered and I suspect it will take all your wiles and the influence you have with her, to convince her that it must be done before the settlement takes place."

* * * * *

Venus was at peace.

The basic selections had been made. That part was over.

Gaia had scheduled the next committee meeting for nine the next morning. It would have to do with the structure of a progress plan for the preparation for the introduction of Humanoid life on the new planet and as such, would require a great deal of thought and discussion, she was sure.

She recognized there was much more to learn and little time to accomplish it. But now that Gabe, Juno and Sebastian were safely aboard the ship, she was confident that any task she might be required to undertake in the future would not prove insurmountable.

She was asleep shortly after she rested her head on the pillow.

* * * * *

Juno and Gabe had been provided with separate suites that had an adjoining door. However, having just been faith confirmed as life partners, they had no intention of being separated, even for a few minutes.

They happily settled into a single unit and after sharing a hot, relaxing bath, immediately sought out the nearest bed.

Sebastian, who was not surprised by that fact the young couple would want to be alone, made himself scarce. Begging the need for a good sleep, he had quickly retired to his own rooms for the night.

After accustoming himself to what Almie service was on offer, which seemed to be limitless, he arranged for a meal and then a drawn bath before he retired.

CHAPTER TWENTY-TWO

- Looking Ahead -

The next day Gaia explained to the committee that it would be necessary for the three Olympoians to follow the same process that the other prospective settlers were undertaking with regard to the memory-cleanse.

In view of her daughter's obvious attraction for the young Neanderthal, Gaia had expected Venus to challenge the need and had been prepared to argue the matter with some force but was surprised when Venus, in front of all the committee members, in a short but unapologetic statement, dismissed the matter almost out of hand.

"I will admit that I have very strong feelings for Gabriel. I have made no attempt to hide that fact from anyone here. However, over the past few months I have matured and grown well past that basic phase in my development. I can no longer afford the luxury of trivializing my life and being self-indulgent. I've realized that I have a duty as an Atlantian to get well beyond that type of interaction.

"I pushed to have Gabe, Juno and Sebastian included in the colonization of the new planet. I did so with the full understanding that I was doing it in response to what they had done for us. If there was an opportunity to do so, I was determined to give them a second chance at life.

"It was the right thing to do.

"But that was not the only reason I did it. It was not even the major reason.

"The much stronger motivation to include them was the fact that, as an Atlantian and part of this committee, I very much want this new world to be the best one ever and I know that the inclusion of Brother Sebastian, Juno and Gabe, among the settlers will raise the odds of that happening.

"They are all simple people but they are strong, conscientious and independent thinkers all. Each will bring to the new planet a fair and inclusive view for the future. I am confident that once in their new world, whenever a choice arises or a decision needs to be made and they are present, the outcome will be one tailored, not toward any narrow personal improvement but only one that leads to the path of the common good for all living Humanoids.

"I have no difficulty in accepting the fact that they must take only faded memories of what they left behind on Olympos. Common sense dictates that, in order to develop their own unique world, they must make their own discoveries and over time, make their own way on the new planet. Many of their past memories would make that difficult, if not impossible.

"You have explained that their individual characteristics will remain. That only memories that might lead to a limited course of action and not to one of free unfettered choice will be adjusted by this process. That no memory will be completely erased but only made extremely vague in order to ensure that each step they take in their new world is primarily of their own creation and not based on the reliance of what they have previously experienced.

"The three of them have a right to know what is going to happen to them and be provided with the reasons why. It should not be something that is arbitrarily done to them. It will have to be presented in a positive sense and it will have to be made acceptable to them.

"With that in mind, I would like your permission to adjourn our current meeting and reconvene in the morning. I know time is short but I think Jonah and I owe them a fulsome explanation of what is to come."

It was agreed unanimously that the request be granted and without further discussion, Jonah and Venus took precious time off from their tasks to spend a day with Juno, Gabe and Sebastian.

A half hour later they were carefully explaining the necessity of their temporary placement into a state of suspended animation to allow the memory cleanse to be carried out. Without going into explaining the actual process in too much detail, they gave them a basic understanding of what the process entailed.

The concept was, at first, more than a little daunting and understandably alarming for the Olympoians, but the necessity for such a process to take place if they were to be given a fair chance at succeeding to create a new life in a new world, had been clearly presented. They understood that to do otherwise would obviously endanger the whole project and admittedly with little enthusiasm, but firm commitment, they all agreed to have the procedure carried out.

That accomplished, Venus and Jonah went on to the more positive prospects of what the future held, a basic explanation of how the new planet would be created.

Jonah began by describing what would happen first - the shift in the position of the two planets, Olympos moving away from Solar into a new orbit and the other shifting in to replace the position around Solar that Olympos had previously enjoyed.

"It all begins when a new planet is formed by accretion from the solar nebula. It is not necessary for you to understand how or what that is. It will be sufficient for you to comprehend that it takes billions of years for this new planet to develop to a stage where it has evolved to the point where the necessary liquid water and atmosphere, which is a prerequisite to the support of life as you understand it, is possible."

Venus, who had been observing the three of them over Jonah's shoulder, noted the blank expressions and the sagging shoulders. She frowned and placed her hand on her brother's arm.

"Hang on a moment Jonah."

He paused and looked up at her and she picked up on what

he had been saying.

"It isn't important for you to know the how or why of it all.

"To be honest, it's hard for Jonah and I to comprehend the complexities of it and we were much better prepared to do so than you could ever be.

"Suffice to say that the fact that all this is going to take billions of years has no real consequence for any of us in practical terms and that is because Atlantis is a starship and she can travel rapidly through not only space, but also time.

"Because she can journey or warp into the future through time, time itself, even billions of years of it, has no real meaning to us.

"You already know that we Atlantians can transport through space in the blink of an eye, moving from the ship to Olympos and back whenever we wish and you know that we can take you with us when we do it, because you have already experienced that.

"Due to the fact that the ship can also travel through time and into the future, although it takes more than a blink of the eye, but not much more, we can also travel in this solar system to any point in time in relationship to the development of the new planet that we so choose, and we can do it very quickly.

"Over the next few days, Atlantis will raise her shields and back away from Olympos to a safe point. Once there, we will briefly view the movement of the two planets into their new orbits around Solar. We will remain there only until we know that the exchange of positions has been successfully completed - that everything is going as it should and then we will time-warp into the future to various points over time, observing and aiding in the process of physical devolvement for the surface of the new planet.

"We have already made our selections for what the various life forms will be from the individual species available to us here on the ship. It is amazing what variations we had to choose from.

"Once the planet has reached the stage of development where it has formed the necessary liquid water and atmosphere necessary for the sustenance of life we will begin putting the final touches on your new world in preparation for Humanoid colonization.

"Despite the fact that this whole process with take billions of years, you will in actually be transported to your new home in a matter of, what you understand to be, days.

"Because you will have completed the memory cleanse just prior to transport, you will have only extremely sketchy memories of what has come before your arrival. That way everything will be new to you.

"You will find yourself in a wonderful world with everything available that you will need to live and enjoy a new existence, the future of which you will then mould yourselves - one that you will then pass on to your future generations."

The blank looks had slowly faded as she spoke, although there remained a reflected uncertainty in their facial expressions.

Jonah grinned.

"Hey! Don't sweat it you guys. It will all be over before you know it. In just a few days you will be starting your new life."

Sebastian nodded and shrugged.

"Well, lets face it. We all committed to this whole idea in the first place, so there is not much point in worrying about the details of how it all comes about it. The way I look at it, when we get there everything is going to be brand new and Solar knows we could sure use a new virgin world, a world bereft of all the mistakes Olympos has had to endure."

Both Juno and Gabe found those words very soothing and smiles broke out on their faces. Gabe vocalized what both of them were feeling.

"Good point Brother."

He shifted his gaze to Venus and Jonah.

"Am I to understand that everything living that will be on

our new world has already been selected from examples already in existence here on the ship? And if so, do we get a chance to have a preview of what we can expect to find when we arrive in our new home?"

Venus and Jonah shared a glance and they both shrugged and then Jonah nodded.

"We'd have to clear it with the committee first of course, but in consideration of the fact that you will go through a memory cleanse before you transport down to the new planet, I can't see any practical reason why not."

CHAPTER TWENTY-THREE

- *Wonders* -

It would set a precedent.

As such, Adon, Gaia and the other members of the committee tended to be hesitant to grant the request. However, in the end they accepted the observation that precedent setting decisions were quickly becoming daily occurrences and that the addition of this particular one, while a definite precedent, was probably simply due to the fact that a new broom was sweeping through the ship.

Both Venus and Jonah had belaboured the fact that the memory-cleanse would look after any observations made during a tour of the secret inner core by the three Olympoians and all had to agree that the excursion would very likely provide them with a brighter outlook of what their future held.

Venus had put it succinctly.

"Anything to help put them at ease at this point seems logical."

The decision to go ahead with the inspection of the secret areas was passed on to Sebastian, Juno and Gabe by Venus, along with the suggestion that they all retire to their beds and get some rest before nightfall, as the primary viewing had to take place after darkness fell and it would take several hours to complete.

She took note of the fact that when she mentioned beds, both Juno and Gabe flushed slightly and she realized that it was quite unlikely that either of them would be getting much rest before Solar set.

Sebastian on the other hand seemed sincerely excited at the upcoming prospect of taking a brief look at what his future world would hold and quite eager to get a good rest as a precursor.

They agreed to meet for dinner again in the small dinning room situated just off their segregated personal quarters.

* * * * *

Once they had entered the cavernous chamber and the big door had closed behind them, Venus equipped everyone with night vision helmets. When all had become conditioned to the initial eerie effects brought about by the use of the night vision apparatus, Jonah, unsure of exactly how the floater operated and exactly where they would have to travel in order to repeat the tour that they had received earlier from Gaia, wisely detailed Sal to operate the vehicle.

Surprisingly his little Almie buddy, who had been sulking for days now, after what he'd considered as having been put upon and much abused during the retaking of the ship, took up the challenge with some eagerness.

Jonah, who had to bite his tongue to stop from making some kind of supercilious comment, decided the best approach would be to let sleeping dogs lie. He restricted himself to a brief chuckle.

The rest of them piled into the back and as they settled in the three Olympoians began to experience similar first impressions to those that Venus and Jonah had undergone on their earlier introduction to the massive chamber.

The sheer size of it was overwhelming.

Their senses filled with the sight, sound and smell of it.

Comfortably warm and embracing, despite the darkness. Seemingly endless skies and horizons. Earthy, vegetation-rich scents drifting on a gentle breeze, intermingling with the sounds of a country night.

Living sounds.

Life aboard the other areas of Atlantis belied the possibility that anything like this could exist here. It was like being in a whole other world, alive with a menagerie of nightlife, the sensation of breathing in clean oxygen-rich air and the view of a stunning array of stars overhead in a clear sky was simply amazing to find here, deep in the bowels of the ship.

Sensing their reactions, Jonah gave them a few moments to take it all in, then he silently instructed Sal to drive on.

As the floater began to move slowly ahead, Venus's voice filled the earbuds built into their helmets.

"We are now in a central hallway which runs down the middle of this entire chamber. The hall walls on both sides are constructed of one-way glass. You will be able to see inside of each of the various sections, but any living thing inside will not be able to see or be made aware of our passing.

"After the new planet settles into its fresh orbit, over billions of years it morphs through several cycles which eventually lead to it being terraformed.

"It is at this stage that water and atmosphere appear and the basic lifeforms begin to develop. These evolve over time and many early forms are very simple. While we have examples of those early forms here, they need be of no particular interest to you, as for the most part, only the much advanced lifeforms will be present at the time of your colonization.

"Therefore, it is only the species that will be present at the time of colonization that we will specifically draw your attention to.

"The two Humanoid sections which normally contain both the Neanderthal and Human species are now empty as their recent inhabitants are currently undergoing their memory-cleanse process in preparation for colonization. However, you will be able to view other such species under development in that area, those that we decided not to include in the colonization of your new world.

"Additionally, as we progress through the assorted sections, you will be able to look in on all the lesser living creatures as well as the types of vegetation from which we had to choose from. While for several reasons we did not select all of these various species, I will try to point out to you the ones that made the cut as we pass them. That should help to give you a basic concept of what you can expect to find when you make the transport down to your new home.

"After seeing all that stuff you just showed us firsthand, I'm all right with it, but before that I really had no idea of what it to expect and it's far less worrying for me, in fact I think it's going to be kind of neat.

"I don't know about Juno and Sebastian, but after our little tour, I'm feeling much better now about what we are going to find in the new world.

"The only other thing that I'm now seriously concerned about is this memory changing stuff. I can't help but wonder what it entails, and I would really like to have a better idea of what it's all about before I undergo it."

Jonah and Venus exchanged looks and Venus nodded.

"No problem. You've been cleared for the entire secure area. C'mon. We'll head there now. It's just one floor up."

CHAPTER TWENTY-FOUR

- Hominoid Genetic Perfection -

The five of them took the elevator up to the next level and Venus led them down the hall toward the *'Cleansing'* unit. As they walked, Jonah had continued the previous commentary.

"As Venus mentioned earlier before we began the tour, we have already completed the selection of Humanoid species that will share the planet with you in the initial stages of the new world's species development. Those chosen have already been placed within the service capsules that will fulfill the cleanse function and maintain life in suspended animation until the new planet is ready to receive you all.

"Once inside, you will be able to see for yourself what it all looks like. Its kind of like sleeping in a bed of warm enveloping water. You can see what the setup looks like and get a basic idea of how the system works.

"There is nothing to worry about. This procedure has been used again and again for the same purpose for quantum entities and has never failed to deliver perfect specimens when the time came for rejuvenation, which comes just prior to colony placement."

Before palming the door lock, Venus did her best to prepare them for what they were about to see.

"Before we go in, I should tell you that Jonah and I only viewed the actual chamber for the first time very recently and I can honestly say that neither of us really understand - all the mechanics of how this is possible and that the first sight of it was, for me at least, rather other-worldly.

"Suffice to say we had a thousand questions, but by the

time we'd left, I had personally concluded that despite the obvious complexity of it all, it appears a harmless and very peaceful process.

"Each of the Humanoids in the chamber is secured within a capsule and at complete rest. You can see that when you look at their faces, they are all at absolute ease.

"The individual capsules themselves have a good many tubes and monitors hooked up to them and the sight of it all can be a little unsettling at first but these are absolutely necessary to provide all the essentials that each specimen needs to sustain life until it is time for them to be awakened and prepared for their direct transport down to the new planet.

"I guess what I am trying to convey to you is that at first glance the whole idea is more than a little disconcerting. But once you have spent some time in the room, I think you will feel much more comfortable about the whole thing.

"I'm betting that you will feel as reassured as I did before we leave it today."

Jonah grinned and clapped Gabe on the shoulder.

"On the flip side Gabe, the initial experience is far from all bad.

"They are all nude in their glass-enclosed capsules and there are no ugly ducklings to be seen. No crap buddy, every single woman picked is a peach and there is a whole herd of really awesome-looking females in there. All in their mid to late teens and only the best of the best my man. Every one of those girls is built for loving and they have been very amply provided with all the necessary equipment needed to stimulate a male.

"Any man worth his salt and for sure, a Neanderthal with all those extra androgen things running around inside him like you have, is going to appreciate what's on offer.

"It's kind of like being a little kid locked in a candy store. Trust me, you're going to enjoy this."

A distinct frown formed on Juno's face and she tightened her grip on Gabe's hand, which she had been lovingly holding as they walked.

"You can look. As a matter of fact, as I gather half of them are male, so will I. But don't even think about ever doing any more than that."

Venus kicked Jonah in the shin and shook her head at him. Jonah let out a yelp.

"What the hell was that for? I was just trying to lighten things up a bit before we went in. Solar knows we could all use a little jocularity these days."

Venus gave him a scathing look.

"Don't be so crass. This is very important. Can you never be serious? Try to put yourself in their shoes for a moment. This is all very new to them, and we have asked them to trust us here. Be serious, for once in your life."

She abruptly turned her back on him and faced Juno as she nodded.

"That aside, point well made Juno. What is good for the gander is good for the goose, after all. Despite his chosen topic being distinctly demented, I must admit that my brother is right about the quality of the Humanoid specimens that are on view inside.

"Ever male in there is worth several second looks. They're honestly quite superb in every way; eye candy for sure. As well as all being very handsome in their own right, you can take my word for it; they've not in the least bit, been shortchanged when it comes to amazing male physical characteristics. Not to put too fine a point on it, they radiate robust health and virility.

"But there is no need to be overly concerned about the kind of thing you mentioned as necessarily becoming a problem. All the subjects chosen have already been pre-paired and to all intents and purposes can be considered as mated.

"It will of course be very important that a vigorous and fulsome procreation of the Humanoid population be ensured within the colonies in order to guarantee that the species expand rapidly. While that fact is something which may well suggest that each relationship already held may not be deemed as necessary to be maintained as monogamous, once those involved have become acclimatized to their new home, it is not particularly likely that this will occur.

"Rules about things like that will be determined through laws reached by way of a developing structure of functional guidelines for daily life, once you all reach the planet."

Juno arched her brows and turned to look up at Gabe.

"I'm sure that won't be something either Gabe or I would even consider. Would we Gabe?"

Gabe flushed slightly and did his best to shake his head vigorously and in a manner that he sincerely hoped was convincing.

"No, no, of course not."

Jonah smiled knowingly and winked at Gabe over Venus's shoulder.

"Well, time will tell of course, but after you've all had a look you might change your minds.

When I alluded to the fact that only perfect physical specimens had been chosen for the purpose of colonization, I wasn't kidding.

"There is not one woman in here that I wouldn't happily share my pillow with and, although she would never admit it to you, when we went through earlier, my dear and oh so prim little sister was absolutely drooling over the males."

Despite the somewhat frigid atmosphere, which had followed both Venus and Juno's earlier comments, all three of the Olympoians laughed.

Venus pressed her hand onto the locking control panel. The door rolled silently open.

As they entered, led by Venus, Jonah, taking up the rear, chuckled and quietly piped up with,

"Take note. She didn't deny it, did she?'

The brightly illuminated, all-white chamber, was quite large. At first impression, it was blatantly sterile and functional in appearance. There was almost complete silence. Only a soft, barely perceptible hum emanating from the individual life support systems could be heard.

The general ambience did not encourage speech.

All present seemed to sense the fact that any new sound introduced into the chamber would be likely to upset the atmospheric tone currently in evidence. Their nostrils filled with a muted but clearly antiseptic odour, to a certain degree, reflective of a medical institution previously visited.

Several worker Almies, wearing stark white coveralls, moved about between the separate capsules, carefully scrutinizing each in turn, in what appeared to be a continuous cycle.

Despite the chamber's instant aura of efficient practicability, its profusion of cables and tubes attached to each individual capsule, it was nevertheless a little chilling to anyone at first glance. That sensation however, was short-lived and very quickly shifted to an appreciation of what was quickly understood to be one of clinical, but efficient nurturing.

It took a few minutes of evaluation before each of the Olympoians realized why that was.

The well-spaced freestanding holding units, each ten feet in height and standing on a square polished metal base, clearly nurtured their charges who were floating inside easily, suspended in a clear fluid.

Each capsule was round and formed from seamless glass, allowing for easy three hundred and sixty-degree inspection.

Mainly however, it was the appearance of the specimens themselves, enclosed within the transparent containers, who conveyed the easily realized sense of relaxed warmth and tranquillity.

As crudely as Jonah had expressed his earlier evaluation of those residing within, he had not been misleading. For all present, the appreciation of what was on view within those capsules was undoubtedly stimulating in that very regard. However, the overall impression was far from being solely one of a lustful appreciation.

In fact, that specific instinctual preliminary appraisal was rather fleeting, although it certainly could not be denied. That these particular specimens were destined to be prime breeding examples was immediately obvious to anyone who entered the room. Even from a distance, each individual was very much more then just impressive when viewed. They were individually unique in that regard and yet if distinctly different, each held the shared example of being of perfect physical configuration.

The experience was mesmerizing. One could not easily shift his or her gaze from one to the next. It was not necessarily so much the initial sexual response that they elicited, but more a realization that their naked perfection itself could not be overlooked.

More importantly, it was the facial expressions that demanded the strongest attention.

Their serene expressions facilitated a sense of blissful harmony that was immediately transferred to anyone looking at them. The sensation was so potent that it seemed to be almost tactile in its composition.

Since entering the vast room, Venus had been surreptitiously observing the Olympoians' features and body language in an attempt to evaluate their individual reactions to what they were seeing. As the minutes passed, she began to feel less and less worried about how it was all going over.

They spent almost two hours silently moving about the chamber, taking the time to reflect upon the living contents of each individual suspension pod. And by time they came upon the final row consisting of empty capsules, three of which would obviously be used for their own later suspensions, it became apparent to her that each, if in awe, was by this point completely at ease and fully relaxed about that prospect ahead.

She smiled and spoke softly.

"If you have seen enough, Jonah and I would like to share a meal with you now. That will give us all an opportunity to further discuss what the future holds for you."

CHAPTER TWENTY-FIVE

- *Choices* -

The meal, held in the small dining room attached to their restricted quarters, was unhurried and in a tone befitting of what they had just seen. Despite receiving answers to all their questions, the Olympoians were, quite understandably, still primarily focused on what their futures would hold. And, in consideration of that focus, there remained within them a persistent, if by now significantly muted, sense of unease that could not be dismissed out of hand.

Venus purposely targeted that remaining nugget of concern as they went on to enjoy several cups of hot and freely fortified, honeyed tea. She intentionally pointed out to the three of them the fact that it was unrealistic to expect that they would be able to completely dispel some sense of unease at what they were about to experience. After all, they were each being asked to trustingly make an astounding leap of faith. Therefore, apprehension was normal, healthy and reasonable in the circumstances. In fact, it was a given.

Having everything out in the open accomplished Venus's goal. The Olympoians quickly realized the accuracy of her assessment and as they did, the majority of the residual tension seemed to flow silently out of the room.

Everyone relaxed.

The topics of conversation then changed completely.

Gabe, Juno and Sebastian pushed any lingering concerns aside and the five of them shifted easily into reminiscence and review of their shared past adventures.

By the time Jonah and Venus had to leave them, each of the Olympoians appeared relaxed and at peace with whatever was to come. As they gathered at the doorway in preparation to call it a night, Gabe, who had gone quiet over the past few minutes, spoke.

"So, we won't see you guys for a while then. I know we've been over this, but could you just give me and idea of what exactly is going to happen to us between now and when we get sent down to the new world. I'm pretty sure that its all in my head somewhere by now, but its just sort of spinning around in there and I'd appreciate it if you could kind of – step by step - lay it all out again for me."

The big Neanderthal was obviously a little embarrassed about asking. This resulted in a short lull in conversation. Having sensed this, Venus smiled and before she responded, she sent out a strong wave of warmth and affection to all three of them.

"Of course.

"This will be our last meal together for some time. In a few hours, we will raise our shields and begin to back off from Olympos until we have reached a safe viewpoint, one well clear of the shifting planets.

"In your time, it will only be a matter of a few days before we have been able to satisfy ourselves that the change in planet orbits has gone as expected. Atlantis will then begin its time-hops into the future, in stages.

"We will do that at intervals, until we see the eventual formation of liquid water and atmosphere. Once that happens we will begin to terraform the planet to our design and then start the process of developing life.

"All of you will be included with each step along the way. We will seek your input and value your assistance in helping in the additional choices we make. Eventually the planet's evolution will be complete to the point that Humanoid life can be colonized and that's when you will play your prominent part in the whole scenario, by way of joining in on the initial settlements.

"Experience tells us that these changes will take billions of years in real time but because we time-warp, that is of no real consequence to those of us aboard the ship and that includes each of you. It will be only a mater of days in your time before it will be time for you to transport.

"We Atlantians will all be very busy over this period and Jonah and I won't be able to spend a lot of time with you. But as I said, the Atlantian timeframe for it all is relatively short, since the ship is able to time-warp ahead at will and very swiftly.

"You have a couple of choices as to how you wish to spend those days.

"You may join your co-settlers in the memory cleanse capsules immediately if you wish. That way you would have no waiting whatsoever to endure. You would simply be reawakened once the planet is ready to sustain you and be immediately transported to the surface to begin your new lives.

"Or, if you wish and you don't think you will find it too boring, you can remain in your quarters until the planet is ready for you and leave your memory-cleanse for the last minute.

"If you should choose to do that Venus and I could bring you up to the main computer room and let you observe what has occurred each time we slip into a wormhole and warp forward in time. That will occur whenever the cooling and resulting changes on the new planet have reached the various levels of development that will require us to must make adjustments.

"In that way, you would have a chance to view the progressive development of the planet over time, and act as an advisory group to our committee as we fine-tune the progress of creating the right circumstances necessary to support the canonization of the Humanoid portion of its development."

Sebastian, sensing how difficult it had been for Gabe to ask for a review of what was to come and wanting to shift attention from his friend, was the first to reply.

"I for one would vote for the second option. Despite the

fact that I gather we would have no memory of having done it in the end, we would be given a once in a lifetime chance to observe the birth of our new world."

Venus nodded.

"Yes, those particular memories would have to be removed."

Juno locked eyes briefly with Gabe and when he nodded, she made it unanimous.

"Yes, the five of us as working as a team again. Let's all share the wonder of watching it be born and develop together."

* * * * *

Well guarded, manacled and under the watchful eyes of both Adon and Gaia, Marduke and a containerized Bellum were escorted down to the transporter bay.

His period of incarceration had left Marduke listless. His spirit was completely broken.

As the others cleared the area in preparation for the transport down to Olympos, Adon remained.

He looked sadly on what little stature and substance remained in his old friend. He was but a shell of what he had once been.

Adon spoke gently and without rancour.

"Since we were children, we've always competed for positon and responsibility. That said, until you relinquished your trust in our mission, I could always expect an honest challenge from you whenever our positions differed and when that challenge was offered, I accepted it with a certain pride and respect.

"I called, and considered you, my friend.

"I feel no pleasure at what I must now do, but you have given me no choice. Demeter has recanted your foolhardy venture and she will remain with us, but there is no longer any place on Atlantis for you. You relinquished that right when you chose to cast aside your duty and align yourself with a colonist progeny and a madman to boot. It is only fitting that you now join him and share his fortunes, whatever they may be.

"Atlantis will begin to pull away to safety once we have fished this transport. Our shields will be up and as we will be moving, no return transport will be possible, even if you were to find some way of attempting it.

"Your fate is sealed.

"I will leave you shackled. However, the code for the unlock is on this tablet, which I will now place in you pocket. You will be able to free yourself relatively easily, although I see little reason for you to care to be free under the circumstances.

"I feel nothing but sadness and disappointment in seeing you like this, but you and you alone are responsible for this ending."

Marduke slumped down onto his knees.

He did not look up as Adon left the chamber and the big door slid into place, sealing the room.

Adon stiffened his shoulders and did not look back as the transport began.

CHAPTER TWENTY-SIX

- Shifting Planets -

They had been following the six ships at a safe distance for several days. During that time there had been no indication that those aboard the vessels had spotted the low flying airship following in their wake. In darkness the entire fleet was brightly lit.

Jacob had made good use of the looking glass and from his observations, he was confident that the formation was indeed an Eisen invasion fleet.

As evening fell, he ordered the speed of the flying machine increased slightly and lowering the glass, he nodded at the helmsman.

"It would appear that fate has delivered our enemy into our hands. We will continue a complete blackout of the airship. Ensure that we show no light and slowly increase speed as it grows darker. I would like to overtake them at about two in the morning. Their crews will be inclined to be less observant at that hour and that fact combined with the benefit of surprise, should give us considerable advantage, at least in the short term.

"I'm betting that Eisen is on one of those vessels. That creature is so full of himself that he would want to personally lead this invasion. We have a limited number of the explosive devices at our disposal. However, if we drop one on each ship as we pass over them, and we are accurate in our drops we may well be able to sink them all. If not, we will turn about and use what we have left to hopefully finish the job.

"Stiffen your resolve, brothers, as you ready yourselves for the battle. It would seem that the outcome of our holy war may well depend on what we do this night.

"For if we succeed in our endeavours, the threat as we know it could be completely removed."

* * * * *

Adon had raised Atlantis's blast shields and ordered the abandonment of orbit and swift movement away from Olympos the moment Marduke's transport had been completed.

He and Gaia had immediately joined the elders in the main control room and were watching the withdrawal from the planet on the large screen by the time that the young Atlantian committee members arrived to join them.

Venus and Jonah had already advised that the decision had been reached to have the three Olympian's take part in the event and had garnered acceptance of their plan to involve them in this and ongoing observations of what was to come.

The space leap, using a previously defined worm hole was just about to take place when the latecomers arrived and when it did the view on the massive screen shuddered, blurred and faded to darkness. Moments later as they slipped out of the tunnel-like time warp the screen reformatted, defining Atlantis's new orbit as it provided a changed perspective, showing two much smaller planets in the center of the shot.

Venus whispered to the three Olympoians whose mouths were agape.

"We have time warped and are now much farther away. What you see on the screen is very highly magnified.

"Of the two planets in view, the one on the left is Olympos. They have not begun to change their orbits yet, but when they do, each will move further away from Solar and in time the other one will take up Olympos's original orbit. As Olympos shifts away from Solar, it will begin to die and the other will commence cooling and with our help, will soon be transformed into your new home.

"Atlantis will remain at this distance until the planets have settled fully into their new orbits and then we will travel the same worm hole in reverse and begin our periodic warps through time to observe the pace of the freshening and with it, the new planet's changing structure."

* * * * *

As darkness settled over the sea, lookouts aboard the invasion fleet reported a strange phenomenon - one of the three moons had disappeared from the clear night sky.

Feldmarschall von Jaeger left the bridge and stood on the foredeck looking upward for some time. He had expected to find that some type of cloud cover would be involved, or some other reasonable explanation for the sightings would occur to him.

It was not to be. The reports appeared to be well founded. Where one would have normally expected to find the three moons, there were now only two.

He considered drawing this conundrum to the attention of his leader, but Eisen was once again seasick and had already retired to his quarters with orders not to be disturbed.

Von Jaeger had no particular desire to challenge those orders and he shrugged and returned to the bridge, advising his subordinates that there was no doubt some type of temporary spectacle occurring mid-ocean had made one of the moons difficult to see. He suggested that it would probably be short-lived and that the hidden moon would reappear before the night was through.

The lookouts found that explanation a little hard to swallow, however. Uneasy, they had difficulty in keeping their eyes peeled for anything other than the specific spot high in the sky where the missing moon should by rights, be shining brightly.

* * * * *

The Devi was in her office chairing an early evening discussion on defensive measures with several of the military leaders who had arrived from afar with their troops in preparation for the holy war when one of her staff entered and delivered her a note.

The missive was short and straight to the point. One of the moons had disappeared from the night sky. Aabha knew what it signified. Her heart missed a beat and she suddenly felt cold, very cold.

So, it has begun.

She quietly sucked in a deep breath and when she raised her eyes up from reading and looked back to those siting around the table she smiled dismissively, casually crumpling up the note and surreptitiously shoving it deeply into the pocket of her robe.

* * * * *

Brother Jacob craned his neck in order to look up into the starlight sky.

There were only two moons out there all right. Solar only knows why. Must be an eclipse of some kind. Whatever it is, we don't have time to worry about it now.

He pulled his neck back in and doing his best to appear unconcerned, shrugged in the direction of the helmsman.

"No need for concern. We've all seen eclipses before."

He turned to a brother standing near the hatch leading to the rear of the aircraft.

"Spread the word. It's an eclipse. Ignore it and concentrate on our preparations. In a very few hours we will likely be deeply imbedded in the battle of a lifetime.*"*

When the hatch had closed behind the brother, Jacob swiveled around to stare out through the windscreen and into the darkness. His raised the glass to his eyes and peered toward the still distant, but brightly glittering fleet of ships stretching out toward the horizon.

I pray Solar that this missing moon is a good omen, but

why can I not shake the feeling that it is anything but. Time will tell.

CHAPTER TWENTY-SEVEN

- *Divided Loyalties* -

Unable to sleep with worry over what was about to befall Olympos, the Devi relinquished her bed and, clad in only her sleeping robe and slippers, made her way to her private chapel, where she spent the remaining hours of darkness praying and seeking guidance from Solar.

By daybreak she had achieved a certain, if hesitant, inner peace and had fortified her earlier decision to dismiss the knowledge of what was to become of Olympos. Buttressed in her commitment to the fulfilment of her promise to keep the matter private, she hardened herself and put her worries aside, turning her complete attention to the resumption of her duties as spiritual leader for the impending holy war.

After a light breakfast she convened her first meeting of the new day. By nine, Aabha was in conference with the military leaders of the newly arrived forces from the states of Kaina and Narain.

She had already hosted similar meetings for the commanders of state for the forces from Neru, Akad, Umma, Loma, Saibutan, Marcus Kalam Billan, Marrad, Dumuzi, Nippur and Lishana.

Those troops from the more distant states, being Ozalta, Kilia, Bora Mesa, Kish, Dorosar and Kaina were en route but had as yet failed to arrive. The two leaders from the island states of Sutra and Kuru, due to their size and close proximity to Indus, had sent notes of apology, asked for her blessing and declared their neutrality in the upcoming battle.

The current meeting had no more than commenced when her secretary interrupted and whispered in her ear. The colour drained from her face briefly as she listened, but she quickly recovered herself and turned to address her two guests.

"Gentlemen. A matter of state I'm afraid. I would ask you to excuse me for a few moments. "

She stood and, out of respect, they rose with her.

"I have ordered refreshments for you and beg that you forgive this interruption. I will rejoin you as soon as I can."

With that she followed her secretary out of the room and once the door was closed behind them she turned to face her.

"Where is he?"

The sister raised her hand to indicate the Devi's private apartments and Aabha nodded.

"Thank you. Arrange for food to be brought in to the two generals in my office. Ask one of the Mitra-Varuna to join them and keep them occupied until I return. It matters not which one, whomever is readily to hand will do."

Aabha turned abruptly away, crossed to the doorway and entered the small chamber opening into her official apartments. The brother of the golden ring waiting therein had obviously been pacing. His robe was wrinkled, his boots mud-spattered. He had a grim expression on his face.

For a brief moment she was unable to place him. He was new, a massive Neanderthal country boy who had very recently joined the order.

Benedict, yes that was it, Brother Benedict.

He had proven himself in intelligence gathering and been selected for his new position only a few months previously.

Aabha managed a smile.

"Brother Benedict, you have news, I understand."

"My apologies for interrupting you, Your Holiness. We have a situation of some importance."

He moved to drop to one knee and Aabha placed one hand under his elbow to prevent the completion of this move to submission.

"There is no need for you to use my title, nor to pay public deference, when we are alone. You forget that you are now a member of the only order that holds that specific privilege.

Please be at your ease and tell me what the problem is."

He stood stiffly to attention and nodded.

"It's the generals, those of Neru and Akad. After a night of drinking together, they fell out over which one of them was the senior and one thing led to another. At dawn they fought a duel down on the docks. Members of your police, supported by myself and another brother, managed to break it up, but before we could do so, both were injured seriously enough to require medical attention. The fool from Neru will likely die.

"We no more than got them off the docks, when lesser officers and common soldiers from both their camps began to arrive. They were only trading slurs and profanities when I left Brother Tonkin to observe the situation in order that I might report to you, but I must say that by that time the gathering members of the two armies were beginning to seriously outnumber the quantity of police that were available and attempting to keep them apart. I fear that if something is not done, they will soon be hacking each other apart right there on the dock.

"It is more to do with boredom than anything else. The city is extremely overcrowded and the foreign soldiers do nothing but drink and carouse from morning to night. As I'm sure you are aware, Neru and Akad went through a brief territorial war last year and there have been several escalating border confrontations between them since you negotiated the cease fire.

"While I'm concerned as to your wellbeing and am not suggesting that you physically intervene in quelling the ruckus, I believe that this incident may require your personal intervention behind the scenes, if we want to check it before it gets more out of hand than it already is."

Aabha nodded and let out a sigh.

"I understand, Brother Benedict. I was afraid of something like this.

"Both the King of Akad and the President of Neru have travelled here with their troops. I will see them immediately and deal with the situation.

"You return to brother Tonkin and observe. If it looks like it is going to get completely out of control, you return here and report to me immediately.

"In the meantime, I will read the riot act to the leaders of Neru and Akad and then dispatch the two of them down to take control of their respective forces. Once they have accomplished that, I will then banish the lot of them. In light of this foolishness, they and their troops will be ordered to leave the relative comfort of the inner compound and they can camp rough on the plain to the west until we are ready to meet the enemy.

"Perhaps it will serve as a lesson to any of the other leaders who cannot keep their men under control."

* * * * *

Juno and Gabe joined Sebastian in the small communal dining area that made up part of their small complex, for the first meal of the day. The monk had risen earlier and was already tying into the hearty farmers' breakfast he'd ordered from the two worker Almies that staffed the day shift, seeing to their wishes.

He looked up as they entered the room and smiled broadly.

"Well, top of the morning to you late risers! These little beggars can certainly whip up a good meal. I'm going to have to work out more often if I don't want to pack on the pounds."

Gabe laughed and rubbed his tummy.

"Good to hear. I could eat an ox."

Sebastian helped himself to a slug of mead to rinse his mouth and once he'd swallowed, he turned his gaze to Juno and then nodded toward Gabe.

"He won't have to worry about extra exercise though. You'll see to that I'm sure."

Due to the dark pigment of her skin, it was hard to read the flush rising from Juno's neck and flowing into her face, but Sebastian knew her well enough to pick up on it.

Juno was made of stern stuff. He hadn't intended to embarrass her and was genuinely surprised that he had done so.

The smile faded from his face and he quickly moved to dispel any further embarrassment by way of a complete shift in topic.

"You two got any idea how we should pass the day? This sitting around waiting is driving me nuts."

Gabe, oblivious to Juno's discomfort, responded as he dropped into the chair across from the brother.

"Ya, I know what you mean. I'd heard of cabin fever before but now I know firsthand what it's all about. How long do you think it will be before they let us out of here again?"

Juno instructed one of the hovering Almies as to what she and Gabe desired to eat and then glanced over at Sabastian.

"I don't know, but I think the three of us should spend some serious time together working on what part we want to play, if they are serious about us advising them on stuff for the new planet."

Gabe shrugged.

"I imagine we have plenty of time to do that. What's the rush?"

Juno began to speak but Sebastian beat her to the punch.

"You raise a good point Juno. If they are serious, and I see no indication that they are not, we should be prepared to offer sound advice. After all, it will be us who are going to have to live there for the rest of our lives."

Juno, completely recovered and with her normal self-confidence at the fore, spoke up.

"Yes, I've been giving it a good deal of thought. If we are to be consulted on how the planet is set up, we should be ready to voice a joint and firm proposal on whatever topic arises. Anything less will demonstrate an ineffective point of view and hold no sway.

"We need to discuss in depth any points that are important to us, reach a shared perspective on what our response should be when questioned about it and be prepared to argue and strongly support our opinion on it, if necessary."

Sebastian lowered his fork to his plate and wiped his mouth with a napkin.

"What you say makes a good deal of sense. If we hope to offer valuable council and more importantly perhaps, if we want to be taken seriously enough for them to continue to accept us around the table and allowing us to remain in the loop, we'd better be ready to offer significant input."

Juno, pleased they were on board with her idea, smiled.

"We also need to make a list of points that we want to raise. Be prepared to put new ideas onto the table, if we want to play an ongoing and significant role in what is to become of this new world."

Gabe thought for a moment and then nodded his head in agreement.

"Better than sitting around I guess. After we eat then, lets get down to it."

CHAPTER TWENTY-EIGHT

- Planning -

The committee of young Atlantians were gathered in the small meeting room. Gaia would be joining them shortly and while they waited for her arrival, they discussed general topics pertaining to the development of the new planet.

Venus had opened the gathering with a simple statement.

"We Atlantians have to take a whole new approach to our direct involvement in the day to day activities once the Hominid colonies have been established. We must not repeat the mistakes of previous efforts. Consider the mess that we have on Olympos now. A world war. Surely we can do better."

Jonah and Enoch met each others eyes and Jonah nodded confidently.

"Ya, Enoch and I have been doing some thinking on that, at least about what types of military gear they will have access to. From personal experience, I will say that we can go back to the period before Olympos was created for insight, of course, but as our generation personally played a very integral part of what was done on that specific planet, we can certainly learn from our personal knowledge of what occurred there.

"Enoch suggests, and I agree, that one of the big problems was the poorly planned and executed provision and deployment of weapons technology, especially in the later years. Put simply, you can't have a world war on a planet without advanced weaponry. If, in the case of the new planet, we are careful not to provide the tools of war on a large scale, it's not likely that it will happen again for us, or for those who follow."

Venus shook her head and sighed.

"Men and their weapons. Boys and their toys.

"What you say is correct of course. This current world war on Olympos could not have come about if Marduke had not provided the machines with which to accomplish it. But to suggest that war is the only, or even the biggest problem we Atlantians created on that planet, is very short sighted, in my view."

Both Jonah and Enoch were obviously affronted by the curtness of Venus's delivery of the statement and it was left to Persephone to smooth the ruffled feathers.

"What Venus has pointed out has a good deal of merit. When we create the circumstances for the development of Hominid life on this new planet, we need to broaden our assessment of what has come before if we intend to improve our creation over that which took place on Olympos. While the mistakes made with regard to the military situation are very obvious to us all, they are certainly not the only mistakes that were made by us Atlantians during the period of our caretaking."

Enoch moved to help reduce the tension.

"That makes sense."

Jonah, still smarting a little at his sister's put-down, shrugged.

"Alright Sis, why don't you explain to us simple-minded males exactly how we should fix all the problems that we Atlantians created when planning for the advancement of development on Olympos?"

Venus paused for a second and then raised her eyes and looked around the table.

"Obviously I don't have an answer to that.

"All I'm saying, and I apologise if I put it poorly before, is that we need to have a very different approach than what was chosen for Olympos if we want to do a better job than those who came before us."

She pursed her lips and struggled for a moment, looking for the words she wanted.

"I guess we could start by taking a little more care about how and when we interact with the new Hominid colonists, to ensure that we don't make too many decisions for them or push them too fast and too far. Perhaps we should let them find their own way more often than not and avoid the temptation to *'mother-hen'* them too much."

Enoch raised his eyebrows.

"You know; you might have something there. Once they are in place, consider spending more time watching and listening and less advising and directing them."

He glanced over at Jonah, who hesitated for a second and then shrugged his shoulders.

"I suppose there is the argument that too many cooks spoil the broth sort of thing."

Persephone smiled and nodded.

"Something to think about for sure."

Venus laughed.

"I think you've hit the nail on the head, big brother of mine.

"I don't know just how far we could take that concept. but perhaps we should go so far as to at least not directly interact with the new colonists to the degree that we did on Olympos.

"Sort of just observe from afar and stay away from the planet itself, at least in a physical sense. Let them make their own choices and decisions. Keep out of the picture unless a very serious situation arises, and maybe even then, only intervene indirectly and never one on one. Let them think they are creating their own domain so to speak."

Enoch bobbed his head.

"Why not. It is their world after all, not ours. Let's talk to Gaia about it. No direct intervention in what advancements or weapons they chose to develop. Leave them to their own devices. I'll bet its never been done that way before but I think if we could accomplish it, that type of approach could have a lot of advantages overall."

The sound of activity in the hallway beyond the room drew their attention and all three looked up to watch as Gaia, followed by *'Two'*, bustle into the room.

She smiled as she crossed the room to take her seat at the table.

"Good morning all. Don't let me interrupt. Carry on with your discussion please."

Venus glanced around at the others who nodded silently in agreement.

"We've been tossing around an idea and we would like your input."

Gaia found a comfortable spot on her chair as *'Two'* moved back against the wall behind her and shifted into rest mode.

"Oh yes, what is it then that you'd like to do?"

Venus took a few seconds to gather her thoughts before speaking.

"We think that on Olympos there was too much direct involvement by us Atlantians, once the Hominids had colonized the planet. We are of the view that with the new world, we should not directly involve ourselves in their day to day lives. That we should let them progress at their own speed without a great deal of involvement from us. In fact, just before you arrived we had concluded that there should probably be no direct physical interference with life on the planet at all by Atlantians, that they should be left to their own devices."

Gaia placed her hands together and looked from one to the other as she weighed the suggestion in her mind.

"You are suggesting that they never physically interact with any of us. That they remain unaware of our existence and that whatever we do involve ourselves in, appears to them to have been something that they either thought of themselves or originated on their own then?"

Persephone nodded.

"Yes exactly. Let them develop at their own pace. Stay out of it if at all possible and never show ourselves in a physical sense. Let them believe that everything that they accomplish has been managed completely on their own."

Gaia leaned back in her chair and clasped her hands in her lap as she evaluated the concept.

"Well, I can say that I do not believe that anything like that has ever been tried before. Why do you suggest it, what is the reasoning behind it?"

Surprisingly, it was Jonah who spoke up in response.

"We think that a good deal of what was negative on Olympos was due to the fact that we acted like a bunch of gods, helping them and bailing them out all the time when things got tough."

He nodded toward his sister.

"Venus brought the concept to our attention and we've kicked it around pretty thoroughly. I have to admit that I was a naysayer at first but the more we talked, the more I realized that she was right. It's their planet after all. Whenever possible, they should evolve at their own pace and be responsible for their own decisions."

Enoch put in his two-flakes worth.

"It seems to us that we Atlantians have the primary responsibility to prepare the planet in readiness for Hominid colonization and of course, fulfill the responsibility of overall caretakers.

"However, we see no reason why while doing that, we have to hold some omnipotent-like supervisory position, when it comes to how they choose to evolve on a day-to-day basis."

Gaia nodded.

"All right, if that is what you wish. So be it."

* * * * *

In the darkness, the airship had begun to close with the brightly lit ships ahead.

The gathered brothers located in the dimly lit interior of the bridge, held their silence as they prepared themselves for the battle to come.

Brother Jacob took one last look at the ominously missing

moon before turning his attention back to the horizon.

That be-damned moon.

Was it an omen of some kind?

Should I be rethinking my plan as a result?

He let out a deep sigh that audibly reverberated throughout the bridge.

"Helmsman. Cut back the power. Let us widen the distance between us."

Keyed up as the others were, they all turned to look at his shadowy silhouette.

Speaking to no one in particular he gave voice to his thoughts.

"We know where they are going and we have almost twice their speed if needed. We will postpone our attack. Instead we will allow them to pull away and when they do, we shall change course for the nearest land. There, we will drop off a brother to carry a message to the Devi.

"Traveling across land on horseback, with fresh mounts along the way and the blessing of Solar, he will reach the Holy See in time to give forewarning of this enemy armada.

"It is possible that we will not succeed in stopping all these ships in our attack. That being the case, we must at least attempt to give Her Holiness warning of the ships headed for Almeca.

"Once we have dispatched our messenger we can return to this course with all speed and then close and carry out our strike against them."

CHAPTER TWENTY-NINE

- *Internal Bickering* -

Bracketed by Brothers Benedict and Tonkin, the Devi stood on her private sundeck and let her eyes follow the long line of troops proceeding through the main gate of the enclosed compound of the Holy See. She had held true to her word.

The armies of both Neru and Akad had been banished from the city.

As she watched the tail end of the procession turn sharply right to follow the roadway leading into the open fields to the west, she observed the growing billows of rising dust begin to settle back down onto the rooftops of the buildings below.

Benedict spoke, breaking the silence.

"Thanks be to Solar, you managed it. Perhaps now we will have some peace."

Aabha shook her head and sighed.

"Yes, they are leaving but despite my condemnation of their foolish infighting, before they would actually leave the two leaders had the affront to get into an argument as to who would be the first to go. I had to intervene yet again at the last moment to settle the matter with the toss of a coin.

"This type of stupidity does not bode well for the battle ahead."

Tonkin, another new member of the order, a tall strongly built human who had been recruited primarily for his fighting skills, nodded solemnly.

"You have the right of it. We've not heard the last of those two ragamuffin hordes. They are an undisciplined lot, with no real leadership to shepherd them. Unless I miss my guess, they will be back at each others throats again before nightfall."

Benedict watched the Devi's shoulders slump and moved to soften the dismal picture that brought to mind.

"Well at least they will not be terrorizing the citizens twenty-four hours a day."

Tonkin humphed.

"No, but they'll definitely soon be hacking away at each other again if this war doesn't soon get underway."

Aabha suddenly felt very tired.

With full knowledge of the big picture, the apocalypse to come; what did this infinitesimal incident really matter?

We on Olympos have an unfortunate history of infighting, pettiness, greed and little regard for our fellow man.

Solar knows that we have little enough to be proud of.

Perhaps our fate is exactly the end we deserve, after spending eons making such a mess of our world.

* * * * *

They had remained in the small dining unit, using the table which the Almies had now cleared and wiped clean.

Juno had a blank pad and pencil in front of her and as they talked, she was making copious notes as they discussed various points.

In opening, they had decided that there was little informed input they could offer the Atlantians when it came to the physical creation of the new planet is self. Once everything was in readiness for the first Hominid transport however, they could offer suggestions based upon their personal observations over the time they had spent on Olympos.

With that in mind, the first area they addressed was related to the specific concept of how the deployment of the colony of Hominids should be initially structured.

In order to do this, they agreed to rely on the hands-on experiences each had shared over their time spent on Olympos. They began by trying to pinpoint ways to remove what they jointly considered as likely obstacles to a successful long-term colonization of the new planet.

Having only their first-hand knowledge and experiences to rely on, they looked at refining the Olympos model, looking at finding a better overall initial settlement structure, during the first stages of the exercise. From there they moved on to evaluating the various developmental phases of Hominid living conditions on the new planet. They hoped all of this would lead to an improved model for the initial stages of entrenchment by the neophyte races.

After a couple of hours, the first wave of ideas had begun to wane and it became obviously to all three of them that it was time for a rest.

Juno put her pencil down and lifted up the pad.

"Right, before we take a break let's just go over the topics we've already covered so far to be sure I've got them clearly recorded.

"No Shapeshifters or Trolls. They either threatened or provided little advancement of the Hominid species on Olympos.

"Human colonization should consist of a limited number of groups made up of fairly large numbers for self-protection and should be located in widespread groups. The more independent Neanderthal settlements should be situated in a more compact area, with each individual unit consisting of much smaller numbers than that of the Human communities.

"Ideally the three of us would settle in an area between the two races, as a sort of buffer. That would allow us to monitor how each is developing and keep a record of their unique advances and accomplishments.

"Generally speaking, we feel the two races should be entrenched in spots where they are relatively distant from each other in order to minimize territorial disputes, but close enough to be able to intermingle periodically if they so choose.

"Situated between them, we would also be positioned to guide their development. Additionally, when the need arose, we could encourage expertise sharing and trade between them as we deemed it advisable."

Venus appeared in the small room just as they were wrapping up.

"The two planets have begun to move. I thought you might want to come up top with us to take part in the review my father will be giving. He will be providing a good deal of background information for us in preparation for our fist warp. His talk will cover what has occurred so far in the creation and development of the new planet we will be going to colonize. Once he has delivered his missive, we will hit a new worm hole and then time warp ahead and visually confirm that both planets have in fact settled into their new orbits."

Juno scooped up her pad and smiled.

"We've just been putting together some thoughts on what we think might help at the time when we colonize. I'll bring our notes with us and perhaps we will also have an opportunity to share those before we advance through time."

Venus nodded.

"Yes, by all means. There won't be a great deal to see on the first warp. It will be just to confirm that the new orbits for both have been achieved, but I'm sure you will find it interesting."

Sebastian frowned.

"I for one am not so sure I want to see Olympos begin its road to destruction. It's one thing to know that it is going to happen, but something else to see it first hand."

Venus crossed to him and placed a comforting hand on his shoulder.

"The initial changes to both planets as seen after this first warp will be miniscule. They will have just entered into their new positions when we make this first time jump, but you will have some idea of what we have previously discussed, once you see it for yourselves. Any changes that have already occurred on the two planets will be small, as they will have just entered into their new positions when we come out of our warp. You will have a better idea of what I'm talking about once you see them in their new positions with your own eyes.

"Don't be overly concerned about seeing any negative adjustment in the condition of Olympos when we arrive on this occasion. There will be some minor changes occurring at this early stage, primarily due to a drop in temperature caused by the greater distance from the sun, but these will not be readily apparent from afar.

However, if you think it still might make you uncomfortable, you certainly don't have to join us."

The monk shrugged.

"No, it was just a passing thought. You're right, this is a once in a lifetime opportunity. I committed to this concept and now I have to see it through, whatever uncomfortable situations that may entail."

Venus looked from him to Juno and Gabe.

"You two alright with this?"

They nodded in unison and she smiled.

"Right, let's head up to the control room then, they're waiting for us."

CHAPTER THIRTY

- *Expanded Solar System* -

The lowering of the young brother down from the airship had taken longer than Jacob had anticipated.

It was the weather more than the actual procedure that had made the process so difficult. Over the past half hour there had been an unexpected and sudden drop in temperature of several degrees, accompanied by a bewildering increase in the prevailing winds and choppy seas. Once over land they'd had to clear a heavily forested area along the coast where the huge trees were being whipped about, their tops visibly shredding in a steadily worsening gale, to seek out a small valley bereft of large growth.

He heaved a sigh of relief as he watched the wiry figure release himself from the rope and wave back up at the awkwardly hovering airship.

It was done. Hopefully now, with Solar's blessing, the Devi would receive at least some warning of what was headed her way. There was little more he could do to ensure that.

It was time to return to course and overtake Eisen's fleet.

He turned from the windscreen and spoke to the helmsman.

"A direct course to overtake the ships. If at all possible, I want to be in a position to attack by nightfall."

* * * * *

Additional seating had been arranged and as Venus led the three Olympoians into the massive room they were greeted by a full house. All the remaining Atlantians on board the space craft were already present and seated in front of the huge screen.

The assemblage rose as one as the young trio entered and Adon, standing in front of his control terminal, turned to face them.

"And here are our guests. Let's take this opportunity to not only welcome them to our midst, but to thank them properly for the part they played in our successful return to Atlantis."

A resounding round of applause filled the chamber.

Venus stepped back a few paces from the Olympoians in order to allow them to exclusively bask in the heartfelt affection being expressed from the floor.

All the Atlantians were of course dressed in their normal attire, that being the universal sleeveless white formfitting body suit. Gabe was wearing a simple shirt and pants constructed of coarse broadcloth and Sebastian was attired in a dark blue robe of the Faith. Both methods of dress were by now common enough to all aboard the ship, in view of the fact that all the Atlantians had spent at least some time on Olympos.

Of the three, it was Juno upon whom the majority of the visual attention was currently being centered.

Diminutive in size though she might be in comparison to the others in the room, Juno, simply being Juno, had that morning chosen to clothe herself in a skin-hugging bright red leotard, which left absolutely nothing to the imagination. She stood out like a single spring flower surrounded by a bed of snow, a vibrant splash of intense colour, colour strongly accented by some very clearly defined and exceptional feminine attributes.

The males in the room, especially the younger Atlantians, couldn't take their eyes off her and the majority of the females, if for different reasons, were paying her heed as well.

While being the centre of attention embarrassed Gabe, who immediately began to flush, Sebastian appeared unabashedly pleased and Juno, who had been a little concerned about how the trio would be received by the other Atlantians, especially the elders, was ecstatic and beamed brightly.

Gaia had saved seating in the front row for the new arrivals and she stood up and crossed to them, welcoming each individually, before she and Venus led them to their seats.

As they took their places the applause halted and the Atlantians sat down. Adon then turned back to face his terminal. He worked the keyboard as he spoke.

"While the elders are generally aware of what is currently taking place in our solar system, the younger members and our guests have little real knowledge of what an astounding development has come to pass. In order to bring everyone up to speed, I will do my best, in laymen's terms, to explain what we are about to see as I provide some background to what led up to it and what we can expect to occur in the future."

The massive screen which had been blank when Venus and the Olympoians had entered the chamber, now changed from a blank blue to reflect a snapshot of the newly positioned planets in the solar system.

"In order to assist you in comprehending what we will shortly be observing, I will first supply a rough idea of how the six closest planets now revolving around Solar are situated in relation to their distance from that wonderful source of life."

Now reflected on the big screen was a depiction of Solar and fanning out from it, five spheres representing planets.

Adon touched the keyboard and a black 'X' appeared at the bottom of the screen and moved up to rest on the largest sphere.

"This is Solar. As you can see, it is very much larger than the other planets, all of which orbit around it."

The remaining spheres differ in size considerably, the closest to Solar being the smallest of the six, followed by a larger planet. The next is larger yet. The fourth is smaller than the third and the remaining two are relatively large spheres."

The 'X' shifted off solar and settled itself onto the fourth planet away from Solar.

"This is the planet we know as Olympos."

The 'X' moved again coming to rest on the first planet from Solar.

"This little guy has just been created and has now taken up what used to be the orbit of the second."

The 'X' now began to move from planet to planet, outward from Solar.

"All six planets reflected on the screen moved further away from Solar after the new planet was formed. Each replaced the orbit of the other in order to accomplish this. Olympos has moved further out from its previous orbit around Solar, and the new planet, as yet unnamed, has moved to replace Olympos's position.

"It is on this new planet that we will be colonizing new life. Historically, we Atlantians have always reserved the privilege of naming their new home to the members of the first colony of Hominid life to appear on its surface."

Adon waited a few moments before using the keyboard again to turn the screen blank.

"There are many more planets in our solar system than the six that were depicted on the screen, but that is not of concern to us. What is of importance is the fact that the repositioning of each of the six, their resulting new distance from Solar specifically, is what provides us with the raw material needed to create a new world.

"The easiest way for me to explain that fact is to ask you to consider Solar as a massive ball of fire. As such, it radiates tremendous heat outward. The planet closest to Solar is therefore also quite hot, but as we move outward from Solar, moving from planet to planet, the effect of its radiated heat lessens for each, as the specific distance away from that source of heat, increases.

"Only a single planet in the lineup I just displayed is in an orbit around Solar that will allow for a temperature range that, over time, will allow the formation of life. Until recently that planet was Olympos, the planet on which we of Atlantis last helped to create life.

"A new planet has now taken up that exact orbit and it is here that we will next go through the life creating process. That progression, in real terms, will take billions of years. However, our ability to time warp will allow us to follow the complete transformation required, both by Solar's reflected heat and our steps to terraform, in a matter of weeks.

"The physical changes that are required to ready the new planet for the part we will play in its transition into an incubator for life will be primarily provided by Solar by way of a series of changes in temperature that will now take place on this planet over time.

"I think that will be enough information for our younger members to absorb for today. So if there are no questions specific to what I've related, I suggest we move on to making our initial time warp into the future and have our first look at both the new orbit of Olympos and more importantly, that of our new prospect for Hominid colonization."

* * * * *

Thunder clouds had begun to form over the bay shortly after Aabha had watched the procession of troops leave the city. With them came whitecaps on the previously placid surface of the water below the palace and a definite chill in the air.

None of this helped her generally depressed state.

As the first raindrops, unsettling and completely out of season, began to drop she dismissed the two brothers and returned alone to the privacy of her chapel. There she sought direction from Solar in dealing with the growing weight of her despondent state of mind.

She received little satisfaction in her attempts to seek solace and guidance.

Her God seemed to have abandoned her.

What had been a sunny day had transformed into a herculean downpour and as the rivulets of water forked their way down the big window above and in front of her, the sudden darkness frightened her.

She lit candles for light and tears formed and began to roll slowly down her cheeks.

Despite her efforts to fight it, she felt her previously unbridled faith beginning to slip away for the first time in her life.

An earlier thought reoccurred with terrifying clarity.

Perhaps it is the end we deserve, after spending thousands of years making such a mess of our world.

CHAPTER THIRTY-ONE

- *Time Warp* -

Using the keyboard, Adon lowered the main lighting system in the control room. As the illumination dimmed, the spatter of conversations around him dissipated rapidly. There was a shifting in chairs as all present turned their attention toward the large main screen and silence imbued the chamber.

Adon worked the keyboard again and the screen came to life, turning a soft, even hue of blue.

"We are entering the worm hole and beginning our warp now. What you next see will be a view of Solar and the six planets in their new orbits, as they move around it. In order to be protected from the intense heat radiating from the closest planets, we will be at some distance from them as we slip out of the worm. As a result, we will require some magnification before we will be able to study the individual planets with any real intensity."

There was little to indicate that the starship Atlantis had begun to move; nothing more than a slight hum as the ship's powerful engines rose to full power.

Adon had no more than finished speaking when the screen faded to black momentarily. Then as the faint hum slackened and then disappeared entirely, the image on the screen firmed up, shifting to a pixilated blue and then filled with the scene he had described.

Although at considerable distance, and therefore appearing as tiny spheres, each of the planets could be clearly seen. A shared and spontaneous expression of amazement and delight filled the room as the image firmed up. Murmured conversation replaced the silence. When the image was crystal clear Adon spoke again.

"As you can see a new planet has formed next to Solar and the orbits of the remainder have each shifted outward. The further the individual planets are from Solar, the less radiated heat and illumination they receive. Having moved away from Solar, Olympos will now begin to cool down. As that process occurs the atmosphere will collapse and conditions will deteriorate fairly rapidly and in time Olympos will lose its ability to sustain life..."

As that fact registered on everyone, the room became silent once again. The younger Atlantians and especially the three Olympoians became lost in their own thoughts. Adon had anticipated such a reaction and he continued.

"...Our main concern from this point on, is the planet that has taken up the orbit that Olympos held before the shift. Until the shift outward occurred it received far too much radiated heat from Solar to allow for the formation of the necessary attributes that would allow for lifeforms to exist. To a much lesser degree, it will also now begin to cool and over time will reach a mean temperature that will allow for the creation of the atmosphere and liquid water necessary for us to begin terraforming and making the other preparations for the future colonization."

Adon fingered the keyboard and the scene began to magnify.

"I will bring the screen image up to full magnification and as I do so, Solar and four of the planets will slip off the screen. We will then be left with only the two that concern us at the moment. Keep in mind that due to how far we are from them, our ability to see a perfectly clear depiction of each planet will be impossible."

The shot of Olympos and the planet that had replaced its orbit began to grow in size perceptively as the others planets slipped off the screen. Adon made an adjustment, which caused the image to centre only on Olympos and the planet that had replaced it. He then backed the magnification off slightly until the two planets were as clearly depicted as he could make them.

The result was much better than it had been, but the image was still somewhat fuzzy and far from perfect. Olympos showed as a sphere, the surface of which consisted of scatterings of blue, white and green blobs of colour. In contrast, the new planet showed as a yellowy-brown collage.

"That is the best image I can offer from this distance. As the two planets go through their cooling processes, we will be able to warp closer to them on each successive occasion and with each shift closer, we will get larger and clearer studies of both."

Along with all the elder Atlantians, Adon was very conscious of the concern, fear, and sense of loss emanating from their Olympoian guests and that of the four young Atlantian committee members. Aware of the depth of their unease and anxiety brought on by the physical viewing of the changes, knowing what it meant for the dying planet, he had no wish to drag it out. He shut the screen down and raised the main lighting to its normal brightness.

"Atlantis will hold this positon for four hours. During this time, we will all have a chance to individually appreciate, rationalize and hopefully find the strength necessary to accept what the shift in these planets truly signifies.

"We will meet back here again in four hours. We will then spend some time in enlightenment as to exactly how our solar system was created and what will take place on the new planet between this point and the time for colonization. This general overview, the mental trip back in time and the glimpse into the future, will bring us all up to speed on how it all began and what is ahead for the new planet. Once we have benefited from this overview of events, both old and to come, the committee of young Atlantians, supported by our guests from Olympos, will commence the first of their many combined planning meetings for the future development of the new planet. In view of the decision to have Jonah and Enoch switch their advisory roles, from now on Enoch will have to spend the majority of his free time with me with a view to his eventually stepping into the lead position for the development of the new world. Jonah will join us as he will have to take instruction from Enoch with regard to his new posting as military advisor and he will also assist me in helping Enoch prepare for that change as well. Venus will spend her unstructured time with her mother, fine-tuning her studies to take up the responsibility for the construct and overseeing of the love and beauty to be displayed among the Hominoids, who will colonize the new planet.

"Until it comes time for the terraforming of the new planet, the elders, with direct responsibility for the advisory roles and their relevant successors, will continue to fulfill these positions, supplying advice to the committee members as required."

He then extended a flow of warmth and support to those who might have had difficulty with what they had seen depicted on the screen and it was soon amplified by that of the other Atlantians in the chamber.

Shortly thereafter, the chairs emptied as groups and individuals left to seek a few hours of quiet reflection before the next gathering.

* * * * *

The intense drumming sound of the airship's motors flooding the bridge had become the norm and no one any longer paid it much attention. They were flying at top speed and as Solar began to settle over the horizon all eyes were glued on the windscreen, the progressively heavier seas and steadily darkening skies ahead. Coming very close to dropping the looking glass, Jacob braced himself as yet another shudder rippled along the length of the craft.

Over the past few hours, the winds, and it seemed by this time rather silly to call them that, had raised from blustery to squally to absolutely insane. They ship was now being hammered by repeated gusts that were increasing in intensity with each succeeding wave. Thunderous rain had been falling for the last hour and now as Jacob searched for signs of the fleet ahead, the rain turned to sleet briefly before morphing into freezing pellets that were soon sticking to the outside of the large window.

The helmsman, who had been struggling to keep the craft on course, shouted in frustration and growing apprehension.

"She's becoming heavier, Brother Jacob! I'm at full power and still having trouble keeping her level! If this keeps up much longer, we're going to ditch!"

With a great deal of effort on his part, Jacob was able to respond in a calm monotone.

"We must be close to them. Hold your speed, brother. Remember, we have Solar on our side in this holy enterprise."

A younger member of the brotherhood, struggling to keep his footing spoke without thinking.

"Has anyone noticed that we can no longer see Solar for the blackness of the clouds?"

Jacob lowered his eyeglass and turned to face the man.

"Enough. We have our duty and we will fulfill it, or perish in the attempt."

* * * * *

The seas were raucous, some individual waves sweeping entirely over the straggling procession of ships as they struggled to make headway.

Eisen had been unable to keep anything down for the past twenty-four hours.

The Rector was so seasick; he was completely incapacitated. He hovered in and out of consciousness and refused to see anyone but his doctor. He was far from the only one aboard the battered fleet to have succumbed to the fury of the raging storm. The ships, mere specks in the massive body of rampant vehemence, were being tossed about like infinitesimal flotsam and jetsam.

In the minority, Feldmarschall von Jaeger was not seasick, but he was frightened out of his wits and had retired to his cabin in an attempt to preserve his position of command.

No one on board the fleet was any longer thinking about the supposed battle ahead. They were all simply praying for deliverance from the clutches of the cataclysmic hurricane-like weather.

* * * * *

Brother Benedict attended the Devi as a result of a message delivered by a sister. He found Aabha in her office, shoulders slumped and standing at the big window looking out over the thrashing waters of the protected bay. Engrossed as she was, the Devi did not hear him enter the room and the young brother cleared his throat to alert her to his presence. She let out a deep sigh and turned to face him.

"Have you ever seen weather like this? Has anyone?"

Benedict shook his head but gave no other reply. Aabha steeled herself and forced her shoulders back.

"What is the situation with the armies? Have they all arrived now? I have heard no reports of problems for the past few hours."

Benedict didn't fully understand why his Devi was so down at the mouth. However, he could clearly see that she was suffering and he strove to offer encouraging news, what little of it there was.

"All have arrived, although the latest are a bedraggled-looking array due to the extraordinarily bad weather. For those who were already here, that same weather has taken all the excess energy out of them. They are all huddled in their encampments and quarters, waiting out the storm. We had pulled back all but a few of the police as there has been no bad behaviour reported over the past few hours."

Aabha laughed, if half-heartedly.

"I suppose we can say that it has a silver lining then, this completely unseasonable, unexpected, unexplained and otherworldly deluge. Massive winds, pounding rain, then snow and now freezing rain. The likes of which no one on

Olympos has ever experienced before, whatever the season. Solar preserve us, when will it stop?"

The brother grimaced.

"I don't know Holy Mother. I will say though, that no army can fight in conditions like this. So if it is war that we face, our enemy must have also come to that realization. Mother nature has loosed this fury upon us and no mere being can stand against her. Perhaps it is the work of Solar in aid of our Holy war against the fascist threat."

Aabha did not respond to the statement. She knew better.

Solar had nothing to do with what was happening on Olympos.

CHAPTER THIRTY-TWO

- *Solar System* -

The group of advisors, young Atlantians and the Olympoian guests, had re-formed in the main control room.

Adon waited until all were seated and the burble of muted conversations had died before he set to work at the keyboard. Once again the main lighting receded to a dull glow as the large wall-mounted monitor came to life before the seated audience.

As the first image filled the big screen, Adon began to speak.

"The biopic being presented has been handed down from generation to generation since the star ship Atlantis began her mission for this galaxy. It provides an overview of the origin of this galaxy and the specific events that had brought about the cyclical creation of each life-sustaining planet, within its confines.

"Based on what we have witnessed during the period that Olympos formed we can expect that our new planet will, develop along similar lines.

"This planet is currently approximately one-third of the age of the universe and an enormous amount of geological changes, accompanied by biological changes, have occurred over that time span. It was formed about four and one half billion years ago by accretion from the solar nebula.

"Volcanic outgassing created the primordial atmosphere and then the ocean; but at that time, the atmosphere contained almost no oxygen and so would have been toxic to most of the lifeforms we see on Olympos, and that would include Hominids. Much of the planet was molten because of frequent collisions with other bodies which, in turn led to extreme volcanism. Over time, Olympos cooled, causing the formation of a solid crust, which allowed liquid water to form on the surface.

"The early development of Olympos is referred to as the Hadean eon. This was the era before life began on Olympos and covers the period of its birth and early development, which ended approximately four billion years ago.

"The Archean and Proterozoic eons followed the Hadean. They produced the precursors necessary for the formation of life on Olympos and then onward throughout the evolution of this early life.

"The succeeding eon is known as the Phanerozoic. The Phanerozoic consisted of three unique component eras, the Paleozoic, the Mesozoic and the Cenozoic, which evolved into the subsequent development of the dominant mammals which now exist on Olympos.

"Hopefully, with this knowledge as background, you will find it easier to understand the new planet which has now taken up Olympos's orbit. What Olympos went through during its very early stages of development is what this planet has also experienced and will experience until we begin to interact with it in order to a help create a new world that is also able to support life.

"I will narrate during the presentation."

All eyes were glued to the screen which depicted a protoplanetary disk.

"What you see here is a rotating circumstellar disk of dense gas and dust surrounding a young newly formed star, which can lead to the creation of a solar system. This proto-planetary disk may also be considered an accretion disk for the star itself, because gasses or other material could be falling from the inner edge of the disk onto the surface of the star itself.

"Protoplanetary disks are thin structures, with a typical vertical height much smaller than the radius, and a typical mass much smaller than that of the young central star.

"These disks consist of a turbulent envelope of plasma,

which is called the active zone. This envelope encases an extensive region of quiescent gas which is referred to as the dead zone. The dead zone is located at the mid-plane and can slow down the flow of matter through the disk, which prohibits achieving a steady state."

Gabe, who for the past several minutes had been propping up his drooping head with one arm, his elbow resting on the armrest of his chair, suddenly lost the battle in his attempt to remain attentive to the lecture. As his eyes closed, a trickle of drool glistened at the corner of his mouth and he began to snore softly. A couple of minutes later his head slipped off his hand and landed on Juno's shoulder.

Relatively speaking, it was a soft landing. However, being totally absorbed in what Adon had been saying and as unexpected as it was; the contact was enough to cause Juno to let out a surprised yelp.

The sound, coming at a moment when Adon had paused and was just about to continue, was magnified by the acoustics of the room and all eyes turned to see what had brought it about.

Embarrassed, Juno raised a hand to her mouth and did her best to sink lower into her seat.

Jolted back to consciousness by her startled squeal, Gabe's eyes had snapped open. He uttered a strangled snort. Momentarily off balance and with arms flailing, he struggled valiantly to maintain his seat.

Sebastian, who had been watching the entire incident unfold with some amusement, found himself having to duck his head to avoid being struck by a wayward elbow, which he'd then grasped firmly in order to steady the big Neanderthal.

This intervention only served to deepen Juno's embarrassment while adding to the growing attention of the others in the room.

Jonah, who had also been gleefully aware of Gabe's flagging interest and had watched it all unfold, burst into laughter as Gabe, now very much the centre of attention, flushed profusely and sheepishly blurted.

"I'm all right, just a little cramp in my leg is all…"

Adon's train of thought had vanished completely.

Venus smiled and silently messaged her father, who was standing with his mouth open staring out at the assembled group.

"Father, perhaps we should take a little break to let everyone stretch their legs."

* * * * *

Gabe, Juno and Sebastian, accompanied by both Venus and Jonah, were sitting around the table in the dining quarters of their apartment complex. Still flushed with mortification, Gabe was being teased unmercifully by the others. He was not amused.

"…Look, so I dozed off. For the love of Solar, who could blame me. Nothing personal, but he does go on and on. I know some people enjoy detailed scientific explanations, but people like me would appreciate a little summarizing – you know, maybe taking a long paragraph and whittling it down to a sentence or two. Would that be asking too much?"

His sympathies at least in part with his Neanderthal friend, Jonah managed to wipe the smile of his face.

"He can tend to get very absorbed in his topics. No argument there."

Venus nodded and looked from Gabe to Juno and then Sebastian.

"Yes, but this stuff is important. While I can see Gabe's point and would venture to guess that he is not entirely alone in his opinion, you have to remember that the primary audience for this information is the younger Atlantians, not specifically you guys. This is a very big deal for us. We need all the information we can get to ensure that what we do with the new planet has the benefit of all the knowledge we can garner in preparation for the creation of a better world. You could argue that under the circumstances, the three of you do not need the intense depth of data that we do, but you have to recognize that you were given the option of being part of the process from the get-go or choosing to instead simply sit it all out in the cleansing chamber until it was time for you to join the colonization."

Sebastian responded.

"Yes, and in fairness your father has made it perfectly clear that we can still select that option. I guess it just boils down to us making a firm commitment either way."

Juno let out a sigh.

"In my opinion it would be dumb for us to take the easy way out. I'm with Gabe as to how hard it is to sit listening to all this stuff. To be honest, I think most of it is going in one ear and out the other, but maybe, just maybe it's worth the effort to stick it out. Who knows what we will remember after our cleansing? Apparently some things will still be retained and they might go a long way toward making our lives easier once we are down there for good. And even if that is not the case, by doing this we ensure that we can be part of the process of organizing what is to come for the new planet and that has to be of some importance. After all, it will be us down there living under the conditions and in the environment which the current planning process is going to put into place."

Gabe shrugged.

"Maybe if we can just have shorter sessions. I mean, he can be as detailed as he feels he has to, but at least give us regular breaks so we can get a chance to shake the cobwebs out of our heads before the next stint"

Venus smiled.

"I'll have a word with him before we go back in."

* * * * *

True to her word, Venus corralled her father and mother in the hallway outside before they went back in to continue the discourse.

Initially Adon was somewhat surprised to hear that the three Olympoians were not totally absorbed in the information he was providing. After a little prompting from Gaia, he soon accepted the fact that, although completely enthralling to the young Atlantians, some of the material he was offering could well leave the Olympoians out of their depth.

He agreed to shortening each session, delivering the content in simpler terms wherever possible, and providing for longer breaks between each recital.

* * * * *

Gabe did his best to make himself invisible as he entered the room after the break. Although he didn't actually see any, he was sure that there were a at least a few surreptitious glances being directed toward him as he took his seat. Adon made no specific mention of the earlier incident, but announced that in consideration of the intense nature of the subjects, from this point forward the sessions would last for no more than an hour and would be interspaced with breaks of a half hour.

As Gabe sat down he muttered under his breath.

"Solar, give me strength!"

The words were no more than out of his mouth when Adon started in again.

"We were discussing a proto-planetary disk...."

"The mass of a typical proto-planetary disk is dominated by its gas. However, the presence of dust grains plays a major role in its evolution, as these serve to shield the mid-plane of the disk from the energetic radiation generated from outer space. Protostars mainly form from molecular clouds consisting primarily of molecular hydrogen. When a portion of a molecular cloud reaches a critical size or density, it begins to collapse under its own gravity. This is called a solar nebula. As it increases in density, random gas motions originally present in the cloud, average out in favor of the direction of the nebula's net angular momentum. This instigates the rotation to increase as the nebula radius decreases, causing the cloud to flatten out and it then takes on the form of a disk. The initial collapse took approximately one hundred thousand years. At the end of this transformation, the star reached a surface temperature which is approximately equal to that of the main sequence star of the same mass."

Gabe let out a soft sigh and sat up as straight as he could and then leaned over slightly to whisper directly into Juno's ear.

"He's going to put me to sleep again..."

She promptly kicked him in the shin and then ignored him completely.

CHAPTER THIRTY-THREE

- *More Solar System* -

Adon was consciously attempting to keep his audience receptive, varying the modulation of his delivery and whenever possible, keeping the technical references to a minimum.

"…accretion of gas onto the star continues for another ten million years before the outer disk disappears. The resulting form is called a T Tauri star and with its creation a planetary system or, what we on Atlantis call a *'Solar System'*, begins. Our ancestors coined that phrase when they named our very first newly formed star *'Solar'*.

"Once a T Tauri star has formed, electrostatic and gravitational interactions combine to cause the dust and ice grains within the disk to accrete into planetesimals. This process competes against the stellar wind, which drives the gas out of the system, and gravity or accretion, which pulls material into the central of the T Tauri star. Additionally, planetary moons form from smaller, circum-planetary analogs of the protoplanetary disks. The formation of planets and moons in geometrically thin, gas and dust-rich disks, causes the planets to be arranged in an ecliptic plane."

A depiction of the planet that replaced Olympos and its single moon appeared on the screen and Adon continued.

"Tens of millions of years after the formation of this new Solar System, it contained dozens of moon to small planet-sized bodies. These were accreting and consolidating into the terrestrial planets that are apparent today. The single moon that is the only natural satellite of the planet we will be eventually colonizing is larger, relative to its planet, than any other satellite in our solar system. It was formed tens of millions of years after our solar system was created when a body as large as Olympos struck our soon to be new world a glancing blow. That collision released a tremendous amount of energy, enough to vaporize some of the planet's outer layers and melt both bodies. When it occurred, it caused a portion of the mantle material to eject into orbit around the planet and this material was depleted of metallic material. This new moon then condensed into a single body within a few weeks and under the influence of its own gravity, became spherical in shape."

The image on the screen shifted as the planet became centered and magnified in size.

"This process of changing began when it was first formed and will be ongoing until its end. The stages of these changes are known as eons. Two of these occurred before the planet moved to replace Olympos's orbit. Now that this planet has taken up its new orbit and has shifted further away from Solar it begins to cool and morph more seriously in a physically sense.

"The first of the eons was the Hadean and it was a time when the planet was much hotter than the Olympos we all know and completely inhospitable to all forms of life. It was a period of intense meteorite impacts and severe volcanic activity due to the large heat flow and geothermal gradient. Be that as it may, it already had liquid oceans or seas at that time.

"In the second phase, the Archean, the planet cooled significantly. Life forms as we know them on Olympos could not have survived on its surface, because the Archean atmosphere lacked oxygen and therefore had no ozone layer to block ultraviolet light. That being said, primordial life had begun to evolve by the early Archean.

"At this point in time, heat flow originating from the interior of the planet was forcing its way up to the surface. This is called mantle convection and is the process that drives plate tectonics, which is the creation of rigid tectonic plates at mid-oceanic ridges. These plates are then destroyed by subduction into the mantle at what are referred to as subduction zones.

"During the early Archean eon, the mantle was hotter than it is now, around three thousand degrees and as a result convection in the mantle was rapid. The initial crust, formed when the planet's surface first solidified, had totally disappeared by this point, due to these plate tectonics and the intense impacts of large scale bombardments of meteorites. The first large sections of continental crust, which were a product of differentiation of lighter elements during partial melting in the lower crust, appeared at the end of the Hadean eon. What is left today of these first small fragments has formed the cores around which the current, much larger continents shown on the screen, grew."

The image on the screen faded back to blue and Adon turned to face his audience.

"As you are all aware, life as we know it cannot be sustained on any planet that doesn't have two things: the right atmosphere and liquid water. Currently the planet that has taken up Olympus's old orbit has both.

"I think we have all absorbed enough for the moment. I suggest we take a half-hour break now and seek some light refreshment."

A single thought went through Gabe's mind.

"Praise Solar for small blessings."

* * * * *

Jacob, using the looking glass, was the first to spot the trailing ship in the convoy.

The image was anything but clear due to the intensity of the storm and the icing of the windscreen, but he'd caught just the impression of something cresting a humongous wave and then it was gone.

"We've caught them!"

He used his left hand to gesture.

"Off to the left a little. We're almost on top of them. Get

the explosive devices ready. We won't be able to maintain this speed much longer against these headwinds."

The helmsman, now supported in his task by two muscular brothers, was fighting the wheel in an attempt to bring about the slight change in course, as Jacob continued to scan the tumultuous waters ahead.

The battered ship crested the next wave.

"There! At the top of the wave! Can you see them…directly ahead of us now? Put us right over her and hold that position."

* * * * *

As they made their way to the exit, Gabe, animatedly favoring one leg, frowned at Juno.

"What was that kick for? I was only commenting, and it hurt."

Juno continued to move and didn't respond.

Sebastian arched his brows and addressed Gabe.

"What kick, did I miss something?"

Juno answered for him.

"He was whining at the start of the lecture and I nudged him slightly with my foot to shut him up."

Gabe snorted.

"Nudged! Nudged my ass. Here - look for yourself."

He moved to the side of the hall to let others pass and promptly hauled up his pant leg to show the monk his reddened shin.

"There - look at that. Nudged indeed."

Sebastian grinned but did not respond.

Juno didn't give Gabe the satisfaction of inspecting the shin. Instead she picked up her pace and the two of them had to do likewise if they wished to keep up with her.

Obviously not about to receive any sympathy from either of them, Gabe let out a sigh and let his pant leg drop back into place. When he and Sebastian had caught up to Juno, Gabe addressed her.

"What's the hurry babe?"

Juno frowned.

"I just want to get some exercise. I wish we could get outside for some real fresh air. Being cooped up on the ship is getting to me I guess."

Sebastian nodded.

"Well we've got a half hour before the next session. Let's find something interesting to do then."

Gabe perked up at the idea.

"Ya, how about we do some exploring. Let's go down to the chamber with all the animals and stuff and see what we can find."

Juno's frown faded and she smiled.

"Yes, some of the animals we saw earlier were really interesting. Now that we've chosen those that will inhabit the new world with us, it might be a good idea for us to go back and have a look at the specific species that we selected."

Sebastian retorted.

"Good thought, considering that we are going to have to deal with at least some of them on a one-on-one basis once we have colonized. Some for food for sure. We should spend the time to find out what they are like - their habits and such."

Juno laughed.

"More importantly perhaps we should make ourselves aware of which ones would be likely to use be interested in using us for food."

Gabe nodded.

"Let's do it."

Five minutes later they had made their way to the massive chamber and headed directly for the area housing the various animal species. Juno, who had memorized the species selected for the planet, led the way as they began moving along the hallway, peering through the one-way glass.

They viewed several of the smaller species, taking advantage of the small monitors that were affixed beside the windows of each separate enclosure. A simple touch of each of the screens would bring up a detailed description of the animal or animals in question.

They were enjoying the change in pace and time passed quickly. The had just managed to observe and read the descriptions of most of the animals on the list for the new planet and were looking in at Mastodons when Juno checked the time.

"We'd better head back. If we leave now we will just make it in time."

Gabe, fully absorbed by what they were doing, frowned but nodded.

"If we have to, but let's come back and finish during the next break."

CHAPTER THIRTY-FOUR

- Atmosphere and Water -

The audience returned to their seats in the main control room.

The majority of the Atlantians appeared refreshed from indulging in some light sustenance and taking a short walk. Gabe, Juno and Sebastian were hyped after spending their free time observing and learning the habit of the various animals.

Once the initial fidgeting had settled down, Adon picked up where he had left off.

"The correct atmosphere and liquid water are the two necessities for life to form and exist on any planet.

"Over time our new world will progress through three different atmospheres, beginning with one with a low oxygen content and morphing in two later stages, first to one with a slightly increased oxygen mixture and second, to one with a fairly high oxygen content.

"The first atmosphere this planet experienced was captured from the solar nebula. It was composed of a number of light elements from that solar nebula, primarily consisting of hydrogen and helium. Over time, a combination of the solar wind and the planet's own heat drove off this atmosphere.

"During and after the impact which created the moon, the molten planet released volatile gases, and additional gases were released by volcanic activity. Many of the volatiles were initially delivered during accretion by a process known as '*impact degassing*', in which incoming bodies vaporize on impact. This resulted in the formation of a second atmosphere, which was rich in greenhouse gases, but still very poor in oxygen content.

"On two occasions as this planet developed, it experienced ice ages, during which the entire surface was frozen. When the last of these melted it released bacteria and methane gas.

"The third atmosphere resulted after this bacterium began to produce oxygen. The result of that injection was the current atmosphere of the planet, which is rich in oxygen.

"The solar nebula that created the planet was far too hot for ice to form at the time of conception and the hydration of rocks by way of water vapor would have taken too long. The source of the liquid water on the new planet was supplied by the bombardment of water-rich meteorites from the outer asteroid belt and some of the larger planetary embryos from beyond range. Comets also contributed to this development.

"As the planet began to cool, clouds formed. Rain followed and initiated the system of rain cycles. Oceans had begun to form on the surface by the start of the Archean eon.

"Six hundred million years before Olympos was the planet we all recognize, the temperatures on that planet was about ninety-five degrees. While life was already blooming under water where the high level of radiation then being delivered by Solar's rays could not reach it, life on the surface of the planet remained barren with the exception of a few patches of algae.

"Thirty miles above the surface, at the point where the destructive rays entered the atmosphere, a change was about to occur, as the increasing oxygen levels interacted with the Solar radiation. The resulting chemical reaction produced another kind of gas, ozone.

"Over the next one hundred and twenty million years this new gas began to form a blanket around the entire planet, absorbing the lethal radiation. As it thickened, it eventually prevented the majority of the damaging rays from reaching the surface of the planet, thereby tipping the balance and allowing life to spring forth on the previously barren rocky surface.

"Initially only small mossy lumps formed but as they began to multiply, they produced more oxygen and levels of this important gas begin to soar in the planet's atmosphere.

"At a point three hundred and seventy-five million years before we left Olympos this transformation saw the beginnings of the future Hominid race. Over time, these early forms of life evolved into dinosaurs, birds, mammals and eventually the ancestors of the Hominid species. Over the same period, procreation of plant life on the planet evolved from using spores to that of seeds for procreation and, unlike the preceding spores, these seeds could survive for much longer periods without water.

"The seeds spread like wildfire over all the land masses and soon the previously barren rocks were rife with plant life. The result of this manifestation of greenery pumped out a vast additional supply of oxygen into the air, raising the level of oxygen in the atmosphere to levels even higher toward the end of the planet's life and bringing about the blue and green gardenlike quality that benefits Hominid existence.

"At this point in time on Olympos, the two initial requirements for the beginning of life were now finally in place.

"Also of interest is the fact that stars get brighter as they age. At the time of Olympos's formation, Solar would have been emitting only about fifty percent of its current power. We expect this will also be true on the new planet and anticipate the rays to become thirty percent brighter, between now and the time we begin our colonization."

Adon paused for a second, taking a sip from the glass beneath his keyboard, before changing topics.

"The earliest lifeforms on this new planet, which has now taken up the old orbit of Olympos, will be formed during what we refer to as the Eoarchean era and after a geological crust has begun to solidify upon the surface following the earlier molten or Hadean eon.

"These first living forms, derived from photosynthesis should begin on the new planet just as they did on Olympos, between two and three billion years ago and at that time began the process of further enriching the atmosphere with oxygen.

"We are not speaking of anything like Hominid life here. The early lifeforms on Olympos were small and microscopic. It wasn't until about a half a billion years ago that complex multicellular life began on Olympos. It then developed over time, and culminated during what is referred to as the Cambrian Explosion.

"The Cambrian Explosion was a very important step in the development of the planet in that it drove a rapid diversification of life forms on Olympos. It also marked the end of the Proterozoic Eon and the beginning of the Cambrian Period of the Paleozoic Era.

"Many of the resulting species which developed during Olympos's time, over five billion of them in fact, became extinct before the planet underwent its recent shift in orbit. It can be anticipated that our new world will go through a similar pattern of change. Just as geological change has been a constant of Olympos's crust since the time of its formation, and biological change since the first appearance of life, so it can be expected to be on the new planet.

"Species will continue to evolve, taking on new forms, splitting into daughter species or going extinct in the process of adapting or dying in response to an ever-changing physical environment. As the new planet matures, the process of plate tectonics will continue to play a dominant role in the shaping of its oceans and continents and therefore the living species they harbor.

"Of primary interest to us is the introduction of the higher lifeforms, those of the Hominid, on the new planet.

"What was done by our ancestors with regard to the development of Hominids, as was carried out on Olympos for example, was to leave their development to the eventual natural process of evolution on the planet to create this range of species.

"As you are all aware, we have now chosen to separately

create our own groups of these species on board Atlantis. The specimens developed by us are intended to be used to supplement the natural supply of Hominids which evolve on the new planet.

"This method of adding to the natural process has never been done before in this solar system. We decided to make this change because we were not totally satisfied with the result that had been previously attained on Olympos, when the evolution to the higher lifeforms was left to its own devices. It is our intention to make certain that the higher lifeforms inheriting the next new world would be, by definition, by far the finest possible specimens.

"In order to accomplish this, we decided early on to choose breeding individuals from the best of the best of what Olympos had produced naturally, and we took that process one step further by genetically modifying these original selections to do our best to remove all negative characteristics and thereby produce an end result of vastly superior examples of each type.

"Additionally, we then used selective breeding of our in-house stock over a long period in order to tweak and improve on each subsequent generation. The result is a pool of exceptional, genetically adjusted examples, which we intend to use as a core group to improve on those that will have been created on the new planet through the natural process. In so doing, we expect to be able to provide a vast improvement in the Hominid raw material available on the planet, which will then lead to the end product of superior progeny over the long term.

"Most of you are generally aware of this program and those of you who have had a chance to examine the results can attest to the perfection of the representatives of the two species that we have now chosen to make up our Hominid colonization of this new planet.

"You should also be aware of the fact that, as it did on Olympos, the addition of Hominids to the mix already sharing the planet will bring about changes in the biosphere it enjoys. These changes will be brought about by Hominid activity which will, over time, produce significant effects on the atmosphere and other systems of the new planet's surface. It is quite possible that the result of this change in activity will lead to an eventual negative effect on the integrity of the ozone layer, and the proliferation of greenhouse gases on the planet. These in turn will be reflected in many ways, especially with regard to the deterioration in the conditions of productive soils and clean air and water."

Adon paused to take another sip from his glass, letting his eyes run over those seated to visually assess how his delivery of information had been received. Satisfied that it had sunk in, but noting the odd yawn emanating from Gabe, he smiled.

"I sense that you have absorbed enough for the time being. I do not wish to overload you with too much information at any given step of the way. You now have a good general understanding of what has and what will take place on the new planet prior to our colonization.

If any of you have any questions about the topics I have covered so far, please feel free to ask them now.

Once that is out of the way, we will move to another worm hole and make our next warp ahead in time."

There were a few questions, none of them originating from the Olympoians.

Gabe seemed to have suffered through without too much trouble this time and Juno, who had been watching him from time to time during the session, chocked it up to the fact that they had found something to actively stimulate the big Neanderthal during the earlier break.

After the final question had been answered, Gabe offered up only one comment.

"I feel like I'm bloody well, back in school again!"
Juno rolled her eyes.

"If memory serves – you didn't like that much either!"

CHAPTER THIRTY-FIVE

- Irony -

Beads of sweat had broken out on the helmsman's forehead and had formed into rivulets which were dripping off his chin as he fought against the raging storm, bravely struggling to hold the ship against the fluctuating fury of the onslaught of wind-driven ice particles.

Their target was now directly below them.

Brother Jacob had personally come to his assistance and was now furiously working the engine controls in an attempt to hold the airship in position at a sufficient height above the wildly bucking ship to avoid a collision. Their target was bouncing about like a toy in an unrelenting barrage of massive waves.

The two brothers were now alone in their labors on the bridge.

The remaining members of the team had moved aft to shift and position the explosive devices next to the gaping open hatch at the rear of the gondola. To a man their cassocks were drenched and quickly stiffening under the steady inclement blast of freezing rain pellets which now filled the skies around them as they surged through the yawning opening.

Learning to handle the large cylinders safely in good weather had been demanding enough. Now that the time had come to put training into practice, it seemed like what had come before had been no more than laborious child's play in comparison.

The icy onslaught sucked in through the open hatch seemed to be welcomed by the heavy metal cylinders which readily embraced and held it in a thick slippery wrapping.

With the added weight from this frozen coating, what had taken two men in training, now required four. Complicating the maneuver was the fact that visibility had shrunk to little more than a few feet and they were unable to clearly keep their target in view as it thrashed about below them in the raging seas.

There was nothing for it. They had to simply have faith in the fact that Brother Jacob was playing his part and holding the big airship directly over the trailing ship in the fleet line. Their confidence in that faith-based expectation suffered a serious blow when, after releasing the first of the explosive devices, no detonation had resulted.

They had waited expectantly after the drop, but had been rewarded with no sound other than that of the raging wind filling their ears.

Struggling frantically to shift the next cylinder in line, they let a second device fall.

Almost instantly, a huge flash below caused them to raise their hands to shade their eyes. This was soon usurped by a thunderous rumble that temporarily deafened each of them, quickly followed by a shockwave that thrust the heavily ice-laden airship upward twenty feet.

All of them were knocked off their feet and the brother closest to the open hatchway cried out in helpless terror as he lost his perch and was instantly swept through the opening. Briefly, his pitiful wails could be clearly heard over the raging tumult and he disappeared from sight into the cloud of oily black smoke that was rising up above the raging inferno created aboard the fatally struck ship that now shuddered below them in her death throes on the raging sea.

Both Jacob and the helmsman on the bridge had been thrown to the side as the shockwave from the explosion below blew the airship upward and slightly sideways. The wheel spun wildly, twisting crazily from one side to the other. As soon as they were physically able, both struggled to their feet and retook their positions.

At the point of the impact from the shockwave, all the

colour had drained from the younger brother's face. Now, as he fought to bring the big craft back under control, it suddenly began to return. Speaking in a strained and hesitant voice, he turned to face Jacob.

"It's a miracle Jacob! She's rising. We're no longer losing altitude. Mother of Solar, she was about to ditch for certain before that explosion lifted her."

* * * * *

The dropped explosive had landed on the deck just afore the wheelhouse of the ship, exactly where an overload of light ammunition, stacked high under tarps, had been lashed down in order to transport the supplies needed for the invasion.

The resulting chain-reaction detonation had literally torn the ship in two. Hit by a massive wave seconds after the blast, the bow section was instantly overwhelmed by its intensity and went to the bottom almost immediately. As it split away from the rest of the ship, the stern initially tilted upward at the front, and then slowly settled back down allowing a tsunami of water to rush into the gaping hole that remained.

Eisen was comatose when the blast took place. An hour before, he had ordered his doctor to inject enough drugs to keep him that way for several hours. He wasn't even aware of his impending death when the grim reaper took him in hand.

Feldmarschall von Jaeger was one of four men on the bridge at the time of the explosion.

As the windows shattered and blew back into the cramped space, he suffered broken eardrums and hundreds of ragged lacerations, some of the shards slicing through his eyes rendering him blind, and many more cutting to the bone.

He crumpled to the deck like a puppet who'd lost its strings and as the aft end of the ship began to rapidly take water he knew his end was near.

Despite that fact, and suffering massive pain, a hint of a smile formed on his face as a last thought drifted through his darkening mind

"What wonderful irony. Eisen, our glorious, all powerful leader, destroyed by use of the very super weapons over which he had obsessed and from which he'd expected to achieve world domination."

* * * * *

On his departure, the Rector had given clear instructions to the skeleton crew of guards he was leaving behind on his home base that they were to ensure that no one was permitted into the compound until he had returned from his victory. The warehouse was still chock full of various types of military weaponry and he'd made it quite clear to each of those holding the fort that he fully expected to be able to avail himself of some of it in the future, should the need arise.

The co-ordinates Adon had entered into the transporter had delivered Marduke and the capsulized Bellum down to the planet's surface, specifically to a point on the tarmac roadway, approximately a mile outside the gates of Eisen's military compound on Indus.

Awkwardly raising himself to his feet, an already dispirited Marduke was further demoralized to find himself in the middle of some sort of unseasonal blizzard. He was being pelted by a wall of freezing rain and snow. Despite the deluge, he was able to orient himself and although he sensed that the gate to the compound was some distance away, he was determined to fight his way forward.

He managed to work his manacled hand over to the pocket in which Adon had placed the code and after an agonizing struggle with chilled, fumbling fingers he was finally able to pull the tablet free and insert it into the locking mechanism.

The resonance of the resounding clicks, coupled with the release of pressure as the manacles dropped to the roadway, gave him a little boost of hope and he raised a hand to his face to brush aside the frozen buildup on his eyelashes as he began to make his way toward the gate. Leaving the capsulized Bellum behind, he trudged his way through the wintery gale toward his goal.

* * * * *

There was an air of anticipation in the room as Adon again lowered the level of the lighting and the large screen in front of them filled with a uniform warm blue colour once again.

"We are just about to warp through a new worm."

The intensity of the now familiar hum began to build as Atlantis picked up speed.

"This time, when we exit, we'll be quite a bit closer to the planets. I have maintained the magnification we last utilized and as a result, we will now see only the two planets on the screen - Olympos and the new one.

"On this hop we are able to get closer because, in real time, in excess of one billion years has passed since the initial formation of this new planet and, as a result of it shifting away from Solar, it has cooled enough for us to safely bring Atlantis nearer than on the last occasion."

The screen went fuzzy for a few seconds and then faded to black momentarily. The hum of the starship's engines died away just prior to the image of the two planets appearing. As Adon had predicted, the impressions of the planets were much larger this time, filling the screen without additional magnification.

"At this point in the natural evolution of the planet, the first stages of life should be forming. This will have likely taken place near the warm alkaline vents on the seabed or in open water. We have no way of knowing if that has happened, of course, but based on historic evidence we can assume that it likely did.

"If it has, some of these early microorganisms will have evolved a method of using the energy radiating from Solar to produce sugars in a process known as photosynthesis. As these continue to develop over time, they will morph to the point where they will begin to release oxygen as a waste product and in so doing will begin to have a positive effect on the overall oxygen content in the new planet's atmosphere.

"You will notice that the land masses apparent on the planet's surface at this point are very large and relatively few in number. Over the next five hundred million years, plate tectonics will take place and as a result, several new and clearly recognizable continents will begin to form.

"Approximately two billion years after this new planet was created, the bacteria that have learned to harness the light radiated by Solar to make sugar from carbon dioxide and water will begin to actively pump out very slightly higher and higher levels of oxygen as a waste product. This will in turn begin the process of the first major incident of distinct oxygen enhancement of the atmosphere.

"A side effect brought about by this initial process of atmospheric change will be the creation of the first of two 'Snowball' conditions, which will hopefully manifest themselves on the planet over time. This first blip in the oxygen content of the atmosphere, as small as it is, will ultimately cause the entire surface of the planet to become encapsulated in a solid and very thick sheet of ice. That said, this first incident of blanket ice forming will not bring about a significantly large enough change in the atmosphere to enable the planet to sustain animal or human lifeforms. That will not happen until after the second 'Snowball' formation takes place.

"Our next warp will take us to the time of that first freeze and we will find out then if the normal processes for planet development, as previously experienced by the earlier members of the Atlantis crews, has been repeated again on this new planet, upon which we hope to create new life.

"Having reviewed the information needed to understand what we will be seeing after this warp and of what we will hopefully see on the next, let's now take the time to examine what is up on the screen and discuss the changes that have come about so far on our new world."

CHAPTER THIRTY-SIX

-Dying Planet -

The young Brother of the Golden Ring that Jacob had chosen to serve as messenger was a muscular, hardy Neanderthal lad, who had been born and raised in the snow-filled northern regions of Neru.

He was a good rider and knew horse flesh well. He was now on his third mount, having already burned out two powerful beasts in his quest to deliver his missive to the Devi.

He'd fully expected to have reached Almeca City twenty-four hours ago, but the weather conditions had grown steadily worse from the moment he'd begun his race to the Holy city and the snow was now a uniform three feet deep and was drifting in massive banks which made many of the roadways he faced all but impassable.

In his home state he'd never experienced a snowstorm of this intensity. It was a whiteout without respite.

By this point he was leading his horse more often than he was astride, picking the path of least resistance. The exhausted animal listlessly following behind him was bathed in sweat, breathing heavily and struggling to keep moving.

The Brother, head and shoulders bent into the fury of the wind, was coated in a thick layer of freezing rain and snow, a ghostly figure, purposely placing one foot before the other, as he blindly pushed forward.

He had been shivering uncontrollably for the past hour and could no longer feel either his fingers or his toes.

* * * * *

They'd had a brief reprieve due the fact that the concussion from the first bomb strike had been powerful enough to shatter the ice which had formed around the airbag. Prior to the detonation, the thickness of the frozen crust had reached the point where it made the ship too heavy to remain aloft. As the shockwave hit and raised the airship, the encasement of ice had cracked and fallen to the sea, lightening the craft instantly.

They successfully targeted two more of Eisen's ships over the next thirty minutes. However, conditions had worsened considerably and now in order to keep the airship relatively centered above the next bobbing warship in the line, Jacob had to continually adjust the power to the engines in a sustained tussle against the fury of the gusting wind.

Ice pellets had pitted and cracked the windscreen in several places. These fractures, coupled with the ever thickening layer of ice covering the glass itself, reduced what little visibility the storm allowed. Jacob turned and shouted at the helmsmen to be heard over the roaring sound of the engines and that of the raging storm that engulfed the ship.

"Good, that's three down and number four directly under us. We are icing up again and running out of time I'm afraid. We've only four of the explosive devices left now, so for the love of Solar, hold this position."

* * * * *

As he had on his last visit, Brother Benedict found the Devi with her back to the door, her shoulders slumped. She was standing dejectedly before the large window facing out toward the bay. The balcony outside the window was filled to a varying depth with drifted snow. In several places it was at least seven feet deep.

He could see that Aabha had positioned herself to take advantage of a line of sight that was only covered by about three feet, but that had made little real difference as, due to the intensity of the storm, visibility outside was no more than thirty or forty feet at best.

Benedict found himself wondering what on earth she could be so intently studying, as there was no chance that she could see anything beyond the glass, other than the raging storm itself.

As he'd done before, he cleared his throat to let her know of his presence.

At the sound, her shoulders raised slightly, indicating to him that she had heard him. Despite that fact, she did not immediately turn to face him.

She had read his thoughts.

"Brother Benedict, thank you for coming. You're right of course. I can't really see anything out there but white. Under the circumstances, I find that strangely clarifying."

Aabha sighed and turned to face the young brother, managing just a trace of a smile.

"You think me a little foolish no doubt, and you may be right in that, but the falling snow calms me and helps me to think."

Benedict flushed slightly at having been caught out on his inner thoughts.

"No Holy Mother, not at all. I..."

Her features softened and her smile widened somewhat as she cut him off in mid-speech to save him from further embarrassment at his having been caught at correctly reading her mood.

"You have news for me?"

She started toward her desk and waved him to a chair across from her as she sat down.

"I've ordered honeyed tea. Sit and let us talk, I need to hear the latest."

It had been over twenty hours since Benedict had slept and he could not remember when he'd last eaten. He looked forward to a warm beverage and welcomed the chance to sit.

A secretary knocked and entered with a tray containing a pot and two substantial goblets. He waited until she had poured, placed the steaming vessels in front of them and left, closing the door behind her, before he spoke.

"I did as you asked, visiting several of the encampments. There is much grumbling and several rumours are flying about. The strongest of these is the suggestion that the weather phenomenon we are currently experiencing is simply a localized situation.

"I know that is a foolish conclusion for them to reach, but as all the troops come from outside Almeca, they have no way of knowing that this type of weather is not only unseasonable for us, especially at this time of year, but completely out of the norm in its intensity.

"The majority of the leaders know that to be the case of course, as do some of their officers, but the foot soldiers do not realize just how crazily unusual this storm is for us locals.

"At any rate, it is what they think. Additionally, they do not believe there can be an invasion launched under the circumstances. They are miserably cold and wet and they simply want to forget the whole idea of a Holy war and go home."

Aabha nodded and raised her goblet to drink. She sipped the hot mixture tentatively for a second and then let herself indulge. After a couple of good swallows, she set it down and raised her eyes to meet his.

"It is as I thought then.

"While I agree with you about the weather not being localized, I find myself tending to also agree with their suggestion that, under the current conditions, there will be no invasion. Any invasion fleet attempting to enter the Bay of Angels in this is going to flounder before it reaches our shores.

"I will put pen to paper and officially express this opinion, thanking them all for their response to my call and ordering that the Holy war be rescinded, and that all foreign armies stand down immediately and return to their home states.

"As soon as these can be made ready, you will deliver a copy of my order, under my seal, to the leaders of all concerned.

"Let them return to those they love, if they can and while they can.

"And, once we have finish our tea, I would ask you to send in one of my secretaries as you leave. I must arrange for a meeting with all my Mitra Varuna and advise them of my decision."

* * * * *

For the elder Atlantians in the darkened room, the image on the screen was little more than a reflection of a single step forward in the long process leading to the eventual creation of world renewal.

Of the two planets depicted, their attention rested solely with the new planet.

As Adon had predicted, it was indeed entirely, or very nearly entirely, covered by what appeared to be a layer of ice. This encasement looked to be thicker at the poles and somewhat more like a layer of slush or snow at the equator.

Understandably, this was not wholly the case for the younger Atlantians seated before the screen, many of whom had spent a good part of their lives learning, playing and visiting on the surface of Olympos.

Initially, they contemplated each of the images before them in turn, their eyes shifting from the old to the new and back again in a cycle of shared concern and hope. For them what was depicted on the screen was, in a sense, both a funeral and a birth.

Adon, having anticipated that seeing the change in Olympos would have a strong effect on their three guests, had argued against having them present for some of the early time-warp viewings, but Venus had pushed to keep them in the loop from the onset.

Her reasoning had been persuasive.

It would give them closure. Something that would be absolutely necessary if they were to be actively involved in the developmental stages of the formation of life on the new planet. Before they could turn their attention to that concept, they would have to accept that life on Olympos was a thing of the past and put that behind them.

She did, however, understand and share her father's concern for the feelings of the three Olympoians who would no longer be able to dismiss the preordained termination of life on their home planet. She had specifically asked that he not draw any direct attention to the condition of that planet while the viewings took place, but to let Juno, Gabe and Sebastian make their own assessment and evaluation of what had occurred on Olympos after this and each future time warp.

She argued that it would be easier for them to accept the inevitability of the loss of life, if each was given the individual space and time to do so on their own terms.

The changes to each planet since the last viewing were considerable.

From the instant the images had appeared, the attention of the three Olympoians present was steadfastly locked onto that of Olympos, which now appeared as little more than a cloud-locked sphere.

The thick atmospheric fog enveloping it was obviously impervious and prevented any perception of what the actual current conditions on the planet's surface were. That fact, combined with what they had learned over the past few hours, clearly suggested that the end of life on Olympos had come.

Each readily understood that if the powerful rays of Solar were no longer able to penetrate the atmosphere, all the living species on its surface would be slowly but steadily losing the necessities of life itself.

There could be no disputing what it signified.

Olympos, as they had known it, was no more.

CHAPTER THIRTY-SEVEN

- *Closure* -

To suggest that the mood within the shared apartments of the three Olympoians was glum was a gross understatement.

After the latest time-warp, they had returned to their quarters, weighed down by what they had observed. They were supposed to sleep in order to be ready for an upcoming committee meeting, the next step in the process of preparing for the eventual colonization of the new planet, but under the circumstances sleep was unlikely.

Instead, without actually planning to do so, they had gathered together in the small dining area to share a sparse meal and talk among themselves.

Juno was definitely feeling both depressed and guilty.

Depressed at the massive loss of life and guilty both for being alive when so many were dead and for being happy to be with Gabe and looking forward to starting a new life together.

Overall, she seemed to be faring the best of the three.

She'd had no family left on Olympos when she left her home planet. Memories yes, but without family left behind, it was understandably easier for her to accept the death of the planet.

Gabe had his grandmother to mourn. While he had not known her personally for all that long, in the short time that he'd been with her he'd grown very fond of the forthright and loving old woman.

He would miss her.

Additionally, he and Juno had each other for support.

Juno felt that it was Sebastian who had lost the most and who would need outside support.

The monk was in a disheartened funk.

He did have family on Olympos when he left it. True, it was only extended and none that he had seen in several years. But the truth be told, his paramount concern was for that of his religious family.

His whole life had been spent in the service of the Belief, the vast majority as a personal guardian of its leader. His was the greatest hurt and he was suffering deeply.

To deaden the pain, he'd begun to imbibe the instant they'd sat down and had been keeping the little attendant Almie busy ever since that time, as he'd availed himself of jar after jar of the Atlantian's favorite potent brew.

He needed to talk. Juno understood that and at her suggestion, she and Gabe were primarily acting as sounding boards for him, mostly just letting him talk, allowing him to vent his anger and frustration.

"...and I just don't understand them. They don't seem to give a damn about all those people who died down there. What's wrong with the Atlantians. When that screen came up, they didn't even care enough to take note of what had obviously occurred on Olympos!"

Juno was more perceptive than Gabe, who really didn't know what to say.

It was she who understood that the monk was dealing with the horror of what had transpired with anguished anger in the only way he knew how. She could also appreciate that he felt like he should have done something to prevent what had happened, even though there was nothing he could have done.

Because of that, he needed to blame someone, anyone, for it. It was something he would just have to get out of his system before he could find closure and be able to move on.

She rested her hand on his and Sebastian lifted his eyes to her and shook his head.

"It just isn't fair. I should have stayed. Why should I escape while the rest were left to perish?"

Juno took a deep breath before responding.

"No it isn't fair. But then, life isn't fair really. On the other side of the coin though, we all understand that being alive eventually means dying. Everyone on Olympos knew that truth. And if you had stayed, what would that have accomplished? The leader of your faith wanted you to leave in order to bring the power of religion to the new world and you accepted her challenge to do that.

"That took both courage and faith. You did the right thing."

There was a soft knock on the frame of the door and the three of them looked over to see Venus standing in the doorway. She sent a flood of warmth and support to them before she spoke.

"I couldn't help but overhear…I'm sorry that you feel that we Atlantians did not demonstrate the sadness that we felt over the demise of Olympos. It was my fault that our inner feelings were not expressed to you. I asked the others not to draw attention to it in order to show respect for your heavy sense of loss. I felt it would be easier for you to deal with it if you were left to sort it out on your own.

"I apologize if I was wrong in that.

"Believe me, when I tell you that we share your sorrow for those who had to experience the end of life on Olympos."

Sebastian instantly found himself regretting his earlier words and the impression they had no doubt left with the others in the room. He got up from his seat and crossed to stand in front of Venus, who was still hovering in the doorway.

"Pay my words no heed, Venus. They were both uncalled for and unkind. It was just my infantile way of expressing my frustrations and sense of loss. I know that you and the other Atlantians who were an active part of Olympos shared our sadness in what we saw today and I appreciate that it is through you that the three of us in this room will have a chance at a new life to come."

"Please accept my sincere apology for what I said. It was simply an expression of deep anguish brought on by the knowledge of what has befallen those on Olympos, none of which was caused by you or any members of your race, but was at the will of Solar."

* * * * *

His horse had collapsed behind him and rolled onto its side in the deep snow.

Tears of frustration froze to his cheeks as the young monk knelt beside his dying mount.

The creature's head lay still, eyes wild, nostrils flared from expended effort. Irregular snorts of faltering final breaths left brief, ghostly trails in the frigid air.

With a good deal of effort, the muscular Neanderthal managed to lift the horse's head and then extend and slip his legs under it to act as a cushion. He stroked the big animal as he offered gentle, soothing words of solace.

The monk stayed like that for the time it took the animal to slip away and then, with a deep sigh of resignation, he simply laid back into the soft support of the snowbank behind him.

After a few moments he opened his eyes and looked upward at the falling snow. Then, with a final prayer to Solar, he gave himself up to the ferocity of the storm that continued to seethe around them.

* * * * *

Jacob looked over at the helmsman and nodded as the ice-laden airship shuddered and began to lose altitude.

"This is it, lad. I'm afraid we're for it.

"We have fought the good fight and done what we could. We are all in Solar's hands now.

"Hold her as steady as you can as she drops. Let's give the others every chance possible to take at least one more of the ships with us when we go down."

* * * * *

As Marduke got closer he spotted two men through the small window in the gate house and, despite the fact that he was soaked and very cold, his spirts rose a little.

It's not over yet Adon my old friend. If you could make it back aboard Atlantis by using one of the war machines, then so can I. And this time I will bring a bloody army with me.

Bold thoughts.

Unfortunately for Marduke, a very angry Eisen had specifically mentioned his name as the one person who was very definitely to be placed within the category of *'persona non grata'* at the base.

The Rector had taken it one step further in fact, unequivocally making it clear that, *'if that treacherous bastard dares to shows his ugly face, he is to be shot on sight'*.

Before Marduke could reach the gate, the two figures had exited the gate house and upon recognizing him, had conjointly raised their submachine pistols, quite ironically weapons they could never have hoped to have seen without his personal intervention.

Marduke raised a hand in welcome and in response the two guards, opened fire.

The Atlantian was struck by a different kind of storm, this one the deadly impact of a hail of hot lead pounding into his totally dumbfounded, shuddering form.

CHAPTER THIRTY-EIGHT

- Hominid Evolution -

Gaia and the young Atlantian committee members responsible for the planning for the Hominid colonization of the new planet were once again gathered in the small conference room they used for their meetings.

Six hours had passed since the last time warp and as they congregated now, the original committee had been bolstered by the presence of four additional members, growing to a total of nine.

As previously promised, Juno, Gabriel and Brother Sebastian had joined their ranks to act in an advisory capacity.

Additionally, they had been joined by Adon, who would be offering the substantial necessary background information which would be needed by the committee during this phase of the planning. This would be essential to ensure that the members had a full understanding of what the two naturally developed species would likely consist of, prior to the addition of themselves and the two hundred *'super examples'*, which had already been created on board Atlantis, to the naturally formed mix that would be in existence when the new planet was colonized.

Once a large pot of honeyed tea and sufficient cups had been provided by 'One', and 'Two', Gaia opened the meeting.

"The next topic we will be familiarizing ourselves with will be that of the natural process of evolution which will be taking place on the new planet and will eventually lead to the development of Hominids. As this is probably the most important process that will happen from our perspective and is relatively complex, it will involve a fair amount of explanation. It is for that reason that Adon has joined us."

Gabe sighed softly, so Juno wouldn't hear, and just in case she did, he followed it with a brief whispered comment.

"Well, at least this part should be more interesting."

Once again, she ignored him. Which was alright. His shin could take only so many assaults; he could live with her ignoring him.

Adon nodded in response to Gaia's introduction and then shifted his gaze in turn to the others around the table.

"Before we start, both Gaia and I would like to offer our own personal thoughts of condolence and support with regard to the fate of their home planet to our Olympoian friends who are seated here with us now.

"We share with you your pain and sorrow at what had to be. We know it will take time for the depth of this loss to become bearable to you and we wish you to know that we are impressed with your chosen determination to put those thoughts of reverence aside for the moment, while we get on with our joint responsibility of building a new world."

Venus nodded her head and smiled. It was obvious to the three Olympoians that she had communicated to her parents the comments that she had overheard earlier and they were somewhat embarrassed, but none-the-less, pleased that she had done so.

Adon silently watched the exchange of glances between them and then began.

"An understanding of the initial processes involved in the natural evolution leading to Hominid life, which will hopefully be now beginning to take place on the new planet, is necessary if we want to understand how that evolutionary progression will eventually lead to the emergence of what we recognize as anatomically modern humans and Neanderthals.

"Early life forms comprise the initial stepping stones of this development. Over time, in the Late Cretaceous period, which is nearly four and one half billion years after the creation of a new planet, these simple lifeforms evolve to the point where the first mammals come into existence and from there, diverge and begin to create what we refer to as the 'Primates'.

"Within this primate line, the Ape was an offshoot of the Gibbon family about fifteen million years after that and in turn diverged into the Orangutans and from there to the beginning of the biped era of development during which the Chimpanzees parted from the Gorilla and eventually developed through evolution into what we would recognize as the near ancestors of the Hominid species that we know today.

"Thus this advancement of these primate lines, over time, leads to the eventual creation of the *'genus Homo'* and thence to the first *'Homo sapiens'*".

Gaia had been watching the others carefully and had taken note of the glazed expression that had slowly developed on Gabe's face, despite his earlier comment, as he'd attempted to take it all in. She lightly rested her hand on Adon's, as she silently communicated with him and the four other Atlantians in the room, specifically drawing her life mate's attention by way of her fixed gaze toward the young Neanderthal.

Perhaps that is enough for this first session. A short break and a chance for questions seems to be in order. The young Atlantians are happy enough to absorb what they need to know about the History, but it is different for the Olympoians. It is a lot for them to digest in one dose. At this point, perhaps a brief discussion and then leave it for today.

Adon immediately understood and promptly changed subjects.

"Well I know that is quite a lot of rather dry information to process. Let's take a break now and have some fresh honeyed tea with biscuits and then throw the concept open to questions and discussion."

Gaia smiled and nodded.

"An excellent idea. A little pick-me-up is definitely in order. 'Two', please get a fresh pot while 'One' clears the table of the remains of our last."

The two little Almies moved into action and in short order the new committee members' mugs were again filled with the steaming beverage. Alerted by Gaia, the young Atlantians present sat quietly and it was Sebastian, who had clearly been doing his best to follow what Adon was saying, who broke the silence and asked the first question.

"So, this process that you have been historically outlining, actually took place on Olympos and we are part of the result, right?"

Adon nodded.

"Yes, as it did historically on all the new worlds created in this solar system, but it did not happen overnight. It took approximately eighty-five million years of the evolution and adaption of the initial lifeforms to reach such an advanced stage of development."

Gabe seemed to snap out of his lethargy. As he spoke, he pointed first to Sebastian and Juno and then to himself.

"You are saying that our ancestors started out on Olympos as some kind of small germy things eighty-five million years ago?"

A broad smile creased Enoch's features. He chuckled, breaking the tension in the room. Adon smiled.

"Well yes, I suppose I am. Keep in mind though, that it was a very long and complicated process."

Gabe shook his head slowly.

"But we aren't the same. I mean that's obvious, you can see the differences between us. I'm much bigger than them. I'm fair and they are dark. I have hair covering most of my body, they do not. I mean, we're just not the same."

Gaia interjected.

"No, of course you're are not exactly the same. Every one of us at this table is unique and individual. There are differences between Neanderthals and Humans because their ancestors took somewhat divergent paths at a certain point, but your two individual species share more similarities than they do differences. You are each a species variation of the other."

Sebastian grinned.

"So our ancestors were monkeys and apes, right?"

Adon raised his eyebrows and smiled broadly.

"Well, those two were definitely in the mix all right, but a long way back of course.

"As I said at the beginning, it was a very complicated process and one which is more often than not, hard to fathom. Suffice to say that once the planet had formed, two main things were required for our purposes, those being an atmosphere high in oxygen and liquid water. These two things allowed the evolution on Olympos to begin, which led toward the development of higher species. You three are examples of the end result of that evolution."

Sebastian shrugged and raised his hands, palms upward.

"Well, I am a man of Faith and have been for all my life. What you have revealed to us is not unlike other unusual beliefs I have had to accept on faith and faith alone. I have no reason to doubt what you have told us is true and can therefore relatively easily accede to it as fact through a leap of faith."

Juno's brows raised slightly.

"I envy you that Brother.

"Personally, I need to be convinced of such a possibility before I can take it as fact. I still have questions that I need answered about this evolutionary process undertaken by my ancestors before I will be able to convince myself that it all happened that way."

Gabe laughed.

"To be honest, I'm still at the point of trying to get my mind around the whole concept of it. I don't question Adon's explanation of how it came about, but I would be dishonest if I didn't admit that there are some parts of it I have difficulty picturing in my mind.

That said, I find the idea fascinating and would definitely like to hear more about what this evolutionary process looked like at the various stages of change, and exactly what brought those specific changes about."

* * * * *

The full complement of Mitra Varuna were gathered in place around the larger ornate oval table in the conference room when Aabha entered and crossed to take her chair at its head.

She did her best to give no indication of the depth of her depression over what was taking place outside the room.

There, the storm continued, unrelenting in its intensity.

Knowing what that meant and not being able to share that knowledge with the others seated before her was frustrating; however, she was determined to keep her promise to the Atlantians. Of those in this room, she and she alone would have to live with what was about to befall the planet.

Looks of concern and alarm registered on the features of her trusted advisors and they could not be dismissed lightly. It was she after all, who they now looked to for an explanation and some hope of deliverance from the current state of affairs.

Aabha had decided that she would do her worthiest to put the best face on it and if possible, to leave those in the room with some sense of hope and peace before she left it. Her own features remained placid as she spoke.

"I've decided to send the foreign armies home. It is obvious that any threat of invasion under the current conditions is impossible. I've come to the realization that Solar has seen fit to intervene on our behalf and remove that risk by way of creating weather conditions that will not allow it to proceed.

"There will therefore be no need for a Holy War. Consequently, we have nothing to fear and shall place our faith in Solar to do what SHE feels necessary.

"In the meantime, we shall all return to our normal duties while we wait for the storms to blow themselves out and once the skies clear again, we will pick up where we left off."

Using the last of her strength, she sat up straight in her chair and as she looked around the table from one face to the next, she did her best to exhibit an air of well-founded confidence. She spoke again as she rose.

"Solar willing, it will be to a much better world."

CHAPTER THIRTY-NINE

- *Evolution* -

His acceptance on faith of what Adon had told them had been enough to put his mind at ease. Sebastian had slept well. Juno and Gabe, on the other hand, had questions about Adon's comments that spurred a good deal of discussion between them once they were alone. As luck would have it however, these did not prevent their minds from eventually turning to other, more personal and immediate attention-demanding scenarios. Albeit, a good deal later than Sebastian, they too, when otherwise at least temporarily sated, had eventually given in to physical exhaustion which in turn led to a sound, if shorter, slumber.

After a shared breakfast the three of them made their way back up to the small meeting room and found the others already gathered around the small table. As they entered the room, Gaia delivered a surge of support and peace to them and smiled.

"You all seem well rested. Good. Adon and I have discussed the agenda for today and we've agreed to begin by answering any queries that may have occurred to you since at our last meeting. Please quiz us on anything you would like clarified or expanded upon."

Sebastian stepped up to the plate.

"If I understand this whole evolution deal, the basics of it are that it never ends. Am I right in that?"

Adon thought for a few second before answering.

"Yes and no. Over the length of the process, some of the species that are a product of the evolutionary progression simply die out, going extinct for various reasons. Others, Hominids for example, continue to evolve."

Sebastian frowned and fired back.

"What causes this to happen?"

Gaia responded.

"Frankly we are not really sure. We think that two basic things tend to influence the process. The first of those is the inherent background of the genetic makeup of any given specific species, which plays a large part in what takes place in relation to developmental changes. And secondly, it seems that environmental influences can also have either positive or catastrophic effects on the evolution of any particular individual species. In other words, in response to a radical change in the environment in which they live, certain components will adapt well, improving on their original genetic makeup as they do so, while others appear to be unable to adjust significantly or rapidly enough to exist in a changed environment and therefore they die out completely."

His curiosity satisfied, the monk sat back to give his friends a chance. Gabe spoke up.

"All of this background stuff is very interesting, but I can't help but wonder what purpose it will serve if we are only going to end up with the memory cleansing thing and won't remember any of it anyway."

Adon chuckled.

"Well, that's a good question. Firstly, it's important to understand that the memory erasing procedure will not leave you with a totally blank memory. It will in fact leave you with a good deal of it intact. Additionally, you will also have partial recall from time to time. This will happen in what you might call flashbacks, incomplete to be sure, but still very insightful. As well, you mustn't overlook the fact that before you go through the memory cleanse, you will be taking an active part in structuring the terraforming of the new planet and be playing an important role in the planning stages of the planet's surface areas. Having a sound background in what has already and will eventually transpire over the extended period of the planet's cooling and the development of all lifeforms will be essential to helping you tackle those particular tasks."

Gabe still looked a little unsure but he shrugged it off.

"I'm sure you're right. I'm just getting bored probably. At heart I'm a doer, not a planner. Probably just impatient to get busy doing stuff."

Juno could sense a tinge of embarrassment in her partner over this admission. She laughed.

"Well, we were warned that we might find ourselves bored if we chose to be part of the planning for the new planet instead of simply going directly into the memory cleansing process. I'm sure that plays a good part in what Gabe is feeling. All three of us tend to like to be in the thick of things if we can."

Gaia nodded her understanding.

"Yes, we Atlantians have such a long lifespan that we have become conditioned to spending most of our lives waiting for the next burst of activity to arrive rather than enjoying an active lifestyle. The most important thing in our lives is the possible opportunity to become personally involved in the planning for a newly formed planet. Because it can take several generations before that happens, the majority of us never have the opportunity to take part in that role. All we are expected to do is manage what our predecessors have created, and do our best to improve the planning for the next planet to be created. You three, on the other hand, are used to being physically active. It must not be easy for you to be idle so much."

Persephone picked up on that thought.

"And thank goodness you are physically active and capable of swift physical response. We Atlantians wouldn't even be back on this ship if you hadn't come to our aid and intervened when you did."

Jonah pursed his lips and nodded firmly.

"Ya, we would have been totally screwed without Gabe, Juno and Sebastian's help."

Adon remained silent for a few seconds, allowing the three Olympoians to bask in the warm aftermath of the exchange.

He then returned to the subject at hand by following up on Juno's last words.

"Keep in mind that you three don't have to stick to this idea of taking part in the planning phase. Any or all of you can change your minds and instead join the others in the chamber until it is time for colonization, although I must admit that I have found a good deal of value in your input so far and honestly believe that it will help to ensure that the new world we hope to create will be successful."

Sebastian interjected.

"I can't speak for Gabe and Juno, but I for one want to continue to take part. To my way of thinking it would be foolish to pass up a chance to help plan for a world in which I will eventually be living. If my input will help to make it a better place, I can live with my impatience. I'm in it for the long haul."

Juno looked to Gabe and then nodded.

"I think we all share that desire. We all want to do our part to make our new lives the best they can be."

Obviously pleased with their response, Adon leaned forward and rubbed his hands together.

"Right, well let's get back to it then. We talked about the ancestors of the Hominid species that first inhabited Olympos. I want to touch now on just how they evolved to that state, how they made the jump from what Brother Sebastian has so interestingly coined *'the monkeys and apes'*, to what we now know as Neanderthals and Humans. The big change came with the evolvement to Bipedalism. Bipedalism is the basic adaptation of the Hominids. It is the main source of the skeletal changes which came about and are shared by all bipedal Hominoids. On Olympos, the earliest Hominoids of presumably primitive bipedalism, arose some six to seven million years ago. At that point the non-bipedal knuckle-walkers, the gorilla and chimpanzee, diverged from the Hominoid line. The full biped, ascended somewhat later. These early bipeds eventually evolved into the genus Homo. Bipedalism freed the hands for reaching and carrying food and also saved energy during locomotion. It thereby enabled long distance running and hunting, provided an enhanced field of vision, and helped in the avoidance of hypothermia, by reducing the surface area exposed to direct solar light. Keep in mind that the planet was still cooling at that time and as a result the environment was continually changing. What had been forests, had become savannas. More area could be covered while walking on two legs, as it used far less energy than quadrupedal knuckle-walking. Therefore, there was also more exploration and territorial expansion. This shift to Bipedalism involved a large number of anatomical skeletal changes, not just to the legs and pelvis, but also to the vertebral column, feet, ankles and skull. The femur progressed into a slightly more angular position. The knee and ankle joints became much stronger. The human vertebral column became S-shaped and the lumbar vertebrae became shorter and wider. The big toe moved into alignment with the other toes, making forward locomotion simpler. The arms and forearms shortened relative to the legs making it easier to run.

About three million years ago on Olympos, the first genetic changes in apes led to the development of your Olympoians ancestors, the first representative of the genus Homo. This was *Homo habilis*, the earliest species to use stone tools. Keep in mind these were the very earliest of Hominoids and their brains were only relatively the same size as that of a chimpanzee. It was at this time that the Hominid SRGAP2 gene doubled, bringing about a more rapid wiring of the frontal cortex of the brain. During the next million years a process of rapid enlargement of the size of the brain in relation to total body mass occurred, leading to an increase in the level of intelligence. Throughout the following stages of development, about one and one half million years ago, Homo erectus and Homo ergaster evolved and with that evolution came a doubled cranial capacity as the brain increased in size. Each succeeding generation developed approximately one hundred and twenty-five thousand more neurons than their parents. These Hominids were the first to use fire and more complex tools, and were also the first of their line to leave their initial colonies and begin to spread out to widen their territory."

He looked over at the three Olympoians.

"It is at this point of the evolutionary process on the new planet that we will be adding you and our ship-created Hominid colonies to the new world. All of you of course will be well advanced, genetically speaking, from the naturally evolved species found on the new planet at that time. With interbreeding over time between you and those naturally developing genetic improvements, the pace of both physical and intellectual improvement will advance exponentially. If all goes as it has historically done on Olympos, the modern Hominid as we knew them while we observed their evolution on Olympos, the Homo heidelbergensis, Homo rhodesiensis etc., will have gradually replaced the local populations of early Homo erectus and will be beginning to migrate out of the continent on which they had originally developed. On Olympos, this outward migration took place approximately seventy-five thousand years ago and led to a limited inter-breeding between the Neanderthals and other Hominoid species. All of us here are well aware of the advantages of what that inter-breeding offered."

Both Gabe and Juno flushed at this remark, Gabe far more obviously than his lifemate, due to his lighter skin coloring. Gaia noted the fact and interrupted.

"We've been at it for some time Adon. I think that we've covered enough for now. Let's take a break and meet again in a couple of hours for our next time warp."

Adon nodded in agreement.

"Yes, we've covered what I wanted to accomplish with regard to outlining the Hominid evolution."

* * * * *

Definitely needing to recharge their batteries after Adon's briefing on hominoids, the three Olympoians mutually agreed to make use of part of the break to pay another visit to the wonders of the animal compound. It was while viewing and learning about the habits of the Saber-toothed tiger that Gabe commented.

"I don't know about you two, but I'm beginning to be a little concerned about having to deal with some of these guys holding something as flimsy as a homemade spear. I'm thinking that we should maybe see about getting ourselves something a little more impressive to use as weapons when we land in our new world, something to kinda level the playing field."

CHAPTER FORTY

- Pangaea -

After spending almost an hour with the animals, Gabe, Juno and Sebastian shared a meal during which they exchanged views and opinions about what they had now learned about the historical evolution of Hominids on Olympos. Then, once the little duty Almies had cleared up the remnants from the table, the three of them turned their attention toward the future.

Adon had not told them what the next warp through space and time would mean in relation to the changes on Olympos or on the new planet; however, they shared a general expectation that these would be of significant proportions in both instances.

It was part way through a discussion of what transformations they might expect to see that Juno dropped out of the conversation and fell silent. Both Gabe and the monk picked up on her loss of focus a few minutes later and it was Gabe who challenged her.

"Hey Juno, did we lose you?"

The glazed expression in her eyes wavered. She raised her head slightly and blinked before shaking her head.

"No. I was just thinking. I had a foretelling experience last night and I was trying to relive and clarify it in my mind."

Sebastian perked up in his chair and leaned forward.

"What did you see? Tell us about it."

She nodded.

"I will, when I can sort it out. It was strange, kind of ill-defined, not clear and straight forward like it used to be."

Intrigued, Gabe met her gaze.

"How was it different. In what way?"

Juno shrugged.

"I'm not sure if I can explain it. I haven't had one for so long now it's hard to remember the last one well enough to discern the difference between it and this one. And now I find myself questioning why I haven't had one for such a long time. I was having them pretty regularly a few months back."

Sebastian sensed her frustration and tried to make light of the situation in an attempt to lift her spirits.

"Well you have been a little busy with other things of late. You and Gabe seem to spend most of your time in bed these days."

Gabe frowned at him.

"Ya right. Don't pay any attention to him, Juno. Why don't you tell us what you can remember of it and we may be able to help you figure it out?"

Juno took a deep breath.

"It's worth a try I guess. Don't get me wrong, I don't think it's bad stuff, but it's just kind of fuzzy, like I was seeing it though a fog or something and I don't want to misinterpret it when I tell you about it."

She took a few seconds to gather her thoughts while they impatiently but silently gave her the time she needed.

"It's the three of us, kind of an overview deal, looking down from above at a distance. It must be of us first arriving on the new world when we colonize, I guess. At first, the three of us are no more than small specks in the center of the frame..."

Gabe interjected.

"How can you tell it's us if we are just specks?"

Juno was lost in the telling, concentrating with her eyes closed. She didn't answer him for a second and Sebastian reached over to nudge Gabe in the shoulder. He spoke softly.

"Let her tell it her way, man."

Gabe glanced at the monk, frowned and nodded. Juno continued.

"…because the view zeros in later and it's just us. We are alone.

"But first my vision of it provides an overview of what the place looks like. It is so beautiful that I don't know if I can do it justice in words; you would have to see it for yourselves to appreciate how wonderful it is.

"We are standing on what appears to be a massive white sandy beach in a delta, where a river flows into a huge lake or perhaps an ocean. The water is a very pretty blue-green in colour and it seems to be a tropical setting, bathed in warm rays of light. I think it must be an ocean because a steady cascade of gentle waves softly breaks against the sandy shoreline.

Away from the beach, the vegetation around us on both sides of the river is very thick and lush. The tops of the trees are swaying soothingly and there are many birds in the cloudless sky, who seem to be taking advantage of the rising currents of warm air which allow them to glide effortlessly over long distances.

It is a feast for the eyes - in a word - paradise."

She opened her eyes and smiled.

"And when the frame of the vision specifically zeros-in on us, we look so content, happy as larks. And really healthy. Younger even and like we don't have a care in the world."

Gabe grinned and clapped his hands.

"It means we are going to be alright. Everything is going to work out as planned."

Sebastian nodded his head in agreement.

"Perhaps it was fuzzy looking because, in real terms, it's a very, very long time into the future."

Juno shrugged.

"That could well be it, I suppose."

Sebastian smiled broadly.

"I'm sure that's why. Anyway, fuzzy or not, its wonderful news. I feel like a great weight has been lifted from my shoulders."

Patently relieved, Juno laughed nervously.

"Yes. Yes, it is. I only wish that it had been clearer. That I could have seen more. I hope I experience more foretelling about this fantastic new place before we colonize.

"Oh, and there is one more thing I have to tell you about it. We were all as naked as the day we were born. No clothing, not a stitch."

Gabe's mouth sagged open and then he shook his head.

"Wow! Not looking forward to that. And speaking about being vulnerable, I been thinking about what I said earlier about have better weapons to deal with some of the big creatures we are going to be coming up against. I think we should bring our concerns up to Jonah. He's in charge of that stuff now and I think we could convince him to help us out, without anyone else being the wiser."

Sebastian nodded.

"It's worth a try for sure."

* * * * *

Later that day, the eight regular committee members met with Adon and the other Atlantians in the main control room for the next leap through time and space.

The hum of the increasing power delivered by the starship's engines as they entered the worm hole filled their ears. As the lighting dimmed, their attention centered on the big screen. In a matter of seconds, they had completed the warp and the screen changed from black to blue and then a new image appeared.

It was a large depiction of the new planet. The engine sound died and Adon began to speak as soon as he could be clearly heard.

"To help make what we now see portrayed here more relevant to you, and assuming that the new planet has developed more or less along the same lines that Olympos did, this view should be a near reflection of what Olympos looked like approximately three hundred million years ago.

"The new planet has been cooling for some time now. It

does this from the outside in and the majority of the sphere is still full of molten material. The surface, which is primarily covered by water, has formed a crust of solid substance. Molten material from deep inside seeks weak spots in this thin crust and when it finds one, it breaks through to boil up out through fissures on the sea bed. The resulting outflow then cools and becomes solid. In various locations it builds up layer by layer until it eventually rises above the water table to form small land masses or continents."

He paused for a second before continuing.

"I'm very pleased to tell you that what you see on the screen does look very similar to what historically took place on Olympos. That large land mass or supercontinent which you can clearly see in the center surrounded by a huge body of water, is what is referred to as a Pangaea. It has been formed earlier by an assemblage of several smaller continental units. These have, over time, formed over fissures in weakened areas of the surface crust. On Olympos, this amalgamation took place in the late Paleozoic and early Mesozoic eras. The same thing has obviously occurred on this new planet and the presence of this Pangaea affirms our belief that the new planet is indeed evolving along perhaps not exact, but very similar, lines to that of Olympos. On this jump we will not be physically interfering with the normal processes that are currently taking place on the planet. Our purpose here now is simply to assure ourselves that everything is going as we had hoped and expected. There are differences. For example, you can see that unlike Olympos, the new planet has only one natural moon.

"So far, so good.

"Our next warp will take us forward in time one hundred and twenty-five million years and it is then that we will be making our first hands-on involvement. On that occasion we will simply be testing the planet's terraforming evolvement to see what might be necessary for us to customize in order to meet our standards for the future support of Hominid life. If you have any questions or wish to stay with this image for a little longer, let me know. If not, we will immediately enter a worm and move forward in time."

It was Sebastian who spoke.

"Olympos had three moons and it was not a, Pan...whatever you called it."

Adon smiled.

"Quite right. Olympos actually had only two natural moons. Because we had positioned our starship in an orbit around Olympos as well, we became that third moon you saw in your sky. And while Olympos was not a Pangaea in your time, that is in fact how it started out. Part of our job after this next time jump through space and time will be to decide how many continents we want on the new planet. Beginning at that point in time, we will play our first active role in the customized development of the planet and I think you will find that process very exhilarating and satisfying. Keep in mind however, that while the natural processes of planet development can be tinkered with, it cannot be totally thwarted. The Olympos you lived on was still evolving when you left it. The plates making up the surface of your planet were still shifting at that time and they would have continued to do so if it had lasted longer."

Enoch followed with a second question.

"Is it our intention then to try and mold the continents. Like working with clay?"

Adon's smile broadened considerably.

"You could say that, although the planet will still be very hot and we will have to remain at some distance. We will mainly work with lasers and force fields, as we custom shape each landmass. However, we will also, whenever possible, follow the naturally forming active volcanic crust lines as much as we can.

"As the planet cools over time we will become more and more involved in its evolution and in due course, toward the end of our tinkering, we will spend a good deal of time on the actual surface itself."

The room grew silent as they all studied the image on the screen and then Gaia spoke.

"I think we have done enough for today. We Atlantians still have to spend some time brushing up on our specific areas of expertise before our next warp, so let's meet back here in the morning at the same time as we did today."

CHAPTER FORTY-ONE

- Insight -

The Olympoians had returned to their quarters where they'd spent the first part of the evening talking together. Gabe had asked Jonah to join them when he could. While they waited for him, Juno's foretelling coupled with the excitement of what was to come on the morrow gave them a good deal of fodder for discussion. They were still at it when Jonah popped in through the door.

The three of them had already decided that it would be Gabe who should raise the idea of somehow getting access to some better weaponry before they colonized. The big Neanderthal had been mulling over in his mind what approach to take while they waited and in the end he just went for it the moment Jonah walked in.

"We were hoping that you will help us out."

Jonah shrugged.

"Sure bro, what do you need."

The discussion that followed took the rest of the evening, keeping them occupied until they finally had to call it a night.

* * * * *

Persephone had gone directly from the main control room to her small office and there had begun to research past plans for the early development of trade as a precursor to eventual economic development on a new planet. She knew that in the early stages of the creation of the Hominid settlements, the main concerns for the small groupings would boil down to the basics of life: shelter, food, a reliable source of water and eventually, especially in the colder climes, clothing. In her position, she would have little to do in those early stages of development. While the emergence of trade would be a long way off on the horizon at that point in time, time itself was no barrier to an Atlantian and she wanted to be ready with her own ideas on economic development well ahead of the curve. She felt strongly that trade was a key factor in any form of long-term economic progress. Experience had shown that the prudent use of trade could positively boost an early settlement's development rate and create absolute gains for all trading partners involved. As necessary as trade would be, it had its downsides and she wanted to be sure that she understood these issues. On Olympos she had witnessed how free trade could become individually harmful as domestic infant industries first came into play. As settlements grow and trade develops there is invariably an increase in real integration with a larger economy and export-led growth had historically been a key part of many colonies' successful long-term development strategies. Additionally, poverty reduction in any society is intimately linked with trade. Sustained strong growth over longer periods had also been strongly associated with a reduction in poverty. Trade and growth were strongly linked.

* * * * *

Gaia and Venus had gone to her mother's apartments after leaving the main control room. Venus was listening intently as the two of them shared a refreshing beverage together.

"I, and in time you, have the responsibility for overseeing the basic functions associated with love, beauty, sex, fertility, prosperity and desire in the Hominid species upon the planet we currently nurture. As such, historically we play a very pivotal role in the successful long term growth and evolution of these specific species. We are in somewhat new territory here, inasmuch as you, unlike earlier such Atlantian committees, have decided not to interact directly with the Hominid population of this new world. In so doing, you will have placed the colonists into a structure that will very likely cause them to look at your indirect activity in their lives as surreal or god-like. Part of your role is to advance their sexuality. Sex brings life and is the primal driving force for these genera. In simple terms, these uncomplicated lifeforms will have need to put a face on what they cannot see or touch; in other words, to have some form of faith, in order to make sense of your involvement in their lives. They will need to believe that some higher authority is looking after their needs. They will need a deep faith in the concept of having superior beings overseeing their daily lives in order to explain away occurrences that they have no understanding of and did not create themselves. In basic terms, unless I miss my guess, and because they will not in this instance be able to actually see us from time to time, they will consider and accept that we Atlantians are their gods. That being the situation, you will very likely be one of the most important of those gods. Your place in that Atlantian celestial body will embody sex, love, beauty, enticement, seduction and persuasive female charm, among a larger community of immortal gods with specific responsibilities in their lives. I expect that, at least initially, the separate groupings will see your image somewhat differently, name you, pay homage to you in various unique ways. But due to your importance in their day to day lives, all will pay faithful homage to the superior being they each envision you to be. If it is as it was on Olympos, they will revere you. You will become one of the most widely referenced deities on the new planet, the embodiment of love and sexuality and in time, they will build temples to you and sculpt your likeness in their mind's eye."

Venus's mouth was hanging open and Gaia, try as she might, could not stop from laughing at her daughter.

"What did you expect? That you, as the caretaker of what is probably the largest driving force in their simple world, that of sex, would simply beam blissfully down upon them and hope for the best?"

Venus closed her mouth and shook her head.

"No, mother. I guess I had some idea about doing things to stimulate the growth in the populations. Seeing to good health and...well I just had no idea it was, well you know..."

Gaia grinned.

"Well my child, if you haven't learned by now that sex makes the world go round for Hominids, its time you did. You will be responsible to see to it that your persona on the planet absorbs and tempers the male essence, uniting the opposites of male and female in mutual affection. Your role there will be to create a general sense that, as one untouchable and unseen and thereby godlike, you are essentially assimilative and benign and embrace several otherwise quite disparate functions. Being divine in their eyes, you will have tremendous power over them. You will more than likely be considered as capable of bestowing military victory, sexual success, good fortune and prosperity. In one context, you will be seen as a goddess of prostitutes; in another, capable of turning the hearts of men and women from sexual vice to virtue. As these species evolve, their concept of your image will be found in domestic murals, mosaics and household shrines. Prospective brides will probably offer a gift up to your image, prior to making their commitment in *'life-partnering ceremonies'*."

* * * * *

Adon, Jonah and Enoch had remained in the main control center. They sat together in a corner of the room around a small table to one side of the big screen, which was now dark. For the first hour, Adon had mostly listened while Jonah quizzed Enoch about his new responsibilities as military and police advisor. It seemed to Jonah that with his advisory switch, he would have very little to do in the initial stages after the colonization. While the first settlers were evolving, his input would be slow and simple in the terms of weapons and protection. He was not impressed when Enoch advised that initially there would be little advancement in this area. The idea of introducing stone tools offered him little anticipation; however, he perked up a little when it came to the eventual introduction of fire and the wheel and by the time they'd discussed water craft, spears, swords and gunpowder, he was feeling a good deal better about his prospects.

With a view to adding a little excitement to the rather dull conversation that had taken place up to that point, and knowing that the experience would be stimulated by such a visit, Adon suggested that Enoch take Jonah on a short tour of the armaments storage facility.

Initially it appeared to Adon that Jonah appeared a little taken aback by this suggestion, almost as if he sensed the possibility of some form of hidden addenda. He didn't respond for a moment but then quickly recovered his composure and Adon dismissed the incident without further thought. The two left immediately.

When they returned Adon had refreshments at the ready and noted with some satisfaction that Jonah had indeed brightened after the tour. He invited them to sit, had 'One' pour mugs of the beverage and turned to a new topic.

"While the three of us have the chance we should perhaps touch on something that we can't share with the Olympoians.

We know that historically we Atlantians interacted directly with the colonists from time to time to assist them with their evolution. As the committee has decided that this type of interaction should not take place on the new planet, we have to agree on how we are to go about providing the assistance when it is needed, without that direct contact. I have given this problem a good deal of thought and I would like to suggest a method of accomplishing the task, for discussion between the three of us, before I take it to the other advisors."

Jonah interjected.

"Why can't the Olympoians be part of the planning on this? I thought we were including them in everything."

"Well, since they will be part of the new colonization we have to consider them carefully before we speak of things that will take happen after we have put them in place. This whole new approach to our involvement in the daily lives means that we will have to ensure that they are not aware of how they are being assisted once they are on the planet. Under the circumstances, that would unnecessarily upset the normal evolution as we now perceive it. If we do not want them to know of our existence and to see us only as some superior outside force in their lives once they have arrived on the planet, we will have to do our best beforehand to ensure that their memories do not provide ideas which may serve to disrupt the sequence of advances they achieve. For example, we do not want them to know about gunpowder before they discover fire."

Enoch shrugged and set his mug down.

"How is that going to be a problem. We're putting them through memory cleansing before they go down just the same as the other settlers aren't we?"

"Yes, of course. But the other settlers, the ones we created here aboard Atlantis, do not have any memories of what Olympos was like. They have been living in a controlled environment and have experienced nothing like the Olympoians have. Compounding that is the fact that the memory cleansing operation is not foolproof. All those who go through it will still experience the occasional flashback to what came before the settlement itself. In the case of the others, they have no memories that would seriously affect their normal evolution. That is not the case with the Olympians, who have spent all their lives to this point living on a relatively advanced planet. They too will have flashbacks from time to time and some of these may disrupt their progress. If we do not want them to know of us and our involvement in their daily lives after they colonize, if it is our intent that they do not realize the part we play in their lives, then we must take care to protect them from all knowledge of it."

Jonah sucked in a deep breath and sat back into his chair,
"Now I see why you were initially against including them in the colonization. If the risk is so high that they could throw a monkey wrench into the whole deal, why did you eventually agree?'

"Well I may have overblown the real danger of them retaining information that would be disruptive. We have had no experience with that type of retention of memory since we have never chosen to add our specifically created Hominid to the natural mix of a new planet. Perhaps there will be no problems arising from it or if there are some, they will be minor. Additionally, your mother is working on upgrading the memory cleansing program to improve its efficiency."

Enoch spoke up.

"That is all well and good. But if we are not to be seen as directly involved with them, how are we going to assist in their problem-solving and inventive abilities, if that becomes necessary?"

"Well, Gaia is also working on that. I gave her the problem when we first agreed to avoid directly interacting with them once they had colonized. She had been looking at adding an additional program into the memory cleansing process. She believes she can adjust it to allow for us to have the ability to make future mind contact with any individual settler as necessary. It isn't expected that this will happen often, but perhaps we will be able to correct any unfortunate flashback that may have arisen and also to induce the concept of any invention we feel necessary in order to speed up evolution or to advance living conditions in a needed area. It is an entirely new concept of course, giving us far more power over them than we've had before. Power tends to corrupt. We saw a perfect example of that with Marduke, which is why I wished to discuss it with you before presenting the idea to our peers."

CHAPTER FORTY-TWO

- Changing Landscape -

The full complement of committee members met early the next morning. Adon was pleased to see that they all seemed well rested and could sense the excitement in the air as they kibitzed and helped themselves to honeyed tea before taking up their chairs.

Adon let them settle a bit before he spoke.

"Today we warp ahead to the point where the new planet is approximately one hundred and seventy-five million years younger than Olympos was when we left it. When we arrive, we will begin our hands-on work at terraforming the new planet in preparation for the later Hominid colonization. Terraforming is the process of planetary engineering, specifically directed at enhancing the planet's environmental capacity to advance our Hominid settlements by ensuring that it will support life. Historically we know what we must achieve. We must create an open planetary ecosystem emulating all the functions of the biosphere of Olympos, one that will be fully supportable for our new colonies.

"To pick up on where we left off yesterday, a bit of a recap and elaboration is in order.

Gabe whispered a *"No! Please!"* and let out a huge sigh. Jonah picked up on it and shook with repressed laughter.

The big Neanderthal was instantly rewarded with yet another swift kick to the shins, delivered by Juno who was sitting on the other side of him. He grimaced and opened his mouth to speak but the expression on Juno's face was enough to make him hold his tongue.

Adon was already well into his talk.

"The Pangaea we last viewed was situated primarily in the

southern hemisphere and surrounded by water. Historically, the formation of this type of supercontinent and its eventual breakup, comes about through what we call plate tectonics, and is cyclical. There have probably been many other such creations that have split apart before the Pangaea we observed yesterday finally formed.

"The movement of these smaller formations indicate in which direction the poles lie relative to the reforming rock. These magnetic poles of the planet drift about the rotational pole. On Olympos, there were three major phases in the break-up of Pangaea. The first phase began in the early to mid-Jurassic, when the Pangaea began to rift from the ocean in the east toward the body of water in the west. Each following phase of rifts created separate continents which then themselves rifted and parted as they first broke away from the Pangaea and then from each other. What we saw on Olympos during our last days was the latest result of this activity.

"So, the breakup of the Pangaea happened over a long period of time.

"When we next come out of the wormhole we will be arriving at approximately the time in history when the Pangaea on Olympos had begun to split up, for the most part following fault lines and fissures, and we are going to play just a small part in how the current supercontinent we expect to find on the new planet divides.

"Now, if everyone is ready, we can enter the worm hole and be on our way. Once we complete our passage through space and time, in this case approximately one hundred and twenty-five million years, I will give you an understanding of what we are about to do and then we will undertake some basic testing before we go about our initial shaping of this new world."

At this statement, a suddenly much more attentive Gabe, gave a thumbs up.

"Bring it on."

The vibration of the massive engines began and soon

reached the now familiar hum. The screen shifted from blue to black for several minutes and then, as they slipped out of the worm, filled with a slightly fuzzy image of the new planet and its much smaller orbiting moon. Adon adjusted the settings on the screen slightly, improving the crispness of the picture and then sat down at his work station.

"As you can see, the appearance of the Pangaea has changed since our last viewing. The surface has taken on a variation of browns and blacks. It now appears barren and desolate. Note the numerous zigzagging red fissures depicting the fault lines caused by the molten core as it forces its way up through the weakened areas of the crust.

"The formation of the environment and climate due to the plate tectonics brings about varying climatic pressures which affect the life on the Pangaea. These plate tectonics are paramount in the formation of later land masses, dictating the resulting continent's placement on the planet, as well as the overall climate, environments, habitats and basic structure of each of the newly created continents. Consequentially, animal and plant life will have to adapt to the new conditions.

"Plate tectonics also cause volcanic activity which, on its own can be responsible for extinctions and adaptations. Many of these will have already affected lifeforms on the Pangea, and will continue to do so on the separating continents as they move to their new locations. Tectonic collisions, earthquakes and chasms will cause mountains and valleys to form on these new continents.

"Life has been evolving during the one hundred million years that this Pangaea has existed and during that time many species had fruitful times, whereas others struggled to evolve or died out. For example, plant eating animals did well. Early on, plants of that period, which were dependent upon spore reproduction, had at one point been taken out of the ecosystems and were replaced by the gymnosperm plant, which reproduces through the use of seeds instead. These new plants were also able to transport water internally, allowing animals consuming them to improve hydration.

"Insects including beetles, dragonflies and mosquitos also thrived at one point, then they were hit with a change that brought about a mass extinction. At a different period of time many reptiles, the ancestors of what you would recognize as crocodiles and birds, also flourished.

"In the timeframe we are now seeing on the new planet, Olympos also had a Pangaea and that huge landmass tremendously affected the setup of the Olympos that our three Olympoians knew so well. When the continents separated and reformed themselves on Olympos, it changed the flow, or continental drift, of the oceanic currents and winds - the shifting of the planet's surface directly affecting climate, among other things. Understandably, this caused havoc among living species, some of whom simply couldn't adapt to the radical changes.

"When the Pangaea separated on Olympos, the realignment of the continents changed the function of the oceans and seaways. This repositioning of the continents also interrupted previously functioning equatorial currents, therein altering the distribution of warmth and coolness in the oceans. Warm waters moved to higher latitudes, which led to an increased evaporation and eventually atmospheric moisture, which then resulted in increased precipitation. This increased precipitation caused the development of snow and ice near the poles. These in turn led to an accumulation which eventually became an icecap, bringing about further global cooling.

"Currents in the newly formed southern sea created a circumpolar current, which eventually led to atmospheric currents that rotated from west to east. These atmospheric and oceanic currents stopped the transfer of warm, tropical air and water to the higher latitudes. As the warm air and currents moved northward, it cooled down the area so much that it became glacial.

"This deterioration of the Pangaea led to one of Olympos's major mass extinction events, resulting in the loss of over ninety percent of marine and seventy percent of terrestrial species. There were three main sources of environmental deterioration which played a part in this. The first was a loss of oxygen concentration in the oceans which caused the deep water regions to grow shallower. This meant there were fewer places for calcite to dissolve in the ocean. That, in turn, led to the extinction of carbonate producers such as the brachiopods and corals that relied on dissolved calcite to survive.

"The breakup of the first Pangaea occurring on Olympos, which will also occur for the new planet shortly, was the beginning of anoxic ocean environments, oceans with very low oxygen concentrations. The mix of anoxic oceans and ocean acidification combined with the metal loading led to increasingly acidic oceans, which ultimately brought about the extinction of benthic species, those who lived in the lowest levels of the lakes and oceans.

"Another factor on Olympos was a large volcanic event resulting from the effects of the tectonic movement of an earlier Pangaea. This had several negative repercussions on the environment, including metal loading and excess atmospheric carbon, which blocked out Solar's warming rays. Metal loading is the release of toxic metals from volcanic eruptions into the environment. When mixed with water, they led to acid rain and general stress on the environment.

"The newly exposed portions of the crust absorbed the carbon dioxide from the atmosphere and the toxic metals infringed on the vascular plants which were already in existence, stifling their ability to photosynthesize.

"As the carbon dioxide was absorbed out of the air by the newly exposed rock formations, they also absorbed the acid rain and its carbon dioxide. Over time, that meant that there was no longer enough carbon dioxide in the air to trap and hold Solar's heat around the planet. In just a few thousand years the temperature plummeted to around minus sixty degrees. That produced ice.

"The more ice there was, the more the light rays were reflected back from the crust. As a result, the ice began to move, spreading away from both poles, forcing its way toward the equator and eventually covering the entire planet in ice ten thousand feet thick, leading to an ice age.

"Olympos, which had begun life as a molten sphere had now become a ball of ice. At that point in the evolution, virtually all the planet's Solar-warmth was being reflected back out into space. For fifteen million years, Olympos was simply a vast frozen snowball.

"Eventually, volcanoes began to break free from the crust, spewing forth the intense heat from the molten core as well as billions of tons of carbon dioxide into the atmosphere. Previous to this time the planet had quickly absorbed carbon dioxide from the atmosphere, but now, with those rocks smothered in ice, there was nothing to absorb the gas, so it remained in the atmosphere.

"Like a heavy blanket it began to trap and hold Solar's warmth around the planet, allowing the temperature to rise. As a result, the ice began to melt and as it disappeared, the crust, delivered of it massive weight, began to rise up. This movement created fissures and weak spots and even more volcanoes. These caused the expulsion of more carbon dioxide into the air which pushed the temperature up even higher. The melt gathered more momentum.

"While the planet was frozen, Solar's ultraviolet rays reacted with water molecules in the ice to produce hydrogen peroxide, a chemical rich in oxygen. As the ice continued to melt, the hydrogen peroxide broke down and released massive amounts of oxygen. The level of this gas in the atmosphere then began to rise rapidly.

"Six hundred million years before Olympos met its end, the planet's temperature grew warmer, reaching a level where it was much like what we would call a summer day. At that time, a day was about twenty-two hours long.

"All the water resulting from the melt, combined with the new higher temperature, created a perfect environment for life. In the oceans, some primitive bacteria had survived the deep freeze and now found themselves in an oxygen-enriched ocean. They began to evolve and flourish in their new environment and the cycle of evolving lifeforms, as we know it, began.

"Armed with this historical information based on what occurred on Olympos, we can now hopefully make informed decisions on how we would like to terraform this new planet for optimum benefit to our future Hominid settlements.

"If there are no questions, let's get started."

CHAPTER FORTY-THREE

- Terraforming -

While he'd been speaking, Adon had been keying information into the main computer bank. When he had finished he lifted his hand to indicate the screen.

"I have taken a shot of the screen image and provided it to our large computer bank with instructions to access it based on the current condition of the Pangea. I have asked it to provide an analysis of the activity currently taking place and to formulate several variations of what, using the natural fissures, we could do that would influence exactly how it breaks up. The computer's memory banks will have already registered the natural fissures and volcanic activity as well as the magnetic pole pulls and the active currents that are now in place on this new planet. It has been assessing all the natural forces at play as well as what physical changes we are capable of influencing.

"I will now change from the image of the planet to a new screen shot which will provide us with the options the computer has come up with. As these appear, please keep in mind that our intent is to ensure that a large land mass, one that in a natural process over time will divide itself into smaller continents, comes to rest on the planet's equator. That is where the temperature will be best suited for our future Hominid colonization. Also, don't forget that there will be temperature variations over the expanse of this land mass. It will be warmer at the equator and cooler toward each of the poles."

The image on the screen changed, replaced by six framed windows. Each provided a different end product scenario of a possible Pangea breakup.

Juno was the first to react.

"Four of the projections would be unsuitable based on what you have told us, as they will not end up producing a large land mass on the general line of the equator. Only the second and fourth manage to bring that about."

Adon grinned.

"Very good and quite correct. So we are left with two to choose from."

His fingers played over the keys and the four rejected screens disappeared to be replaced by a larger version of the remaining two, on a split screen.

"The choice is yours to make; which will it be?"

The committee members were all leaning forward eagerly in the chairs, eyes glued to the screen. There was silence for a few seconds and then Sebastian spoke up.

"The one on the left is the best of the two options. It has the largest land mass centered on the line of the equator, with less in the cooler, higher and lower hemispheres, making it best for colonization."

There were several nodded agreements with the monk's appraisal and then Enoch, who had been carefully studying the two images voiced his agreement.

"Sebastian has the right of it."

Adon smiled broadly.

"Yes, I think he has chosen well; are we all in agreement?"

Nods all round.

"It's settled then. I will shift back to the view of the new planet and we can begin our work."

He entered the change on the keyboard and the screen flickered back to the original image reflecting both the planet and its moon.

"We will be operating with two of the starship's strongest systems - first with laser and then with force fields. In order to use these powerful devices, I will have to bring all the engines up to full power, allowing the devices to come on line, so do not be alarmed by the sound and feel of the change in Atlantis's ambience."

This time, the humming sound previously experienced

when increased power was needed, reached a much higher level as the ship came to full power and a gentle but steady tremor, not particularly disquieting, but definitely noticeable, could be felt throughout the large room.

While this was happening Adon entered the selected scenario into the computer banks and went about preparing the two systems to gear up for use in providing the desired adjustments to the natural process of Pangea breakup.

A pin drop could have been heard in the room as Adon began to speak again.

"A laser, which is light amplification by stimulated emission of radiation, is a device that emits light through a process of optical amplification based on the stimulated emission of electromagnetic radiation. The laser differs from other sources of light in that it emits light *'coherently'*. Spatial coherence allows a laser to be focused to pinpoint a spot, enabling applications such as laser cutting. This coherence allows a laser beam to stay narrow over great distances. That is how we will use it today.

We will, as I mentioned earlier, mainly use it to deepen the natural fault lines already apparent in the crust - those fiery lightening-like red lines you see zig-zagging over the rock face. The computer will now automatically use the shipboard laser to fulfill the design that we have just chosen."

He keyed in the execute instruction and the thin beam appeared at the edge of the screen and shot quickly out toward the planet, immediately impacting one of the fault lines at the top of the screen where the land mass met the water.

What had already been a thin red line began to widen and as the laser began to move along, it visually expanded its width.

Those watching appeared hypnotized as the beam started to follow the fault along through the land mass, shifting as needed to stay in the groove until it worked its way back to the shoreline.

Adon did not have to raise his voice as he spoke.

"The laser is adjusting as it moves, going no deeper than necessary at any point at this time. The piece of crust that has now been treated from shore to shore will not actually break off until we utilize the power of a force field on it. The beam will now shift to the next land area that it wants to select."

He had no more than uttered the words when the beam disappeared for an instant before reappearing, again on the coastline to, begin to work its way along a different set of fault lines.

"The computer will work its way around the entire shoreline first, selecting the areas of crust that border on water. Once that has been accomplished it will be time for us to bring the force fields to bear in order to complete the breakaway of those sections. That done we will again use the laser and the force field to work in from the newly created shorelines and repeat the process until we have separated all the sections of crust needed to meet the screen selection we choose."

No one commented. They simply watched with wonder.

It took only about a half hour to complete the entire cutting task and when it was finished the now separated sections began to find their point of buoyancy. Then, with the help of the ship's force fields, they slowly began to move out and away in various directions from the remaining mass. The largest chunk, in the center, was massive and it did not move, but instead remained positioned, centered on the line of the equator.

A shared exhalation of held breath emerged and Adon, himself relieved to see the operation go so smoothly, laughed.

"And so, our entry into planet modification begins. So far, the development of this new planet had followed pretty much in step with what took place as Olympos developed and evolved.

"Next stop for us will be a leap ahead in time to the point

where we can expect to see the first real signs of Hominid development."

The screen faded to blue and then black.

As the overhead lights came back to full power, the hum of the engines faded away and Juno spoke tentatively.

"I wonder…would it be possible to have one last look at Olympos before we call it a day? I know it's silly of me, but I would just like to assure myself that…well, hopefully just get some closure I guess."

Gaia looked to Adon who nodded solemnly.

"Certainly, if you wish it. But understand that what you will see will not be pleasant."

Gabe reached over and rested his hand on Juno's shoulder.

"We have all accepted that. I also think it would be a good idea for all of us to fully understand that Olympos, as we lived it, is no longer a reality."

Sebastian added his agreement.

"Yes, if it is not too much trouble, I too, would like to see how it has been transformed."

Adon turned his attention to the keyboard and the screen lit up again, first turning to blue and then displaying the image of Olympos and its two moons.

The picture was stark and left no doubt as to the end of the planet. It was a dry, barren wasteland marked by old volcanoes and impact craters. Currently, almost the entire surface appeared to be scoured by a massive sand storm.

Juno sighed deeply.

"My Solar! That certainly mars any pleasant memories I had about it. There is quite definitely no life left there now."

Gaia frowned.

"No, and there has not been for a very long time."

Adon was aware of the unquestionable finality of what the screen reflected and he worked the keys, letting the image fade off to a blue screen.

"Yes, Olympos has been completely changed. No life could possibly exist under the current circumstances.

"Our next space jump will bring us to a point where, if the

new planet has continued to developed as Olympos did, we should see signs of the ancestors of early human development, that being when the new species first split off from the lineage of the chimpanzees.

"At this point I suggest we make that next jump.

"When we come out of the worm this time we will not only be assessing that stage of the evolutionary cycle, but will also be making tests of the general environmental, atmospheric, and water conditions to ensure that they have reached a point in their evolution that will allow for the natural progression of these very early Hominoid genera into that of the more advanced species."

CHAPTER FORTY-FOUR

- *Chemical Analysis* -

The hum of the ship's engines began to rise again as they entered the new worm hole to make the next move forward through time and within moments the main lighting in the control room faded. The screen flickered to blue, then offered a fresh image of the new planet.

The changes reflected in this latest illustration differed considerable from the one before and Adon, eager to move on from the negativity that had surrounded the devastating snapshot of Olympos, began to speak immediately.

"As you can clearly see, the appearance of the new planet has changed dramatically."

He did not have to elaborate further on that point. It was clear to his audience that a massive transformation had taken place. Oceans and lakes, a vibrant blue in colour, were easily recognized for what they were.

But the largest change was in what had been previously, for the most part, barren rock. A variation in hues of what appeared to be brownish rock and a new vibrant green carpet of vegetation covered almost all of the land masses. It appeared to be marshy in many areas; others were thick and luxuriant, almost jungle-like in form. What looked like small ice caps now covered both of the poles.

"Since the last time we warped, the planet has gone through considerable evolution and with it the life upon it. It is that advancement that we are interested in and if all is going to plan, it will hopefully have led to the development of the first of the evolving bipedal Hominid populations.

"What we expect to have happened is, of course, based on what took place on Olympos as it developed. We will be wanting to confirm that that process has been replicated on the new planet.

"It certainly looks like the planet has come a long way. As we had anticipated, it now looks to be a blue and green world and probably bursting with life of all kinds - with any luck, including that of those earliest of the Hominid ancestors.

"In terms of an age comparison with Olympos as we knew it before leaving, the new planet has apparently kept pace. Homo erectus will have recently evolved here."

Juno spoke up.

"Will we be able to see them?"

Adon smiled.

"Yes, if you wish. We have infrared heat sensing equipment aboard Atlantis that will allow us to pinpoint warm-bodied life forms. It might take a few moments to isolate the exact species, and then we would have to magnify to a high degree, but since we are able to get physically closer to the planet now, we should be able to do that. First though, we will be deploying a pod manned by Almies to the surface to take samples for testing to ensure that atmosphere and water conditions are as they should be by now, if all has gone to plan.

"I will change the screen shot so we can watch that pod deploy from the transporter room and then follow its time-traversing beam to the planet."

Gabe responded.

"Why do you send the little ones? Would it not be possible for some of us to do this work?"

Gaia interjected.

"Not safely at this stage. Until we have tested both the atmosphere and water quality at the surface, it would be unsafe for any of us to land on the planet."

Sebastian picked up on the thread.

"Once the tests have been done and if they prove to be acceptable, would it then be possible for us to visit the planet?"

As Sebastian was speaking, the image on the screen

changed, replaced by a longer view taken from Atlantis. Adon shrugged as he keyed instruction into the control board. An opening appeared in what had, seconds ago, appeared to be a solid rock formation on the surface of the spaceship and a silver orb drifted out from the interior. It held position for a second and then with a blur accelerated rapidly and disappeared.

"Yes, I suppose, although if we did so, we would have to be sure that we did not in any way interact with the existing evolving Hominid lifeforms. We could use the infrared system to scan ahead of time to ensure no contact, I suppose. However, I'm not sure that it would be a good idea at this point in the evolvement of the planet. Perhaps we should wait until one of the future space and time warps.

Jonah grinned.

"That would be cool."

Adon continued.

"We have a location lock on the traverse beam and it has now reached the surface so I will advance the image on the screen and magnify sufficiently for us to view the pod and its passengers as they work."

All eyes were glued to the image as it turned fuzzy for a second and then hardened. As it did there was a burst of exclamations. They differed and came from all sides, but one main thought was common throughout.

It was one of surprised wonder.

It was Venus who expressed her feelings the most succinctly.

"It is beautiful, so lush and colorful!"

Adon laughed.

"It is, isn't it? They have been programmed to land on a shoreline on the equator, at the point where a river flows into the ocean. Conditions there should be near perfect for a future Hominid settlement, although we have checked with the infrared and there is currently no such colony on the location."

The room fell silent again as the audience first quietly

watched the two Almies moving about industriously and then shifted their individual attention to the surrounding landscape displayed before them.

Adon's gaze stayed with the Almies. He watched as they completed their assigned tasks and began to move back toward the little silver pod. As they entered and the capsule hatch closed he turned back to the keyboard.

"Okay, we will be bringing them back now. Once they are safely back on board I will use the infrared system to see if we can localize some of the planet's occupants. It may take a little time to sort through the contacts to see if we can locate a representative of the most advanced Hominid species."

The image on the screen faded into blue and then a larger overview of the planet came into view again. Adon worked busily on the keyboard for several minutes and as he was working, interjected in the shared discussions of what they had seen that was now going on among his audience members. In short order he spoke again.

"They're back on board. They will have completed the testing on the return journey so I expect we will have results from them shortly. In the meantime, I have begun our search for an example of Homo erectus. I probably should point out that if we are successful, please do not expect too much. The evolutionary process for what we would call Human or Neanderthal for that matter, is a very long one and when it comes to this new planet, we are nowhere near reaching that stage of development. If we are right in our expectations and things are going to plan, we might perhaps find a specimen that will bear a striking resemblance to what we consider as modern humans. However, if that should happen, understand that it will be possessed of a brain that is about only three-quarters the size of a modern man's as we know it and that hopefully, it will sport a forehead that is considerably less sloped than that of its predecessors, as well as teeth that are much smaller. Its body also ought to be extremely hairy, more ape than manlike, certainly not anywhere near a mirror image of any of you Olympoians."

A small light glowed briefly on his keyboard and Adon's attention shifted. He depressed the key below the light and then smiled broadly.

"Well, both atmosphere and water have tested well within the range that we had hoped they would. This is wonderful news, as it goes to support our initial expectation that the new planet would likely follow the evolutionary processes that Olympos had before it. It also means that we may very well find the specific specimen that we were hoping would be present."

Conversation in the room dropped to a murmur. Everyone edged slightly forward in their seats.

They did not have long to wait.

Adon expanded the magnification and as it took effect, the image on the screen began to enlarge until eventually it held a shot of a relatively flat area covered in tall grass. The magnification then increased again, telescoping into an area depicting about one thousand square feet.

It was Gabe who first picked up on the movement in its centre.

"Look there, just to the right of the middle of the screen. Something is moving."

Adon made a minor adjustment and the shuffling form filled the screen.

No one said anything for several seconds and then Adon broke the silence.

"That ladies and gentlemen is exactly what we were looking for. Say hello to a prime example of Homo erectus!"

The image depicted lumbered its way through the tall grass and the screen adjusted to follow it.

"As we had hoped, the new planet appears to be replicating the evolutionary process we observed on Olympos. There can be little doubt about that now. Unless something untoward occurs, all that is left for us to do is move forward through time to periodically check on the progress of the evolution of this species until we reach the point when it is time for us to colonize."

Gaia interjected.

"We have done enough for today. We have been provided with a good deal to think about and after our next space warp we will be making some very crucial observations in order to determine the point at which the Hominid population has evolved. In that vein, we will be looking specifically for evidence that will affirm that tools are being used by the advanced species. By this point in the evolutionary cycle, the use of stone tools, which should have already been accomplished for some time by the earlier ancestors of Homo erectus, will now be commonplace for him. We will want to confirm that this is the case.

"Additionally, we will want to ensure that all the lifeforms existing at that time on the planet are those that we have already selected as ideal for our purposes. This will likely necessitate the eradication of some species of plants and the introduction of others.

"Time for us to get a good night's sleep and meet here again in the morning at nine."

CHAPTER FORTY-FIVE

- *Sober Second Thought* -

Both Venus and Jonah had joined the three Olympoians in their apartment complex for their evening meal. Conversation was lively and upbeat, all five of them reliving the wonder of what they had seen after the latest warp through time and space. The phenomenal changes in the planet itself, along with the revelation of the presence of Homo erectus, had provided them with plenty of positive talking points. In was late in the evening by the time the two Atlantians took their leave.

After they'd left, Sebastian suggested a nightcap before they called it a day and Juno and Gabe readily agreed.

When the little duty Almie had duly provided the snifters of steaming liquor, it left them alone in the room.

Still excited, Gabe and Sebastian had been maintaining a deep discussion about the day's events throughout the serving process, but Juno had remained relatively silent after the departure of Venus and Jonah.

It was Sebastian who finally picked up on the fact and addressed her.

"You're awfully quiet. Is anything wrong?"

In response Gabe, stopping in mid-sentence, turned his attention to her.

"You had another foreseeing, Babe?"

Juno, who had been staring blankly down at the drink which she held cupped in both hands, took a couple of seconds to respond.

"No, I was just thinking...this memory-cleansing thing. I know we all agreed to it and its part of the deal we made, but the closer we get to doing it, the less I like the idea. I'm not sure I want to lose all my memories. I mean, everything we've done in our lives, all the stuff we did together...even how we feel about each other..."

Off topic, the comment came at them from out of nowhere and both the monk and Gabe were at a momentary loss for words.

Juno set her drink down on the table and looked up at them.

"They say we will have some memories of our past left, but they will be fuzzy and we may have the odd flashback. The question is, what memories will we be left and what flashbacks will we have? Will they be ones important to us or will they be mindless and without real value? Will we even remember each other?"

Talk about a downer!

Gabe didn't have a clue of what to say in response. He turned to look pleadingly at Sebastian for help. The monk cleared his throat and sucked in a deep breath before speaking.

"I really don't know how to answer that. This whole idea of adding their own specimens and us to the natural colonization mix, is new to the Atlantians. They have no history to rely on. I get the impression that even they don't know what the end result will be."

The expression on Juno's face had been one of concern and that seemed to deepen at his words. Sebastian struggled to give her some solace.

"On the other hand, they did say the process was selective. They must therefore have some means of picking specifics for attention while allowing other memories to remain. Perhaps we should raise the issue with the council members. I can certainly see where you are coming from. It would be nice if we could at least get a better understanding of the process."

Gabe piped up.

"Makes sense. I mean it's probably just certain stuff that they don't want us to remember. Stuff that would be bad for us to know because it would upset the applecart once we arrived on the planet, if we decided to take advantage of it."

Sebastian nodded emphatically.

"Yes, I'm sure that's the case. In the morning we'll ask, but I think Gabe probably has the right of it. Anyway, don't let it get you down, Juno. What we saw today was pretty amazing. I have a good feeling about this whole thing."

The frown didn't exactly leave Juno's face, but she appeared to brighten a little.

"Yes I suppose you're right. But I will raise my concerns in the morning."

Relieved that she was feeling a little more positive, Gabe nodded in agreement.

"Right, you do that and I think, on that note, we should probably wrap this up for the night or we'll likely end up sleeping thought the morning meeting."

* * * * *

All members of the committee joined Adon in the main computer room on the dot of nine the next morning. They found him working at his keyboard and he continued to do so while they made their way to their seats.

Although she was more relaxed than she had been the previous evening, Juno was still apprehensive about the prospect of the memory-cleansing. Encouraged by both Gabe and Sebastian, she raised the subject with the others once they were all seated.

She addressed her initial query to Gaia.

"The three of us were talking last night and we still have some misgivings about the memory-cleansing thing."

Adon overheard her and his fingers paused over the keys and he turned to face them as Gaia replied.'

"Misgivings?"

Juno frowned.

"Well, not misgivings per se I guess, more like a need for a better understanding of the process."

Sebastian stepped in to help her clarify.

"Now that the prospect is looming closer, we had some questions about how it's done and what it will mean for us…"

He paused for a second as he shifted his mind back to the previous night's conversation, and then continued.

"We understand that the basic idea for doing it is to ensure that we do not have the ability to inadvertently upset the normal process of evolution among the native populations when we are added to the mix on the planet. That makes a good deal of sense to us. However, we are a little concerned about just how far it will go in erasing our memories. For example, will we still know each other and recall our shared memories together? Will we still have the strong bond we now have with each other? Will we know who we are, what our names are, stuff like that?"

Gaia smiled.

"Obviously we should have given you a better grasp of it on the tour of the chamber. By your questions, I can see that you have good cause for concern."

She turned to Adon.

"I think we should put off the next time jump until we have this sorted out."

Adon nodded in agreement and swiveled around until he was squarely facing the others.

"You're right, of course. I had no idea we hadn't properly communicated the cleansing to our Olympoian friends and I can see why they might be having some problems with the idea. By all means, let's put the matter to rest before we do the next time warp. You go ahead, Gaia, and answer any questions they have."

Gaia shifted her full attention to the three of them.

"The entire process is handled by the ship's main computer. In simple terms, it will scan your memory banks looking for any information that is not yet likely to be common knowledge to the naturally evolved Hominids who will already be in place on the planet at the time when we colonize. In respect to the other two hundred specimens that we have created here on Atlantis, this process is relatively simple, as we have been very careful to do our best to ensure that they have experienced nothing aboard the ship that would in any way put them in a position of knowing more than the native inhabitants they will be joining. It is a relatively simple programme and it doesn't affect relationships that have already been formed, it simply erases any memory that would not be a known quantity at the time of colony introduction. In other words, it would not produce the results that you appear to be concerned about.

"In the case of you three, due to your modern history on Olympos, we have had to massage that original program to a considerable degree as you have a great number of memories that could conflict with insertion at the time of colony introduction. However, it would not erase the base memories that you seem to be concerned about, only any incidents that would contain facts that would be in advance of the time period involved. As to exactly what that will mean, your guess is as good as mine. I suppose that after you have gone through it, any memories you have that revolve around what we would class as modern elements, might be patchy at best after the culling process has been applied. I do not believe that it will in any way affect your personal relationships - which means that you will still be bonded as friends.

Additionally, I have a gut feeling that you will also retain at least some fuzzy/fractured memories that do contain portions of information that are far in advance of the time period. Hopefully, should that occur from time to time, you will know what has happened and for the sake of the others, keep the epiphany to yourself.

"Does that answer your concerns? Do you have any more questions about it?"

The deep furrows in Juno's brow had faded considerably as Gaia talked, but she wasn't completely at ease with the concept as yet.

"What about communicating. Will they talk when we go

down there. Will we be able to understand them and they us?'

Adon took this one.

"Well no and yes.

"Talk, not as you understand the term, perhaps. But you will be able to communicate. Just before we send our colonies down we will be carrying out a careful study of all of the Hominid groups in place on the new planet. We will be scanning for an understanding of the degree of individual group evolutionary development in relation to a great many things when we do this. I won't go into them all now, but one of the things we will have a look at will be all their various means of communicating. We expect these will vary a good deal. If groups have been intermingling with others, there will be some common areas. If not, each separate grouping will have advanced in their language skills at different paces. The main computer will record these and analyze them all and then later, while you are going through memory cleansing, it will inset into each of your minds a full understanding of any and all the variations currently being used.

"Another function of the memory cleanse is the removal of any recognition of your names. This is necessary as names are a distinct trigger for other memory retention and as such could jeopardize the effectiveness of the other cleansing functions. We will be asking you to select new names for yourselves just before you take the cleanse and these will then be implanted in your minds during the process itself.

Juno interrupted.

"We won't have our own names when we colonize then?"

Adon responded.

"No, we will be replacing your current full names with a single given name. All the settlers we send will have only a single name. It is all that is needed under the circumstances, as language skills will not be advanced to the point of requiring a further unique description of oneself at that point in the evolution of the planet."

Gabe's brow furrowed.

"Well, that's going to be bloody weird."

Gaia laughed.

"Not really. You will know yourselves by the implanted names and use them as if you were born with them. I would suggest that you choose fairly simple ones as they will be more easily understood by the native population when you interact with them."

Adon picked up the thread.

"As you decided earlier, when we colonize, you three will be placed in a site on your own. It will be located between a large settlement of Humans on one side and a similar group of Neanderthals on the other. As a result of the earlier insertion of native language dialects during the memory cleanse, you will be able to communicate effectively with any and all groups of either species, should you cross paths.

"Any other questions?"

Juno glanced briefly at Gabe and Sebastian and then shook her head.

"No, I don't think so, at least not at the moment."

Adon nodded.

"Right, well let's take a little break and then we can enter our next worm hole. I think you will find this next warp very interesting

CHAPTER FORTY-SIX

- *Evolutionary Assessment* -

As soon as they were seated, the rising hum of the engines could be heard and the overhead lights dimmed as they commenced the time warp.

Without looking up from his keyboard, Adon began to speak.

"Ok. I have already keyed in instructions for a heat sensing search to commence once we are through. That will determine the location of all the current Hominid encampments. You will note that we are considerably closer, turning our attention to only the largest of the continents, the one that basically straddles the equator. We know from what happened on Olympos that, for whatever reason, there will not likely be any ancestors of early Hominids currently located on the smaller continents that earlier broke off from that central section of the crust.

"As mentioned before, on this jump we will be looking to confirm that certain markers in the evolutionary cycle of Hominid development have been reached. Our first concern will be to confirm the general use of stone tools, which, based on our historical understanding of what occurred on Olympos, should have already been occurring for some time by the earlier ancestors of Homo erectus.

"If all has gone as expected the use of these should now be commonplace for him.

"Additionally, we will want an overview to ensure that all lifeforms on the planet are those that the committee has previously selected. This will likely require some tweaking by the removal of some species of plants and the addition of others as well as some adjustment in the other animal lifeform species.

"Once we have completed our overview here, two large work crews will be dispatched down to the planet to make whatever changes in flora and animal life that are necessary to meet the standards we've already set. One of these work details will be operating under the direction of Gaia and Venus. It will direct its attention to the animal species. I will be supervising the other, assisted by Enoch and Jonah and we will be concerning ourselves with to the proper balance of the plant lifeforms.

"If you care to, the rest of you will be able to follow our progress on the screen while we work."

The big screen flickered from black to blue and then as the motors grew silent, filled with a large image of the massive continent straddling the line of the equator.

Adon continued to work the keyboard as he spoke.

"I've begun the heat-seeking apparatus previously programmed. It will spot all animal life and begin an assessment of specific species as well as categorize all plant life. As I mentioned earlier, we will be locking in on only the huge landmass which is the remains of the earlier division of the original large land mass.

"The first evaluation will concern itself with the location of the warm-blooded groups. In so doing, we should expect our search to register a fairly large number of hits in the first instance. These will each be marked by a black dot.

"When all of these have been selected, the computer will automatically shift into a secondary, refining program, which will then reject all other targets and retain only those of the Hominid locations, each of which will then be denoted by a large red X. It will take a few minutes to accomplish this task. Once it is completed, we will examine, through magnification, several of the hits at a very close range. At that time, you will be able to clearly see the selected Hominid groups' activities exposed in their natural state for the period."

The large room remained silent as the first few black dots began to form. Soon there were literally hundreds of them.

Gabe couldn't believe his eyes.

"Wow, there are sure a lot of living creatures down there. Hard to believe!"

Gaia laughed.

"Yes, animals of all kinds. Give it a few minutes and let the program work. It will whittle the number down fairly quickly and then the majority of the black dots will disappear and a few red X's will begin to pop up.

There will a great deal fewer of those, I suspect."

Patience not being one of Gabe's strong points, his mind began to wander while they waited.

"Will we be able to go down there this time and have a look around?"

Gaia deferred to Adon.

She was a little surprised when Enoch responded.

"I think it is still a little early for that. Everyone will be busy, either working down there on the flora and fauna challenge or assessing the overview of the evaluations being made by the computer with regard to the level of evolution achieved among the Hominid populations."

Adon, who had been about to respond to Gabe, held his tongue and a smile formed on his face.

The lad was taking his new responsibilities seriously, it seemed.

The first red X appeared on the screen and was quickly followed by a second and then a third. Adon spoke.

"There we go; it shouldn't be long now."

The process of red X's replacing a relatively small number of what had previously been black dots proceeded across the expanse of the land mass in short order. Sebastian commented.

"Sixty-eight of them. How many individuals in total do you think?

Adon shrugged.

"Hard to tell. Some of the groups will number only a few. Others may be quite large. The computer will be working at making a total count though.

Let's do this from left to right."

He keyed in a command and the screen began to telescope in on the first red X, which was located along the coastline on the left side of the gigantic landmass. There was a moment of utter silence and then a shared expression of awe as the first examples of Homo erectus began to come into focus. Looking downward from above, the figures seemed to be gathered on a rocky cliff ledge slightly above a large body of water.

It was a small band, numbering perhaps twenty, almost half of whom were youngsters of varying ages. As the imaged telescoped inward, the adults appeared to be seated in a semicircle while the youngsters cavorted nearby on a lower band of sand near the water.

Gabe was mesmerized and blurted.

"By Solar! Would you look at that!"

Adon suppressed a smile as he turned to enjoy their animated surprise.

"Yes, now if all of you would use your eyes to scan the general area, we are hoping to find some confirmation that they are using some form of stone tools."

It was as if his comment was unheard. As the image became crystal clear, exclamation after exclamation punctuated the silence.

From Sebastian.

"But they don't look like us! Biped or not, they look more like apes!"

Juno interjected.

"Look at their faces. They must spend all their time out in the sun. Their faces are so lined; they seem almost leathery!"

Gabe chirped up.

"They sure are brown all right. The kids' faces aren't so lined. Looks like the adults have a pretty hard life maybe."

Juno responded.

"It's the shape of the head more than anything and the facial features that make them look apelike. I mean they are pretty erect and all that, but they have weak chins, broad, flat noses, wide cheekbones and that low, sloped forehead. Their heads are kind of apelike and from that perspective at least, they do resemble apes more than men."

Sebastian nodded.

"Except that they aren't as hairy as apes. The location and density of the facial hair the men have is similar to ours though, and the pattern of hair on their heads is more like ours than apes. Also, they have less overall body hair than apes by far."

Gaia interjected.

"You have to consider that these are evolving ancestors, far from what you would class as modern man. In real time the new planet, when compared to what you knew of Olympos, is only half way along the timeline of Olympos's overall development at the point you left it. Prior to what we are now looking at, only about three million years have passed on this new planet since its inception. Hominid evolution still has a long way to go.

"At this point in time, the weather conditions should primarily be hot and dry. Hominids will be coexisting with the animal ancestors of what we know as elephants, rhinos, hippos, hyenas and water buffalo. Stone tools should be in evidence. These will be very basic. Perfectly designed rocks if you like. They would be used for killing prey, smashing their bones, stripping their skins and, as such, a concrete indication of the Hominid evolvement in relationship to their cognizance, mental and technical abilities."

Adon gave them a few more minutes before repeating his request that everyone try to spot something to indicate that this small grouping was indeed using some form of stone tools. This time, the appeal seemed to get through and the room returned to silence.

It was Jonah who broke the hush.

"Look...next to that big male sitting on the rock by himself. See that long thing lying beside him. Looks like it might be a spear."

Sebastian frowned.

"Could be, I guess, but it sure wouldn't be much good for throwing, the shaft is too uneven. It would wobble like mad if you tossed it."

Adon zoomed in on the object.

Enoch made an observation.

"I think Sebastian is right. It's a spear all right, but probably used more for stabbing than throwing."

Adon exclaimed.

"Yes, and more importantly look at the tip. It's been roughly fitted with a triangular stone point. Looks like it could be made from something like obsidian."

There was general agreement and, satisfied, Adon backed out the magnification a little so the entire encampment could be seen again. He sensed that his audience didn't want to leave the scene quite yet, and he gave them a few more minutes before he spoke again.

"We'd better move on, or we will be looking at this one camp all day."

They then randomly examined another twelve of the targeted settlements, two of which, both being located in the colder areas furthest from the equator, were relatively small. The remainder varied in size, a few quite large. In four of these cases they found clear evidence of the use of stone tools.

CHAPTER FORTY-SEVEN

- Hands On -

They had been at it for over four hours and had accomplished most of their aims in relation to assessments of the various pre-set evolutionary thresholds as stipulated by the settlement committee.

All lifeforms that needed removal or insertion had been pinpointed.

The two work details, comprising their supervisors and over four hundred Almies each, many working with heavy equipment and portable laser and force fields, had been transported and were working diligently over the surface of the planet, occasionally running into animal life, but always at a safe distance from the previously marked Hominid settlements.

The remainder of the committee, supplemented by several of the senior Atlantians who had joined them to observe the frantic activity on the new planet, had been avidly following the action on the large image-cycling screen throughout. Over that timeframe one of the elders, obviously an expert on the Hominid evolutionary process, had replaced Adon at the keyboard and she had been providing a running commentary as the images came and went in rotation.

For the three Olympoians, it offered a second chance for them to grasp the evolution of the Hominid to date and what could be expected for the future.

Now, as the work crews reflected on the screen began to prepare to transport back to Atlantis, the elder finished her commentary.

"...and if all goes on this new planet as it did on Olympos, early human migrations and expansions of both the archaic and modern humans now in existence in the relatively contained continent we are currently examining, will soon begin across the various continents. Keep in mind, that when I say soon, I mean in the next two to three hundred thousand years of the planet's future development.

"This initial migration should then be followed by the migrations of other pre-modern Hominids and likely include the ancestor of both of what we understand as modern humans and Neanderthals.

"Eventually, the evolutionary process will hopefully follow that of Olympos and if so, Homo erectus will venture out of the populated area we have centered up on the screen, which would correspond in time as that of Olympos approximately two hundred thousand years before it met its end. Through the natural process of evolvement, they should in time be replaced by Homo sapiens, during the following hundred thousand years.

"And, once again, following the pattern we saw on Olympos, forty thousand years later they will have spread over the majority of the habitable areas of the planet. This movement will be necessary due to several ice ages, when expected weather conditions will repeatedly force the various settlements to migrate along by using the resulting massive ice bridges that formed at that time."

The elder then keyed in a series of commands.

"While we await the return of the two crews, I have instructed the computer to provide a loop image of what we have seen over the past four hours. I know that because we covered a great deal of activity in relatively short spot checks during that time, many of you will want to have a second chance to take in the full extent of what was accomplished."

A burble of agreement began among the watchers as the images of what they had observed earlier began to repeat on the screen.

Once the crews were safely back on board Atlantis, those sitting watching the screen decided to break for the mid-day meal, and return to the screen again in an hour's time.

Gabe, Juno and Sebastian, filled with wonder at what had

transpired on the screen, returned to their own apartments for their repast and while they ate, found themselves jabbering like excited children, in a round of spirited exchanges about the specific things they'd seen.

Under the circumstances, the hour passed quickly for them. When they reentered the main control room they found the majority of the Atlantians already seated. In short order the committee members who had earlier been on the planet's surface joined them and Adon took his usual place at the keyboard.

He paused there briefly and then turned to face the group.

"I hope all of you share my satisfaction at what we accomplished today. We have confirmed that in its evolution, the new planet is pretty well repeating what took place on Olympos, something we have been buoyantly anticipating. Having that validates everything we have anticipated and accomplished to date. On this positive note, I suggest that we make good use of the remainder of the day and move immediately into our next time warp. If everyone is in agreement, I will clear the screen and we will do just that."

The small pockets of conversation dropped away to silence and Adon chuckled and nodded his head.

"I'll take that as agreement."

He turned around and let his fingers move over the keyboard.

"Our goal on this next jump will be to evaluate the evolution of the Hominid population in relationship to a specific marker in their advancement, that being their ability to control fire. We will be leaping ahead approximately two million years. As a point of reference, this will take us to the stage of evolution that Olympos had attained approximately six hundred thousand years before it died.

"If, as we sincerely hope, things have continued to develop and evolve as they did during that same time period on Olympos, upon our arrival we should find that our newest Hominids have now evolved to what we refer to as the Homo heidelbergensis. This particular improvement over Homo erectus, is a likely common ancestor of both Humans and Neanderthals.

"If we do find that this advancement has taken place, we should reasonably expect that they have mastered the art of making and using fire consistently. The ability to use controlled fire allowed Hominids to cook their food, obtain warmth during the colder night-hours, and also offered them some protection from predators and insects.

"Homo heidelbergensis exhibit several changes brought about through natural evolution. As a result of this change, we expect to note a new robustness of cranial and dental features and a remarkable increase in brain size over that of Homo erectus. The males should average out at approximately five foot nine inches tall and weigh about one hundred and thirty-six pounds. Comparatively, the females would stand five foot two inches and weigh in at about one hundred and twelve pounds. Envisage these Hominid to be strongly built, and if what we saw on Olympos is repeated, they should be equipped with excellent hunting tools and be well suited to dealing with the climate fluctuations that will now be a common occurrence in their settlements.

"We will be observing only on this visit, checking to ensure that the adjustments we made the last time have properly taken hold and confirming that the Hominid evolution has continued to roughly emulate that which previously occurred on Olympos. An indication that those we view are using controlled fire will help us to ascertain that. In order to make that a little easier for us, we will be initially viewing the respective continents in darkness, about an hour before the dawn, through the use of heat seeking sensors. Once we have evidence of the use of fire, and daylight arrives, we will take some time for closer study of some of the individual settlements in order to ascertain the level of Hominid evolvement that has taken place since our last visit.

"We have entered the worm and are about to induce warp

speed."

Silence was replaced by a wave of excited shifting about, combined with the building hum of the ship's massive engines. As the screen flickered to blue and then to black it attracted all eyes in the room. Unlike what had happened previously, in this instance the sound of the engines at full power appeared to persist for a longer interval. The silence that formed as the engines began to slow bespoke of the shared anticipation filling the room. By the time they exited the worm hole and the hum began to wane, everyone present was unconsciously holding their breath as they waited impatiently for an image to form on the huge screen.

The view, when it appeared, was one depicting the dark half of the new planet. As such, little detail could be seen. Adon spent a few moments working the keyboard and then tuned to face the now intrigued, but impatient group.

"I've activated the heat sensing apparatus and it has begun its work. It will take a few minutes for it to produce the results we are looking for as it has to differentiate between the various heat sources present. These will run the gamut from active volcanoes at one end of the spectrum, to warm bodied lifeforms at the other. It will then diagnose these and separate them, rejecting the higher readings and dividing the remaining lesser readings into categories important to us, in order to produce an overview which will then be reflected up on the screen."

The tension seemed to lessen at his words and several watchers shifted in their chairs, seeking a more comfortable positon as they waited. Moments later a low murmur of conversation could be heard as small clusters began to discuss what they might expect to see later, once daylight arrived.

A plethora of white dots began to form, working their way across the screen from left to right. Once they had finished, several blinked out, and a few moments later the procedure was repeated, again reducing the total.

Adon spoke.

"The computer is working at removing all indicators with the exception of what we are looking for, those being small fires and specific Hominoid hits. We appear to be about halfway through that process. A few more minutes then and we will be able to telescope into specific targets and see if we can find evidence of what we are looking for."

Gabe spoke quietly to Juno.

"I wonder if we will get to see any Neanderthals this time?"

Her brow furrowed slightly and she shrugged.

"I don't think they will have appeared yet. Why don't you ask Adon?"

Gabe shook his head.

"Naw...not with all these people around. But remind me to ask him later when it's just the committee here."

Juno grinned and shook her head.

"That may not happen again. At this point it looks like everyone is interested in seeing what's occurring on the new planet. But I will try and remind you if the opportunity arises."

The number of white dots on the screen had been reduced to what appeared a little less than one hundred and Adon spoke up.

"Okay that looks like it's been narrowed down considerably. Now we can zoom in and have a much closer look at what has been targeted."

Adon began to use magnification, starting on the left side of the continent and moving randomly across to the right, zeroing in on approximately every tenth white pinprick. Several settlements of various sizes came into shadowy focus. However, there was not enough light to identify specific individuals. On the third try the image was much clearer, primarily due to the fact that the prone occupants of the encampment, who were obviously sleeping, were lying in a circle around what was undeniably a healthy blaze.

An explosion of amazed announcements of that fact filled the room and, overwhelmed by the response, Adon laughed.

"Right, well I believe we can definitely class that as a controlled fire. Now if we wait a few more minutes, Solar's rays should begin to show themselves and we will be able to clearly examine the occupants of a few of these others, hopefully to find that Homo heidelbergensis has in fact evolved."

CHAPTER FORTY-EIGHT

- *The Neanderthal* -

Pre-warned of his concern, Juno had taken note of the fact that on this latest visit to the new planet, none of the groupings of settlers viewed had turned out to be Neanderthals. She knew Gabe would be disappointed. So, when Adon pronounced the effort a very satisfactory evaluation and closed down the screen and the rest of the audience, excited and happily offering each other congratulations, began to make their way out of the room, Juno took Gabe gently by the arm and whispered into his ear.

"Let the others go. I've spoken with Sebastian. The three of us will stay behind and speak to Adon in private. And stop worrying. I'm sure that the Neanderthals just haven't yet split off from the other Hominids at this point in their evolution. Anyway, we'll talk to Adon and find out."

Once the room had emptied, the three of them, with Juno in the lead, approached Adon, who was concentrating on the keyboard. Gabe took Juno's elbow and whispered to her.

"He looks busy; maybe we should wait till later."

As if she hadn't heard her life-partner, Juno addressed the elder Atlantian.

"Adon, Gabe is concerned that we have not yet seen any Neanderthals on the new planet. I know that there is probably a reasonable explanation for that, but we wondered if you could give us some idea of what is going on with them."

Adon, absorbed in what he was doing, took a second to register what Juno had said. As it sank in he raised his eyes and one look at the depressed Neanderthal standing just behind Juno was enough to break his concentration.

"The Neanderthals...right. Well, based on what historically took place on Olympos, we shouldn't really be expecting them to show up just yet. I would think by the time of our next jump, which will take us forward in time about another three hundred and fifty thousand years, we should catch our first look at them. So far, everything has pretty much gone according to plan though; no reason to be concerned about them at this point, I'm sure."

Adon noted that the strained expression on Gable's face didn't alter much. Nor had the imploring look being offered by Juno. He realized that more was needed. He got up from the keyboard and turned to face them squarely.

"I suppose my saying that isn't much of a consolation to you at this point. Thinking back on it, we really haven't spent a great deal of time discussing the birth of the Neanderthal. On Olympos it occurred about two hundred and fifty to three hundred thousand years before the planet shifted position into its new orbit. If you have a few moments, I could give you a basic concept of what can be expected in that regard here on the new planet if, as we have every reason to expect, it continues to evolve along the lines of what took place on Olympos."

Gave brightened considerably, stepped forward, and nodded.

"That would be great."

Adon gestured toward the small lounging area to the right of the screen.

"Let's sit over there. It will be more comfortable."

Once the four of them were seated, Adon thought for a few seconds and then began to speak.

"As I mentioned, on the next warp, we will be arriving to view the planet at a point when Olympos was about two hundred and fifty thousand years away from its orbit change. We can reasonably expect to find that the Neanderthals will have made an appearance by then. Keep in mind that Homo erectus was a widespread, polytypic species, with groups persisting longer in some regions than in others. That meant that the advanced evolution of this species was bound to vary from location to location. The Neanderthals or Homo neanderthalensis, evolved as an offshoot of Homo heidelbergensis. This created a second branch of Homo heidelbergensis.

"Homo neanderthalensis retained most of the features of the Homo heidelbergensis after its divergent evolution. Although shorter, Neanderthals were more robust, had large brow-ridges, a slightly protruding face, and lacked a prominent chin. They also had a larger brain than all the other Hominoids. On Olympos, Homo sapiens diverged from Homo heidelbergensis approximately one to two hundred thousand years before the planet shifted orbit. Homo sapiens, who also evolved from Homo heidelbergensis, differed from the Neanderthal in that they had smaller brows, were taller and more gracile, and had a flat face with a protruding chin.

"Later, due to weather changes and the resulting environmental shift, the Homo heidelbergensis migrated out of their original settlement sites to new, more livable locations. The Neanderthals however, who were a heartier bunch, chose to remain where they were, managing to adjust to the worsening conditions. As a result, the two reigning Hominoid populations of that time were, for the most part, isolated during the last of the prolonged quaternary glacial periods.

"As I said earlier, we should find evidence of them on the new planet after our next shift through space and time."

Adon paused and Juno glanced over at Gabe. The worried look had slowly slipped from his features as Adon delivered his explanation and he now seemed a good deal more tranquil.

Juno turned back to Adon and smiled.

"Thank you. That makes the whole thing much easier to understand."

Gabe nodded.

"Yes…will we be able to go down to the planet this next

time we travel ahead in time?"

Adon thought for a moment and then shrugged.

"I don't see why not. We will only be popping in to check to see if the evolvement of Homo sapiens from Homo heidelbergensis has been completed. Once that is accomplished, we can certainly transport a group down to any area that is bereft of active Hominoid communities and give you time to get a feel of the place if you like, perhaps even select the locations of the colony settlement areas we will use for our own ship created specimens, as well as a spot between them where the three of you will set up camp."

Sebastian grinned.

"Now that would be something. I can hardly wait to actually see what it all looks like."

Adon nodded his head in agreement.

"Yes, and I'm sure you are not alone in that. We are all getting impatient to get to the point of our actual colonization. Well, it will not be far off now. In the morning we will enter our next worm hole and once we have completed our mission there, the next warp we make will to carry out the actual colonization. All going well, by tomorrow afternoon you three will be in your memory cleansing cylinders and in a few days at most in our real time, you will be down on the planet and enjoying the wonders of your new permanent home."

* * * * *

Jonah and Venus joined the three Olympoians for dinner that night. All five of them were aware of the fact that it would in all probability be their last meal together before colonization. Emotions were running high.

Juno had been relatively quiet during the meal and several attempts by the others to draw her out had resulted in little change. It wasn't that she was upset about anything in particular, she couldn't put her finger on exactly what was specifically weighing on her mind. After the little Almies had cleaned up the table and a relaxing round of drinks had been supplied, she finally realized what was bothering her.

It was Adon having earlier mentioned the memory cleansing thing. Despite the fact that she was certain that she had overcome her initial concerns about it earlier, some aspect of that process was still nagging at her deep in her sub-conscious. What was it?

As the excited conversation bubbled along all around her, she found herself shutting it out and concentrating on seeking an answer to the quandary. A few minutes later her concentration was broken as her ears picked up the end of what Gabe was saying.

"...and if it cleanses memories of things that we should not have when we colonize, will that mean that I will no longer know how to make myself invisible?"

Jonah, to whom the question had been directed, didn't have an answer. He looked over at Venus for help.

Venus frowned slightly and pursed her lips.

"To be honest, I really don't know. While I understand the basics of it, just as you do, I don't fully comprehend exactly how it works. What it erases and for that matter what if any part of the process we might be able to influence."

That response gave Gabe pause for thought.

"I wonder if your dad could tell us?"

Jonah shrugged.

"Couldn't hurt to ask him."

Juno interjected excitedly.

"That's it...that's what I'm primarily worried about! Will I lose my ability to foretell as a result of having my memory cleansed?"

Silence reigned for a few seconds as they all turned to stare at her.

She had not intended to vocalize the realization and embarrassed, she offered a snap explanation.

"Something about going through that process has been bugging me for some time and for the life of me, I couldn't figure out what is was. I had this vague thought in my mind that I didn't like the idea of losing my memories, but it was kind of fuzzy, you know, nothing I could really put my finger on. But that's what it is; I've begun to trust and count on my ability to foretell and I really don't want to lose it."

Venus nodded.

"Right, well then we'll see if father can allay your fears in that regard before you guys go into the cleanse cylinders."

Sebastian frowned and interjected.

"Sounds good. We won't worry about it for now then, and we'll ask your father about it when we are about to go into those things."

Juno arched her eyebrows and opened her mouth to speak but the monk gave her a warning look and beat her to the punch.

"Wow...would you look at the time. We'd better call it quits for tonight...tomorrow is going to be a big day for the three of us for sure and I for one want to get a good sleep before morning."

Surprised by Sebastian's brusqueness, but having gotten the message, Juno pursed her lips and kept silent.

They said their goodbyes and moments later the three Olympoians were alone and Juno immediately challenged Sebastian.

"What was that look for? Why didn't you want me to follow up on checking with Adon about the mind cleanse thing?"

The monk shrugged.

"Well, after what we've been told so far about this memory cleanse, I get the impression that the Atlantians have kind of inserted us ad hoc into a programme that was originally designed for their ship-bred colonists and that they don't really know for sure exactly how it will affect us. I've got an inkling of how we can avoid the whole thing, so I just wanted to drop the discussion for now."

Gabe frowned.

"What have you got in mind?"

"I'm still working on it. I'll let you know when I get the

details worked out. In the meantime, let's make sure that none of us makes any further mention of concerns regarding the memory cleanse to anyone else."

CHAPTER FORTY-NINE

- *Homo Sapiens* -

Once they had bidden Sebastian goodnight and Gabe and Juno had retired to their own sleeping quarters to prepare for bed, Juno raised the topic of the cleansing with him. She had been uneasy about how the monk had left the discussion on the memory erasing discussion and felt the need to broach the subject again with Gabe the moment they were alone.

"I'm not comfortable with us avoiding the discussion about the memory thing with Adon."

Taken off guard, Gabe, who was rapidly shedding his clothes and had other things on his mind, responded with a questioning look and she shrugged before continuing.

"I know I was the one who raised concerns about the process and I fully agree that we have significant questions that need to be answered in that regard, but the Atlantians have been very open and supportive of us since we came aboard the ship. I think they have been honest and straightforward about everything and it seems to me that we should be able to trust them to have our best interests at heart. To me the idea of surreptitiously planning to somehow thwart their plans seems distinctly disloyal and troubling."

Naked at this point, Gabe pulled down the covers and then sat down on the edge of the bed. Juno, who had been about to strip for bed herself, took one look at his physical state and immediately recognized that her life-partner had been thinking of other things and that at this particular juncture, he was not likely to be particularly interested in reviving the topic of cleansing.

Determined to do so, and realizing that continuing to undress would only serve to further stimulate and solidify his current intentions, she paused in her preparations and smiled over at him.

"Could we just take a few minutes to discuss this before we go to bed? I promise it won't take long. I'm kind of torn by the opposing views."

Gabe met her gaze, obviously more than a little disappointed but sensing her need to talk, he shrugged.

"Sure, Babe. I've been thinking about it too. The more I toss it around, the more uncertain I am about it. For one thing, we don't know what will happen to us in that thing and that uncertainty has to be playing some part in our concerns about it. To tell you the truth, I don't know what we should do. Adon and the others seem to think it will all work out and even if it means that doing it could cause us both to lose our special abilities, maybe that's not a bad thing."

Juno frowned.

"What do you mean?"

Gabe shrugged.

"Well the whole idea of this new world means that we are kind of like, going to be reborn on this new planet. What Adon said makes sense if you think about it. We don't want to start a new life with memories that will just complicate things and screw stuff up for us once we get there. That would drive me nuts. Maybe we're just quite understandably nervous about the process and we should put our fears aside, do as you say and put our trust in the Atlantians to do what's best."

Juno was silent for a few seconds as she mulled it over in her mind yet again and then she brightened and smiled.

"What you say makes a good deal of sense. Let's sleep on it and make our final decision in the morning."

Gabe chin-gestured toward his lower extremities.

"Good, I'm glad that's settled, now let's get back to one of the more important things in life and then try for a good night's sleep."

* * * * *

As soon as the little housekeeping Almie had served them with breakfast and left them on their own, Sebastian reopened the subject of the mind cleanse.

Grinning broadly and keeping his voice down, he laid out his plan.

"Once we have confirmed that there are Neanderthals present and that Homo sapiens have evolved from Homo heidelbergensis, which will hopefully be on this next visit we make this morning, we can ask for one more visit before the actual colonization is to take place. We can tell them we want to make a final visit to the planet in order to select the best spot for our own settlement and I'm sure they will grant that request. And when we go down for that last visit, we'll find ourselves a good place to go to ground and simply not return to the ship."

Juno looked at Gabe and then back to the monk.

"Gabe and I have been talking about it and we decided this morning that we really don't want to avoid the mind cleansing process. Gabe pointed out that we are probably just afraid of the unknown and that it really doesn't matter what happens. We think we should put our trust in the Atlantians to do what is best for us and we've agreed that if, as a result, we lose our gifts, perhaps that is for the best."

Sebastian's gaze shifted to Gabe who promptly grinned and nodded.

"Yup, we talked it out. Either way it goes, we're OK with it."

Sebastian, after having spent a fair amount of time working on his little plan was clearly a little disappointed at having it rejected out of hand. However, the two sitting across from him had obviously made up their minds and he could see no sense in offering further argument.

"Right, well that certainly makes things simpler and if you guys are alright with it now, then so am I. Now, with that out of the way, we'd better get our butts up to the control room. I for one am very much looking forward to transporting down to the surface of our soon to be new home."

* * * * *

The warp went without incident and after an infrared scan had recorded the positions of all the Hominid settlements, just over a dozen of these were examined under magnification and as anticipated, clearly depicted encampments of both Homo sapiens and Neanderthals.

Excited congratulations filled the room and when the exhilaration had waned somewhat, Adon turned to face his audience.

"All is as we expected. We are finished our evaluations for today and are now at the point where we can colonize. That will take place in two days' time.

"Our three Olympoian guests have asked that we allow them down onto the planet before they enter their memory cleanse process in preparation for their transfer to the planet with our other specimens. They wish to view their prospective homeland and I have agreed to their request. The conditions necessary for Hominid life are clearly now in place, which means they will be able to make the trip to the surface without the necessity of enclosed transport. Jonah and Venus will be accompanying them, so I would ask them to stay behind."

With the exception of the Olympoians, Adon, Gaia and their children, the room quickly emptied.

As the large double doors closed behind them Adon smiling broadly, specifically addressed the eagerly waiting Olympoian threesome.

"A big moment for you then, a chance to have a firsthand look at your new home. Once we have selected the desired landing coordinates, Sal and Duanna will initiate direct transport to the surface for the five of you."

Juno spoke up.

"I had a recent foretelling that showed me a specific place

on the new planet where the three of us had an encampment. I believe that I know more or less where it is on the screen. If I point it out, will you be able to figure out the proper coordinates to take us directly there?"

Adon nodded.

"Yes, we should be able to do that and if necessary, once we you get down there, you will be able to refine your positioning if you need to. Jonah and Venus's Almies will be able to manage that."

* * * * *

Juno had indicated a spot on the coastline near the equator, where a large river flowed into the ocean. It was a spot located approximately equidistant between two Hominid settlements, one of Neanderthals and the other Homo sapiens. Adon approved of the choice and quickly configured the coordinates.

Within a half hour the party of five and their accompanying Almies had landed on the massive white sandy beach at the point where the river, a deep blue and flowing gently, made its way into the aquamarine tinted ocean beyond. For a few moments no one spoke as they simply looked around and took it all in. The setting was tropical. Where they stood, just to the south of the meeting of the intermingling bodies of water, and as Juno had foreseen, a steady cascade of gentle waves rolled soothingly in against the sandy shoreline. In small tide pools, crabs and other marine life teemed. There was a refreshing, slight but persistent breeze, which carried a light salty tang, drifting in from the ocean. Away from the expanse of beach, a rock face rose about twenty feet high and above it was a small expanse of plateau upon which thick and lush vegetation covered both banks of the river. It was very warm, strong rays cascading down from an all but cloudless sky. Sounds of life abounded. Bird songs filled the trees - a multitude of feathered missiles overhead, effortlessly riding the rising air currents, others diving into the water and rising with fish in their claws or bills. From what they could see beyond that, it seemed likely that a variety of animal life sheltered and lived beneath the lush forest. It was what Juno had foreseen and yet it was so much more. She took Gabe's hand and squeezed it enthusiastically.

"Yes! Just smell that air – fresh and clean, like after a summer rainfall, and not a cloud in the sky. Just as I pictured it but so much better. Isn't it wonderful!"

Venus couldn't help but pick up on her excitement.

"It's absolutely beautiful. I don't think you could have selected a better spot to start your new lives."

Sebastian grinned and turned toward the tall forested shoreline fronting the sandy beach.

"It looks like there are some caves up on that rock outcrop up there a little further back on the plateau. If we can find a dry one, it would be a great place to shelter us safely during the hours of darkness and during any bouts of inclement weather. C'mon, let's do a little exploring."

He led the way toward the rock face and the others eagerly followed. After a few hastily aborted attempts at finding a natural staircase leading up from the beach to the higher elevation, the monk found what he was looking for and the little line of explorers was soon at the top and headed toward the small grouping of caves. Juno was the one who spotted the little creek that ran along the side of the caves before dropping in a cascading waterfall downward off the rocks and flowing toward the much larger river that could be seen in the distance below. A profusion of fruit, nuts and berries could be seen hanging from branches and bushes along its banks.

"Well, fresh water would certainly be close to hand and what could be edible plant life seems to be abundant."

Together they eagerly entered all seven of the openings, which were haphazardly spaced along the secondary rock face, briefly examining the individual interiors before moving on to the next in line. When they'd finished their inspection Gabe, who had moved into the lead, pointed to the fourth in the lineup.

"That's the best one, completely dry and did you see that fissure in the rock in the ceiling about twenty feet inside the entrance. You could see just a hint of light at the top of it. I think it's open all the way to the top of the cave and its appears to be angled toward the beach, so while no water could come in, smoke from a fire inside should rise through it naturally. We could do our cooking inside if necessary and have a fire at night for warmth. While the cave itself has a relatively small opening, it's pretty large inside, has multiple chambers and looks like a perfect all weather shelter. What do you think?"

As a group they moved back into the cave he'd indicated and within a few moments everyone was in agreement that it was perfect for their needs.

CHAPTER FIFTY

- *Rebirth* -

Despite the sterile, almost clinic-like spotlessness and aroma, the impression offered by the large, intensely illuminated, all-white room was once again a little daunting for the three Olympoians.

For moral support, the full committee had joined them for their entry into the memory cleansing chamber. Adon, sensing their unease from the get-go, immediately led the little group on a short tour down the lines of occupied cylinders in the hopes that a close up view of the inhabitants would help ease the tension somewhat.

His few soft, and almost reverent words of reassurance were easily heard above the only other sound in the high-ceilinged room, the barely perceptible hum emanating from the individual life support systems surrounding them as they moved.

As they had in the previous visit, several worker Almies, clothed in sparkling white coveralls, went on with their various duties, paying little or no heed to the visitors.

More than Adon's soothing words, it was definitely the obvious relaxed and tranquil expressions on the faces of those behind the glass that overrode any last traces of unease the Olympoians harboured. It evaporated quickly as they took in the long lines of nude, gorgeous and perfectly formed specimens peacefully displayed within their individual suspension pods.

When they came to the line of unoccupied cylinders, three of which they would soon be gracing, Gaia spoke.

"Do you have any last questions before you begin the cleanse?"

Juno, who had been holding Gabe's hand firmly during the

tour gave him a quick glance and then smiled and shook her head.

"No, we've come to terms with the idea and the process."

Adon nodded.

"Good. Well, we'll leave you in the capable hands of the worker Almies then. All that will be asked of you once you separate and before you are placed into suspension will be that each privately select a single new name for yourselves which will then be superimposed over your current ones during the cleanse. You are about to be reborn into a brand new world and you will arrive just as any newborn, naked and newly called. You will have your whole lives ahead of you and your progeny will, throughout history, help to master this new planet."

Venus, torn between a sense of impending loss and a premonition of wonders to come, surreptitiously wiped away a tear and managed a weak smile.

"We will miss you my friends, but we will faithfully share your futures, if from afar. Although we have agreed to a policy of not physically inserting ourselves into your new world, we will look to give you aid when you are in need and we will celebrate all your successes."

Adon and Gaia, along with Enoch and Persephone, stepped back from the five who had shared so many adventures together and stood quietly watching the shared hugs and tears aplenty, before the three Olympoians were gently taken in hand by the patiently waiting Almies.

* * * * *

The entire ship's complement gathered in the main control room just before dawn.

There was an air of intense excitement and expectancy among those seated as Adon brought up an overview of the large continent centered on the planet's equator. The screen then went entirely blank for a moment prior to morphing into several separate blank windows, one large one in the center, with several other smaller ones surrounding it.

He had no need to raise his voice to be heard.

"In order to give the settlers a full day to orientate themselves to their new surroundings, the transports will begin just after dawn.

"Using our ship-created specimens, we will be setting up ten new settlements. Batches of twenty couples each will be distributed to diverse areas within the viable life supporting locations, at sites that had not been previously settled by the natural inhabitants. These couples know each other well and have been naturally paired off here on the ship before they were selected for colonization.

"Each of these new settlements will be placed within the proximity of at least one other natural settlement, which has already been assessed and is prospering. It is hoped that these successful natural colonies will be able to interact with our new arrivals within a reasonable period of time. Over time we expect that this will then allow for the likelihood of the eventual inter-breeding of the natural specimens with the progeny of the Atlantian specimens, therein accomplishing the hoped for genetic improvement in the resulting offspring.

"At least initially, we should expect that our new colonists will be somewhat taken aback when they find themselves in their new, much expanded environment, which to them will be radically different from the limited quarters they were used to sharing here aboard the ship. Hence it will be paramount that we monitor them carefully and assist them to reach a plane of acceptance as soon as it possible.

"On the screen you will see eleven currently blank windows, a large one in the centre surrounded by ten smaller ones. As the colonization takes place these individual screens will come alive. They will be used to continually monitor the newly arrived inhabitants in order to assess how they are settling in. I have prepared a roster with Enoch that will insure the control room will be manned twenty-four hours per day until we are satisfied that the members of each are accepting his or her new surroundings and beginning to make their new home their own.

"Moreover, we will be transporting the three Olympoians to their preselected site. We have taken special care to ensure that this site is within a reasonable walking range of four of the other settlements, two of these containing native specimens, one of Homo sapiens and one of Neanderthals. The remaining two will be new settlements from Atlantis, one of each type.

"It is anticipated that Gabe, Juno and Sebastian will thereby be able to make contact with the others as soon as they wish to do so.

"The three Olympoians are to be the last to be transported down to the planet. They will be settled by themselves. We felt this was necessary since they have not been created here on the ship and because of that, we can expect that despite their memory cleanse, they will find their new environment very different from any memories they might still retain. We have done our best to see to it that any obviously confusing memories have been removed in their case. However, despite our attempts to adjust the memory cleanse process accordingly, we believe that there may still be occasions when such things occur. We can expect, therefore, that they could perhaps take a little more time to come to terms with their new surrounding than will our ship-created specimens. Because of our concern in that area, the three of them will be monitored on the large window in the centre of the screen. Venus and Jonah have asked to personally take turns monitoring the Olympoians development for the first few days in order to be able to respond to any concerns immediately, should the need arise.

"For all of the settlers, the first forty-eight to seventy-two hours will be crucial. If all goes well for those first few days, we can reasonably anticipate that the new settlements will soon make themselves at home in their new surroundings and begin to venture out from the safety of their encampments. This will allow them to meet and intermingle with the natural settlements and in time lead to the interbreeding we hope for, accomplishing our original purpose of positively adding to the natural gene pool on the planet.

"The worker Almies are ready to make the first of the transports and if there are no questions I will give the signal to begin."

There were none and Adon turned to the keyboard and made several entries. Within seconds, the first of the small windows on the screen had opened, providing a telescopic overview of a small clearing next to a lake. The newly transported couples could be clearly seen lying together in the centre of the clearing.

"As you can see, the settlers have been sedated and upon arrival will be individually surrounded by a protective force field. That field will remain in place until their incapacitation dissolves and they awaken. Within a few moments of the transport they will regain consciousness and be fully restored, both mentally and physically.

"The members of the committee have each taken responsibility for concentrating on one or more of the specific screens and will begin doing so as the transports progress. I would ask anyone in the audience to be on the lookout for anything unusual as the colonizing progresses and immediately bring it to our attention so that we may intervene as required.

It is hoped that the successful natural colonies will be able to interact with our new arrivals within a reasonable period of time. This will improve the likelihood of the eventual inter-breeding of the natural with that of the Atlantian specimens, therein accomplishing the hoped for overall genetic improvement in the resulting progeny.

* * * * *

The sun had been up for only an hour when the three Olympoians completed their transport.

They regained consciousness within a few minutes and

awoke to find themselves lying on warm sand, a few feet away from the gently rolling waves breaking on the beach.

The freshness of the air filled their nostrils as they raised themselves and stretched. The two young ones unconsciously reached out to each other to hold hands.

Even at this relatively early hour the temperature was comfortably balmy.

At first their consideration was for their surroundings. In turn, each could be seen examining the ocean, the beach, the river, the bluff and caves in the distance and the lushness of the plant life beyond.

That done, their attention shifted to each other.

Each felt a sensation of déjà vu and felt no particular unease or even surprise at finding themselves on the sand. There was a mutual acceptance, a shared understanding that they knew each other as friends and colleagues, although the reason for that feeling was just beyond their grasps.

All three felt warm, safe and full of pent up energy for what was to come.

They were naked. However, that fact, although recognized, seemed unimportant and was immediately dismissed as irrelevant. For the moment at least, there was no need of clothing here.

The older human spoke first.

"I'm sorry, I know we've previously met, but I've forgotten your names. I'm Odin."

The young dark human female responded with.

"Eve…"

The third, a muscular Neanderthal, smiled and extended his hand.

"Adam."

<u>Other books by Patrick Laughy</u>

Murder Mysteries

The Little Black Book
Alumni

Historical Fiction

The 4th Reich series
Books 1-7

Fantasy

Atlantis-Ship of the Gods
A trilogy